SPECIAL MESSAGE TO READERS

THE ULVERSCROFT FOUNDATION
(registered UK charity number 264873)
was established in 1972 to provide funds for research, diagnosis and treatment of eye diseases. Examples of major projects funded by the Ulverscroft Foundation are:-

- The Children's Eye Unit at Moorfields Eye Hospital, London
- The Ulverscroft Children's Eye Unit at Great Ormond Street Hospital for Sick Children
- Funding research into eye diseases and treatment at the Department of Ophthalmology, University of Leicester
- The Ulverscroft Vision Research Group, Institute of Child Health
- Twin operating theatres at the Western Ophthalmic Hospital, London
- The Chair of Ophthalmology at the Royal Australian College of Ophthalmologists

You can help further the work of the Foundation by making a donation or leaving a legacy. Every contribution is gratefully received. If you would like to help support the Foundation or require further information, please contact:

THE ULVERSCROFT FOUNDATION
The Green, Bradgate Road, Anstey
Leicester LE7 7FU, England
Tel: (0116) 236 4325

website: www.foundation.ulverscroft.com

Sara Zarr is an acclaimed author for young adults, a National Book Award finalist and two-time Utah Book Award winner. She has written essays and creative nonfiction for *Image, Hunger Mountain online,* and *Response,* as well as for several anthologies, and has been a regular contributor to *Image*'s daily Good Letters blog. Sara also hosts the 'This Creative Life' podcast. Born in Cleveland and raised in San Francisco, she currently lives in Salt Lake City, Utah, with her husband.

Visit her website at: www.sarazarr.com.

Tara Altebrando studied American Government at Harvard, and has never had a full-time job — her past work has ranged from music journalist to stand-up comedian. A commended author for young adults, she collects spoons, has a trampoline in the house, and lives in New York with her husband and daughters.

Visit her website at:
www.taraaltebrando.com

ROOMIES

When Elizabeth receives her first-year room-mate assignment at the beginning of summer, she shoots off an email to coordinate the basics. She can't wait to escape her New Jersey town (and her mom), and start afresh in California ... Elizabeth's message to Lauren in San Francisco comes as a surprise: she had requested a single. But if Lauren's learned anything from being the oldest of six, it's that you don't always get what you want — especially when what you want is privacy ... Soon the girls are emailing back and forth, sharing secrets even though they've never met. It seems that the only people they can rely on are each other ...

SARA ZARR & TARA ALTEBRANDO

ROOMIES

Complete and Unabridged

ULVERSCROFT
Leicester

First published in Great Britain in 2014 by
Hodder & Stoughton
London

First Large Print Edition
published 2016
by arrangement with
Hodder & Stoughton
An Hachette UK company
London

A catalogue record for this book is available
from the British Library.

ISBN 978–1–4448–2943–3

Published by
F. A. Thorpe (Publishing)
Anstey, Leicestershire

Set by Words & Graphics Ltd.
Anstey, Leicestershire
Printed and bound in Great Britain by
T. J. International Ltd., Padstow, Cornwall

This book is printed on acid-free paper

MONDAY, JUNE 24
NEW JERSEY

Sometimes there are signs. Or things I can't help but interpret as signs. Maybe from fate or the universe or God, if there is one. Or maybe from the grandmother I barely knew but who I've always been told is in heaven.

Watching and judging.

Like Santa.

There are just times when it really feels like some*one* or some*thing* is paying attention. Even to little old me. And right now he or she or it is looking down on me lying on my bed, where I am seething because of a five-minutes-ago fight with my mother about how I am going to spend this, my last summer at home before college. I have plans to meet my friends at the beach tomorrow and she thinks I should be . . . well, she doesn't even know *what* she wants me to be doing instead. Here's a hint: It is probably the exact opposite of whatever I want to be doing at any given moment.

I seriously only graduated last week. The cap and gown are still hanging right there on the back of my bedroom door.

Someone, some power, must see me gripping the bedspread beneath my fingers and he (or she or it) must feel some kind of pity for me because he (or she or it) takes it upon himself (or herself or itself) to trigger someone on the opposite coast, someone named Helen Blake, who works in Student Housing at UC Berkeley, to sit down at her computer and type in my e-mail address and send me a message that makes my phone buzz on the bed next to me and that helps me to calm down, and to release the bedspread, and to remember that nothing, not even living with your mother, is forever, though it mostly feels that way.

Dear Elizabeth Logan, it says. I am pleased to provide you with your dorm room assignment and contact information for your roommate this coming school year. While it is by no means mandatory for you to get in touch, some students find that there are practical issues they would like to discuss before orientation week.

Below the dorm info is a name — Lauren Cole — a snail mail address in San Francisco, an e-mail address, and a phone number. It is enough to make me spring up off the bed and rush to my desk. There is a light, gritty layer of dust on my open laptop's keyboard; I

2

haven't used it since school ended but something about sending e-mail from it — instead of from my phone — feels more official, more serious.

I am nothing if not officially serious about going away to school.

So I type in this Lauren's address — calling seems crazy — and I put Hi Roomie! as the subject; then I think for a second that I have no idea what to say, but it turns out I do.

Dear Lauren,
You don't know me but I got an e-mail from Berkeley telling me that we're going to be roommates. I am so excited to 'meet' you! I've been waiting and waiting. Since I'm moving to California from New Jersey, I'm not bringing that much stuff at all — only what I can fit in two suitcases. Maybe I'll ship stuff? I'll prob-ably pack a hundred times in the next 65 days (not like I'm counting, ha ha), so I can be sure everything I want to bring will fit. My mother says she'll give me money for a mini-fridge or microwave. Are you already planning on bring-ing either of those?

I think about wrapping it up but I am really just getting going so I don't stop. Not yet. I rub my fingers together to get rid of some dust, then dig in again.

I'm so jealous that you live in San Francisco. You must really like it if you're staying close for college. It's cool that you're going to live in the dorms. I swear I've been wanting to go away to college ever since I found out it was possible to do that. It's all I think about lately. Getting out of this place.

I should stop now. No one sends e-mails this long. But as it turns out I am not quite done with the stuff that needs to come off my chest so that I can maybe breathe again, so that I can maybe survive the summer and the move to the land of the Man Who Left, otherwise known as Dad.

This may sound crazy but I've never been to California — even though my father moved to San Francisco a bunch of years ago. I haven't seen him since I was pretty little, and I never talk to him, so it's not like that's the reason I picked Berkeley. Anyway, I promise not to be too annoyingly touristy or anything.

I'm babbling. So yeah. Let me know about the microwave/ fridge situation.

Elizabeth (but everyone calls me EB) Logan

I send it before the feeling of release turns sour. Then I head over to Facebook and search for Lauren Cole. Turns out there are a couple of fan pages for famous Lauren Coles I've never heard of. And one at the University of Florida, but none that looks like she might be my roommate, a fact I find depressing. Who *isn't* on Facebook?

MONDAY, JUNE 24
SAN FRANCISCO

It's a rare quiet moment in the house. When I say *rare*, I'm using it in the real sense of the word: rare like a meteor shower, rare like a white tiger, like a double yolk or a red diamond. Rare as in I use up about a third of this precious silence trying to remember when it last was. Silent. For another fifteen minutes I try to decide how not to waste it. I have the day off from both my jobs. Should I take a nap? Hook my iPod up to the living room stereo and blast it? Make a deluxe quesadilla, which, for a change, I wouldn't have to share?

I opt for a combination of stereo takeover and nap, putting on a mellow playlist at a soothing volume and stretching out on the floor — with a blanket under me so as to avoid Cheerio dust. Finally and blissfully, I'm alone. It isn't long before I make the muscle-twitching, gape-mouthed descent into sleep. After what seems like about ninety seconds, I become aware of the sound of the van idling outside.

Already? No. No.

Sometimes in the moments surrounding REM sleep, you hear things that aren't really there. I forbid my eyes to open. But there's the sound of the van door sliding on its track. (Note that I did not say *minivan*.) My mother's voice. The babbling of P.J.; the cry of Francis; Jack and Marcus fighting. For some reason I don't hear Gertie out there. Soon enough that reason becomes apparent.

'Why are you on the floor?'

Gertie plops onto my stomach. Oof. 'Because I like the floor,' I say.

'Why?'

'Because I said so.'

'Why are your eyes closed?'

'Because it makes the room nice and dark.'

She touches each of my eyelids gently, and I feel her weight shift as she leans over my face, expelling her soft grape-juice-and-baby-carrot breath. She pets my hair and I hope to God she hasn't been picking her nose. 'Are you *dead?*' she asks in a dramatic whisper.

'Yes.'

Gertie is absolutely still for a count of three; then she bounces on my stomach and I'm forced to open my eyes and roll over to get her off me. 'No you're not! No you're not!' She laughs like a maniac. 'Mama says come help.'

The next chance I have to think is five hours later, after Dad's come home, after we've gotten through the ordeal that is dinner, after baths and toothbrushing and all the bargaining and coercion and threat-making that help those things happen, and after Francis is down but the rest of them are living up the twenty minutes before story time and, at last, lights-out.

It's the first opportunity I've had to look at my e-mail in three days. There are two screens of new messages, mostly spam. As I sort through it, I find some stuff from my best friend, Zoe — links to videos and sites I'll probably never have time to look at — and a message from my dad. He sends these one- or two-sentence notes from work when he's bored or thinking of me. This says, Garfield has been violated. Investigating. There's a picture attached of the mug I gave him when I was in first grade. It's got a big lipstick print on the rim. I write back: That is a bold red. Inquire among VIPs.

On the third screen, the page of oldest messages, there are a few from Berkeley. One of them has to be about my housing request. I'll save those to open last; I'm too nervous now. I go back to the first screen to start clicking off the spam and find a message I didn't notice the first time. The subject line is Hi Roomie! and I almost junk it for porn, but when I see the preview of the first line, a chill comes over me.

I open and read it through.

Then I frantically click over to the Berkeley messages and find the one telling me about my roommate.

So it's true. My request has been denied. 'Crap,' I mutter.

'Can I play Dora?' It's Gertie.

I minimize the window — I'm not sure why; it's not like Gertie cares about my e-mail or can understand what she's seeing. She breathes down my neck, her sticky hand already leaving a mark on my desk, which I've just cleaned for what feels like the tenth time today, making use of the industrial-size tub of Clorox Wipes I pay for with my own money. 'No,' I say. 'Can you go . . . occupy yourself or something?'

I try not to sound mean. I'm already in trouble for being 'mean' to Jack, even though he's the one who completely spilled cranberry juice all over my favorite sweater, at some point between the interruption of my nap and dinner. I'd saved up for like a month to buy that sweater. I yelled at Jack and called him a moron, and when Mom found me and said,

'He's six, Lauren. He didn't do it out of malice,' what came out of my mouth was 'I wish I were an only child.' And Mom gave me that look she has and walked out, reminding me to apologize to Jack before dinner. At which point he didn't care anymore, having moved on to the crucial task of making sure his various food groups didn't touch.

So even though I want to physically toss Gertie out of my room, I don't. Because actually it's not my room. It's *our* room — I share it with Gertie and P.J., my sisters. Jack and Marcus are down the hall. Francis still sleeps in my parents' room in the bassinet.

'Here,' I say to Gertie, getting up and pulling my old Mr. Potato Head down from the high shelf in the closet. Her brown eyes widen. I rarely let her touch Mr. Potato Head. Grandpa Cole gave him to me, and all the pieces are there and the box is still in good shape. Mr. Potato Head has sentimental value, so he's one of the few things I'm not forced to share. 'You have to play with this in here. Sit on the bed and be quiet, okay? It's almost lights-out.'

She nods, probably afraid that if she says anything else I'll change my mind.

I get back to the e-mail.

This is what I want to write:

Dear EB,

Already I'm calling her Ebb in my head, even though I'm sure that what she means by EB is Eee Bee.)

I requested a single. All I've wanted for the last decade is a room of my own. Some privacy. A place to be alone with my thoughts where they are not constantly interrupted by someone else making some kind of racket, or even someone else just quietly trying to exist in the same space as me. When I got the full scholarship I knew it would probably be pressing my luck to ask for a single, but the box was there to check so I checked it. A 'roomie' is really not what I had in mind. Really not what I had in mind at all.

Of course, I don't write any of that. It's not Ebb's fault my parents wanted a big family.

Dear EB,
Hey. I hadn't really thought about appliances.

(Where am I supposed to get the money for this stuff? My magic money tree? I can probably find a decent microwave at Goodwill if I look every couple of days. Mini-fridges are harder to come by.)

Why don't you do the fridge part and I'll take care of the microwave.

San Francisco is okay. We live in a foggy neighborhood on the south side of the park so it's not like we have a view of the Golden Gate Bridge and cable cars going by or anything. Only the smelly old Muni trains.

I reread her e-mail. I feel as though it would be polite to acknowledge what she said about her dad, or about New Jersey, or ask a question, or something, but P.J. runs in and lunges for Mr. Potato Head so I wrap it up.

Nice to meet you.

Lauren Cole

"*Tato head!*" P.J. shrieks. I scan the e-mail one more time and I know it looks kind of rudely abrupt, but I have to save Mr. Potato Head. And anyway, I wanted a single.

I click Send, close my laptop, and put it up on the high shelf. Gertie lets out a dolphin-pitched death scream and when I turn around, P.J. has got one of Mr. P.'s ears and is about to run away with it. I grab her by the waist. She screams. Gertie screams.

If Mr. P.'s mouth were attached, he would probably scream, too.

TUESDAY, JUNE 25
NEW JERSEY

That's it? was what I thought when I first read Lauren's e-mail late last night. And now that I'm reading it aloud to my friends, Justine twists her face into a grimace and says, 'That's it?' Even though the end of the school year was a little bit strained, Justine and I have been friends for so long that it sometimes feels like we can read each other's minds.

I toss my phone down onto the beach blanket in front of me. 'That's all she wrote, as they say.'

Justine and Morgan — a newer friend of ours, mostly from senior year — are trying to get me on a strict early-morning beachgoing schedule between now and when I leave for Berkeley, so as to maximize surfing and time together. We're coated in sunscreen and sitting in chairs under umbrellas, reading articles in shiny teen magazines about things like dorm decor and tips for living on your own for the first time, while Alex, Danny, and Mitch surf. Justine tosses her magazine onto our blanket before saying, 'Maybe she was busy. You know. Dashed it off without thinking.'

I shoot her a look that says, *Come on.*

'Well, I tried.' She turns to face the water and I see a smile form at the corners of her mouth. 'What's her e-mail address, Ice Queen at condescending-mail-dot-com?'

Morgan lets out a chuckle but doesn't look up from her mag.

I say, '*That*'s more like it,' and look back at the article I've been reading about the Top Ten Things to Pack for College. A pillow. Headphones. Flip-flops for the shower . . .

I wish I could pack a few friends.

'I wouldn't worry about it.' Morgan holds her magazine out to me but I'm not ready to trade so she tosses hers onto the blanket, too. 'You'll find some super-dorky shrubbery major like yourself and you'll barely be in your room anyway. You'll be too busy planting bushes.'

'It's not called shrubbery,' I say for the gazillionth time.

'You know she's just messing with you.' Justine flashes a smile at Morgan, who returns it.

I let it go. But there's a part of me that's still annoyed that my friends don't get it. That no one in the whole of Point Pleasant gets it, except for Tim at Beech Design — and even he looked at me like I had two heads when I walked up to him while he was working on the Schroeders' backyard last summer and told him, with six-month-old Vivian Schroeder on my hip, that I wanted a job. He said he couldn't pay me and I said I didn't care — that I'd keep my babysitting job to make the money I needed. So he told me to come in the next morning to talk about hours. I'd been watching him and his small staff for weeks — carving up that yard and putting it back together again so that it felt like there were rooms outside, places worth being. I knew I'd found my calling. I'll be a paid full-time employee this summer starting Friday, and I still babysit for Vivian occasionally at night.

'I've never understood why you have to go all the way to California when there's a great program at Rutgers,' Justine says. 'Plus, *I'll* be there.'

'We've been through this,' I say, thinking, *Yes, you'll be there*, and Danny and Alex and everyone else we know, except for Morgan, who'll be a short drive away at NJIT, and Mitch, who's going to Seton Hall. 'Too close to the mother ship.'

'So you say.' Justine gets up and grabs her board.

Morgan gets up, too. 'Coming in?'

I haven't surfed much so far this season — there's no surfing during peak beach hours, which end up generally being when I'm free. And I'm not even sure I'm going to try to surf out in California, though my friends are all convinced that that is secretly part of the whole point of my going west. Bigger waves.

'In a minute,' I say, and they both turn and walk off toward the boys — their boyfriends and mine; Justine, much to my chagrin, likes to call us 'the six-pack.' Then I pick up my phone and read the e-mail again, trying to decide if it really is sort of rude (like I actually thought there were cable cars on her street?) or just straightforward. I'm not sure. But I feel dumb for having told her that stuff about my dad. Justine always says she loves that I wear my heart on my sleeve, but I've been thinking it wouldn't be a bad idea to put on a few layers when I leave for school. I guess I thought it'd be easier to get some of the weird stuff out over e-mail. That way, when this Lauren person and I settle in for our first night sharing a room and I say, 'Oh, my dad's gay' — when I'm forced to tell the whole story, like I inevitably will be — maybe she'll be a little bit prepared. I could do without the 'no ways' and weirdly sympa-thetic 'really?s' followed by those 'not that there's anything wrong with its.'

I honestly *don't* think there's anything wrong with it.

The wrong thing, let's face it, was abandoning me.

I hit Reply and think for a minute about how to respond — whether to even bother — while watching Alex ride a pretty big wave for a good long while. I'm going to miss him and his wild salty hair and goofy laugh, but things have been tense lately so I'm not sure how much.Lauren, I type. And then I go back to the subject heading and delete the Roomie! bit — leaving only the re: and the Hi — because it seems dumb now. We're clearly not going to be e-mail buds.Mini-fridge it is, I type, but what else is there to say? Forgive me for blabbing about my dad? Would it kill you to ask a question, maybe get a little e-mail volley going? Do you eat Rice-A-Roni, 'The San Francisco Treat,' like, every night?

I take a deep breath and write, I'll see you in August!, then delete the exclamation mark and then put it back and delete it again a few times. I sign it Elizabeth.

'EB!' Alex is standing at the water's edge. He cups a hand to his mouth when he yells, 'Come on in!' and for a second, I close my eyes against the sun and see my mother in a black bandeau suit and me as a young girl in a polka-dot bikini — right here on the same beach — and we are happy and playing in the surf and then busy making sand castles and forts and then, later, knocking down those castles and forts and flying kites in the shapes of mermaids and bats and dragons.

That was all when she was happy.

That was all before.

I get up and grab my board and set out in Alex's direction, suddenly very much hoping I didn't send the exclamation mark but feeling pretty sure I did. A wave crashes behind Alex, right at his ankles, and he gets thrown off-balance and has to recover. I think, *I feel like that most of the time,* and when I reach him, I decide I'll kiss him — right there on the beach with anyone watching who wants to — and see if it steadies me.

THURSDAY, JUNE 27
SAN FRANCISCO

I'm breaking down cardboard boxes behind the Financial District deli where I work, imagining a future job for myself that doesn't involve mustard or mixing up five gallons of tuna salad at a time. Of course there's my other job — filing and data entry for an insurance company — but it's not much of an improvement, taking into account paper cuts and keyboard cramp.

I'd like to be in a lab. Sterile, quiet, isolated. Me in a white coat, hair in a bun, sporting some cool retro glasses and holding up a test tube . . .

A roach falls to the ground from somewhere within the thick banana box I'm attempting to crush. I jump back the same moment Keyon comes out of the service door with a bag of trash in each hand.

'Am I that scary?' he asks, tossing the bags into the Dumpster.

'No. Visitor from the Roach Motel.'

This lab in which I'll conduct my future work? Roach free.

20

Keyon takes a pack of gum from his pocket and offers me a piece.

'Thanks.'

'Maybe that roach traveled here all the way from Brazil. On a banana boat. Honor the journey, baby.' Another roach crawls out from under the box. Keyon steps on it calmly. 'And here the journey ends.'

We chew. The late-afternoon sun is warm, which feels great. But then, closing time always feels great. The deli is only open eleven to three to serve lunch to the office workers downtown. During that time it's basically nonstop. At closing it always feels like we've survived some kind of stampede. Instead of wild animals it's anxious humans decked out in business casual.

'Hey,' I say, 'will you finish closing for me if I leave a little bit early?'

'Depends.' Keyon stretches his arms overhead. His T-shirt comes up a little. I look away, because we're sort of friends and it seems unfriendly to ogle his abs, regardless of their excellent condition.

'I want to hit the Goodwill on my way home.'

'You can look, Lo,' he says, patting his stomach and grinning.

I play dumb. 'Look at what?'

Keyon shakes his head and laughs. 'Okay.

So what are you out for? At Goodwill?'

'Microwave.'

He thinks for a second. 'Which store you going to?'

'Irving is closest to my house,' I say, taking an X-ACTO knife to the last of the banana boxes. 'But I usually go to Clement.'

'No, no. Don't bother with that mess. You need to hit Fillmore.'

'It's kind of out of the way. I'm on the bus.'

He looks at his watch. 'If you close up with me, I'll drive you. I got a cousin that works there. Maybe he can hook you up.'

I calculate the time involved, the crowded rush-hour buses from the Fillmore to the Outer Sunset, me carrying a microwave. A ride would be sweet. Still, I hesitate. The reason I say Keyon and I are 'sort of' friends is that I don't really know him that well.

I didn't know him at all, basically, through all four years of school. Science nerds (me) and athletes (him) didn't cross paths often, despite the fact that at Galileo even science nerds have some social power. And the subgroup of athletes who were also at the top of the class academically (him) seemed to have their own thing going on most of the time. It's hard for people with five younger siblings (me) to keep up.

Then, on the last day of school — just a

few weeks ago now, though it seems like ages — we found ourselves in the same cluster of people signing each other's yearbooks, and I was feeling all sentimental about leaving high school and asked him to sign mine.

He stood there with the pen poised over the class page, then looked at me. 'Um, what's your name again?'

'Lauren.'

He nodded, then wrote something and handed it back to me. We were both waiting for other people, so we made small talk and he asked me what I was doing this summer.

'Working, mostly.' I told him I was looking for a second job, because the insurance company wouldn't give me more hours for the summer and warned me they'd be cutting back my existing hours after they computerized the filing system.

'My dad needs someone. He's got a sandwich shop downtown. On Montgomery?'

That would be easy to get to on the streetcar, I thought. 'I don't have much of that kind of experience. I mean, I cook for my little brothers and sisters, but . . . '

Keyon laughed. 'It's sandwiches, not biotech. Show up tomorrow at ten and you get the job. It'll save my dad the hassle of interviewing.'

I showed up.

And for some reason it hadn't occurred to me that Keyon would be working there, too. Me, him, and his dad were basically the lunch crew, with a little extra help eleven-thirty to one. But Keyon and I are work friends, who talk about work, and do work, and then leave work and don't have any connection in between. If he drives me to Goodwill, then we're either going to officially be friends outside of work, or I'm mooching rides.

'Are you sure you have time?' I ask Keyon now.

'Where else do I gotta be? City Hall?'

'I don't know. Maybe you're, like, the special assistant to the DA in your off-hours.'

He laughs. 'You watch too much TV.'

It does feel urgent to get the microwave. Like I need to prove to Ebb or Elizabeth or whatever her name is that I'm into this, I'm on board, as sort of an apology. She was obviously annoyed, or hurt, in her last e-mail. The flat I'll see you in August without closing punctuation left no doubt in my mind that she's already starting to hate my guts. I want to get this stupid microwave, even though I don't need it for another two months, just so I can e-mail her to tell her I found it. A peace offering.

'Okay,' I say to Keyon. 'Thanks.'

He maneuvers his dad's boat of a Chrysler through the city streets. It's awkwardly quiet. After several blocks, Keyon asks, 'Do you have your seat belt on?'

'Yep.'

More awkward quietness. Then we both start talking at once.

Him: 'My dad is obsessed with seat belts — '

Me: 'One time we got pulled over — '

Then we both say, 'Sorry, go ahead,' at the same time, which makes us laugh. He tells his seat belt story, and I tell mine; then we're there and he somehow manages to find a big enough parking spot within three blocks of the store.

The store smells like Goodwill always does, musty and mildewed, a little like my grandma's garage. And it's crowded, even at this time of day, the merchandise looking extra-unappealing under the fluorescent lights. Keyon lifts his arm in greeting to a guy at the register. 'Hey, Mikey.'

Mikey, who is even taller than Keyon and a lot lankier, only nods, counting out change.

'Here,' Keyon says, placing a hand on my shoulder to steer me to the electronics department, such as it is. There are a lot of

25

old TVs, outdated computer monitors, ancient stereo systems. And one microwave.

'It's way too big,' I say, tentatively touching the grimy handle with one finger and then quickly withdrawing it. 'This is like a microwave from the dawn of microwave invention.'

'Yeah, you don't want that. Hang tight a sec . . . ' He goes off toward the front. I look over the toy shelf nearby, seeing if there's anything Gertie or P.J. might like, and do not believe my eyes when I see a Mrs. Potato Head. There's no box, and she doesn't have all her parts, but she's woman enough to make a good companion for Mr. P.

After what seems like a long time, Keyon returns with Mikey. He glances at the Mrs. Potato Head in my hands and raises his eye-brows, apparently bemused. 'Follow us. We're going to the room where they sort new donations.'

'Oh, awesome.' I ask Mikey, 'That won't get you in trouble?'

'My boss is cool with it once in a while. Friends and family. I mean, you're still gonna pay.'

We walk into this massive room in the back and are greeted with a bunch of suspicious glances from the employees who are sorting piles of stuff. 'My cousin,' Mikey announces.

Keyon pats his chest. 'Me.'

'Yeah, I think they got that,' Mikey says. 'Take a look around. I'll be back in five minutes.'

I don't know where to start. Keyon goes straight toward the corner of the room where there's furniture and other bigger stuff. A love seat. An entertainment center. A few dining room chairs. I go to the opposite corner. More TVs and old computers.

How do I tell Ebb that I can't just go out and buy a brand-new microwave, even at Target or Costco or something? There is no 'my mom is giving me money for . . .' in my life. But I can't show up with a gross microwave from the Reagan era. And I don't want to dip into my savings; I don't care enough about food being hot to do that. My priorities are probably totally different from hers in every way, and instead of respecting my frugality she's going to think I'm cheap and tacky. But I *have* to be cheap and tacky because I'll need a new laptop soon; my current model is a hand-me-down from when my dad got a new one for work.

'Lauren,' Keyon shouts out. 'Check it.'

I look across the room and he's holding up a compact white microwave. Score.

One hurdle cleared, for now.

Dear EB,

Good news. I have secured a microwave for our dorm room. Technically, my friend Keyon secured it, and transported it, but it's safe in my garage until moving day. We are now ready to pop many a bag of popcorn.

So that's something to look forward to.

How's the weather in Florida? It's been pretty nice here lately, considering there's barely such a thing as summer in SF.

I should mention I have five younger brothers and sisters. The oldest is six and the youngest is nine months and in between there are twins. Wait, I'm forgetting P.J., who's almost three. Like that's not enough to deal with, I have two jobs so it's always kind of chaotic, hence abrupt e-mail and I hope —

I delete the last paragraph. I hate sounding like a martyr. But also, it's the truth. I put it back in.

— hope all's well over there.

Till later,

Lauren Cole

FRIDAY, JUNE 28
NEW JERSEY

'What's up with you today?' Alex says. We spent the morning at the beach with the rest of the six-pack and now we're sitting on the patio of a boardwalk burger place, just the two of us, having an early lunch. He is leaning in toward the table and drinking his Coke through a straw, without picking up the glass, and for some reason it really annoys me. I mean, *Pick the damn thing up!* Vivian Schroeder has more advanced drinking skills.

'Nothing's up.' Our burgers arrive and I'm suddenly not sure whether I'll be able to eat mine. 'It's dumb.'

Alex shrugs, takes a bite of his own burger. He's apparently okay with letting it go that easily. I, on the other hand, am apparently not; the quick loss of my appetite proves it. 'I e-mailed the girl who's going to be my roommate. She doesn't seem all that interested.'

His mouth is full. 'You're probably reading too much into it. You do that sometimes, you know.'

This is supposed to be funny. Because of the fight we had a few weeks ago at prom, when he made a joke about sex that pissed me off. We haven't had it and I'm happy to keep it that way. He is not. He also thinks it's okay to joke about it — like to say 'EB doesn't put out that easily' when Danny asked me to dance — and then to pretend he wasn't actually talking about sex at all. He claimed I was 'reading into' things, that he only meant I don't really like to dance. I want him to understand that I am not reading into things now.

'She just asked me how the weather is in *Florida*. I already told her I live in New Jersey.' I've been letting the e-mail sit, letting it stew. There's no point in writing back right away. Or maybe ever.

'So make a joke of it.' Burger juice cuts a creek down his hand. 'Send her the link to weather-dot-com. Or a map of the US with New Jersey and Florida highlighted so she learns the difference.'

'Yeah, I'll do that,' I say, super-sarcastically, though I'm tired of making a joke of everything.

'She's a roommate,' Alex says. 'It's not like you have to be best friends.'

'I know,' I say, but my eyes burn behind my sunglasses. Who *is* going to be my best friend

30

in college? Why did I think it was such a great idea to pick a college as far away from Jersey as you can get without leaving the continent?

'You already have a best friend.' Alex swallows and smiles. 'Me.'

I hate when Alex says stuff like that, stuff that makes me wish I were leaving tomorrow, stuff that makes it hard for me to ignore the fact that my feelings for him don't match his for me. I eye my burger and hope that if I take a bite, the sick feeling will go away. Also, I start work this afternoon and I'll most likely be on rock-removal duty, a task that requires a lot of energy and focus, so I really need a decent meal. It still shocks me sometimes how heavy rocks can be, even the ones that don't look like much at all. And I feel like there's some kind of wisdom to be gleaned from that fact — something more than *Looks can be deceiving!* — but I am not sure what it is.

'Did you mention surfing?' Alex asks. 'Maybe that put Florida in her head?' Even though that makes no sense whatsoever, I appreciate that he is trying to help me, that he's taking me seriously after all.

I shake my head and he shrugs, dumbfounded.

I should break up with him, I know. Because we are not going to have sex.

31

Because I don't feel *that way* about him anymore, if I ever did. But it hardly seems worth the effort when college can do the breaking up for me. The path of least resistance is a path I know well, having trod it in circles around my mother for years.

★ ★ ★

When I turn up at the address Tim gave me, there's a guy I've never seen before poking around in the yard out front. Tim never said anything about a new employee, but I'm not exactly his confidante. It *is* true, however, that he has started to take me more seriously now that I'm enrolled in a landscape architecture program. Mostly, he tells me stories about life before he and his wife (who handles the administrative end of the business) had kids, and I like to listen. Apparently, they used to work hard all spring and summer, then spend their winters in places like Belize and Costa Rica when their work dried up for the season. I've never been anywhere, so the idea that my chosen profession might allow me to 'winter' in Central America excites me no end. In my fantasy, my mother even comes down every year and we have Christmases that are fun, like with Rum Runners and Caribbean-sounding music, and not like the ones we

32

have now — with endless televised yule log fires and that feeling of disappointment we share when we realize we've only been awake for ten minutes and have already opened each other's presents and have nothing else to do.

'Can I help you?' the guy says when he sees me. He looks about my age and I'm sort of annoyed that Tim thinks he needs a male intern or employee. The rocks are heavy, yes, but I've never complained.

'I work for Tim,' I say, and the guy says, 'Who's Tim?' He looks like he just rolled out of bed. His hair is jutting in all the wrong directions, his clothes are crinkled, and there's even something cakey near the side of his mouth. Like some kind of frosting or old milk. In spite of all this, he is adorable.

'Landscaper?' I say.

He wipes his dirty hands on his shorts. 'Oh.'

A woman's voice calls out from somewhere. 'Didn't I tell you to leave it alone?'

The guy looks up. 'Yes, *Mom*.' He smiles over at me and rolls his eyes. 'Multiple times.'

I look up and catch a flash of blond hair disappearing into a second-story window and only then really start to notice the house we're working on. How nice it is. How massive. How entirely unlike the condo my mother and I have lived in since my dad left when I was in kindergarten. There are trees around the house that I would kill for. Old trees. The sort that have benches under them and thick knots in their trunks. Trees that weep flowers in spring. There are trellises in the yard that have been strangled by roses in a sort of gothic way, and there is a part of me that thinks that this guy's parents are wasting their money, hiring Tim to update their grounds. Still, I am happy to be able to spend time here. The 'garden' at home is an eight-foot-square lawn beyond a tiny patio, on which sits a grill my mother has never figured out how to use.

The guy says, 'Well, I guess I'll leave you to it.' He walks up a path to the front door, picks a mug up off the steps, takes a sip of what I can only assume is coffee, then turns and says, 'I'm Mark, by the way.'

'Elizabeth,' I say.

I do not say 'but everyone calls me EB.' I do not register the green of his eyes, the smooth skin of his arms, the way his shorts hang a tiny bit too low on his hips. I am leaving. Soon. Leaving Alex, leaving my friends, leaving my mom and this Mark guy, too. There will be no regrets, no looking back, and certainly no weird flirty stuff with a client's son.

Still, I can't resist asking. 'What were you

doing?' I nod at the garden.

'Oh.' He shakes his head. 'It's stupid. But there's this frog that sort of hangs out here. I was going to, I don't know, relocate him?'

Not noticing the way his top lip sort of puckers when he talks and for sure when he kisses, too; not thinking at all about the fact that a guy who'll save a frog while his coffee gets cold is probably a guy worth getting to know, I say, 'I'll keep an eye out,' and he says, 'Cool.'

He disappears inside and I sit on the stoop and don't think about whether he's going to watch me work, from his window, or whether I'll see him again later today or tomorrow or the next day. I don't think about sippy-cup Alex and that burger juice or sex at all. Because things are already complicated enough. So I just sit waiting for Tim and take my phone out and pull up Lauren's latest e-mail. When I reread the bit about popcorn, I think how dull she sounds. Because looking forward to popping popcorn sounds pretty . . . sad. But then I think about all the frozen-dinner or takeout nights I spend at home alone while my mom is on dates and think about the fact that if my father hadn't left — or been gay — maybe I'd have a brother or a sister to watch movies with, and how that would be more fun than watching alone, or with Alex or Justine, and then I realize that I am actually looking forward to it, too. To popcorn and pajamas and maybe even silly pillow fights. And maybe I *am* reading into things. I decide to give her the benefit of the doubt one last time.

Lauren,
Great news about the microwave. Orville

(I Google *orville popcorn* for the right spelling.)

Redenbacher, here we come! Thank your friend Keyon for hooking us up.

Something about typing the name Keyon makes it pop out more and it occurs to me that it sounds . . . black? African-American? I realize that for no good reason I have been assuming that Lauren is white. But I can't exactly come out and ask her what ethnicity/race/ color she is, can I? And also I shouldn't assume she's black if she has a black friend. God, I'm naïve. Which is one of the reasons I wanted to go away to college in the first place. People here seem a little samey and closed-minded sometimes, especially when they hear that I have a gay dad, and I don't want to end up like that if I can help it.

36

I go back and reread her e-mail for other possible clues, then feel dumb — of course there aren't any! — so I get back to my own note.

BTW, I live in New Jersey, but by the beach. The weather here is horribly hot and humid these days. Which sounds an awful lot like Florida now that I think about it.

FIVE younger brothers and sisters? Twins! Wow. It's just me and my mom.

Gotta go!

EB

Tim still isn't there, but it's good to keep things short and sweet. And so I wait. And I go to Facebook on my phone and search for Keyons but between the small screen, the mobile app, and the sun's glare, it's too frustrating and, really, sort of pathetic of me. I decide to take a closer look at the garden to see if I can't find that frog.

SUNDAY, JUNE 30
SAN FRANCISCO

'What is it, P.J.? What? I can't understand you when you're crying!' Actually, I can't understand P.J. at all, anytime, crying or not. She's in that incoherent toddler stage of language, and though my parents seem to understand her, everything that comes out of her mouth sounds to me like a series of wheezes, glottal stops, and pig Latin. Of course, *she's* convinced she makes perfect sense and is therefore red with frustration that I can't comprehend why the food I've served her is totally unacceptable.

'Ga meh ippy geh!'

Wish I could help you with that, Peej.

It's me, P.J., Gertie, and Marcus tonight; Mom and Dad took Francis and Jack over to my grandma Gertrude's in Daly City. Her rule is no more than two children at a time in her house. Smart woman.

'Gert,' I plead, 'do you know what P.J. wants?'

Gertie shakes her head soberly as she threads one piece of macaroni onto each tine of her fork.

'Marcus?' I try.

'Ippy geh!'

'Maybe she wants ketchup.' He slides off his chair and goes to the fridge to retrieve the bottle; then before I can say 'Marcus, don't,' he's squeezed ketchup all over P.J.'s mac and cheese.

She completely loses it. Total core meltdown.

Instead of going right to her, picking her up, talking her through it — which should come naturally since I spend so much of my time doing just that — I stare at her face like I would if this were a research project. P.J., in my kitchen table lab.

My observations:

It's amazing how red she can get. Nearly purple.

I wonder if I ever howled like that, making myself so sweaty with anger that my hair stuck to the sides of my face.

How long can I do nothing before the neighbors start to think I'm torturing my siblings, or before Marcus and Gertie attempt to intervene, no doubt making it worse?

And lastly, the thought I've been avoiding:

What are my parents going to do without me?

I mean, I know it's not like I'm moving across the country, but across the Bay feels almost the same when you're like us and even going over a bridge counts as an exotic vacation. I guess I can jump on BART anytime, then grab the L car and be right here.

But it won't be the same. School is going to be hard, and I'll be working, too, as soon as I can get a job on that side of the Bay, and even if I come by on the weekends . . .

'Can I have ice cream?' Marcus asks, calmly but loudly, over P.J.'s screams.

That snaps me out of it. I take Peej out of her booster seat and carry her through the kitchen, patting her back, while she calms down.

'No.'

'Why not?'

'Because Mom said no dessert tonight. For any of us. You heard her.'

'Why not?' Marcus asks again. Despite the fact that he and Gertie are twins, the only way they're alike as far as I can tell is their love of variations on the question *why*.

P.J. takes in a big, shuddery breath. 'Ippy,' she whispers.

'Why should you have dessert every night? I practically never got dessert when I was your age.' I open the fridge in search of something P.J. might eat.

'Why not?'

'Because Mom and Dad were health nuts back then. They didn't believe in sugar.'

'Why not?'

I close the fridge door. 'Seriously, Marcus, you're not going to break me. You can ask me 'why not' a hundred more times and you still won't get dessert.'

He pushes out his lower lip and flounces out of the kitchen saying something about how it's not fair. Oh, the drama.

Thank God Gertie is being an angel tonight, slowly eating her dinner in peace, even the green beans. I want to kiss her sweet little cheek.

I need to get food into P.J. somehow, then get them all to bed. Then do my push-ups and sit-ups, update my checkbook to see where I'm at, then shoot off e-mails to Keyon, Zoe, and Ebb. What I would also love is a hot bath. However, I showered this morning and when there are eight people in the house it's a little selfish to use that much water twice in one day.

P.J. passes up everything I offer: peanut butter on crackers, baby carrots dipped in pickle relish (gross), ham-and-cheese roll-ups, all her favorites. She mashes her lips together in total refusal.

I guess she won't starve to death in the night. When I carry her into the living room I

41

find Marcus asleep in the beanbag chair. That was fast. After getting P.J. and Gertie washed up and into their beds, I carry Marcus to his and let him sleep in his clothes.

Now, for as long as I can stay awake, it's Lauren Time.

For a scary second, I feel like I'm on the verge of a P.J.-like melt-down myself. That's the thing about having a minute to think around here. Everything you haven't had time to worry about in the chaos of the day comes at you, *whoosh*. If you don't move on to the next task, ASAP, it can undo you. When people remark to my mom how tiring it must be to have all these little kids, she always laughs and says, 'I don't have *time* to think about how tired I am.'

Well, me neither. I'll have to schedule my meltdown for another day.

I open up my bank accounts online. Things are looking okay, considering. I've got about $600 in my checking and nearly $3,200 in savings, which I think of as half of that, because of the laptop situation. Dad's birthday is coming up in September and I want to get him a new gas grill for the back porch. He'll say it's too extravagant, that his little mini-grill is fine, but secretly he'll rejoice. The man does love to put meat on a fire. And the more Dad grills, the less Mom has to cook, and the fewer pans I have to scrub.

I write a short e-mail to Keyon thanking him for the microwave hookup and asking him to send my work schedule for next week so I can plan with Mom when I'll be available for kid-watching.

When I start an e-mail to Zoe, I see she's online so we chat instead. Because of my crazy life, practically our whole friendship is conducted via computers and cell phones when we're not at school, even though she lives pretty close. She'll be going off to Seattle University soon, anyway. In some ways it feels like no big deal. We've had our good years and our bad years and always wind up as solid as ever with no major drama. In other ways, it seems we've already started to say good-bye.

A lot of our conversations are about memories.

Remember the summer we were volunteer zoo docents. Remember how Aaron Goldfarb broke both our hearts in sixth grade. Remember when we thought we lost Jack at the Exploratorium. Remember when I burned off Zoe's bangs demonstrating the chemistry set my parents gave me for my twelfth birthday. (That was one of our bad years.)

Zoe ends the chat with Keep it real, LoCo!, which cracks me up.

My mood comes down again when I start

replying to Ebb's e-mail. I still feel like a major jerk about my last one to her. I'd tried to be more enthusiastic; then I messed up again.

Dear EB,
I can't believe I said Florida. Not Florida. NOT. It's no excuse, but would you believe the far-thest (furthest?) I've ever been from home is Bakersfield? That's a big, depressing city in central southern CA. But you probably know that, obviously being more acquainted with maps than I am.

Yeah, the microwave thing is kind of a funny story. I don't know Keyon super-well. His dad owns the company I work for.

That sounds a lot better than 'I work at his dad's sandwich shop.' Ebb is probably rich or at least upper middle class if she's coming to Berkeley from the other side of the country. And I know that shouldn't bother me or keep me from being myself, but I like the way 'owns the company' sounds. Like Ebb will maybe get a different impression of me than I have of myself. I mean, she's not *here*, she can't see into my life, I can kind of be whoever I want with her for now.

He works there, too. We work together.

44

Reading Dr. Seuss to P.J. has affected my writing style. I backspace over that part.

He went to my school but I didn't KNOW him know him, except in the way everyone knew him because he was this big jock and also really smart and not an ass. Wide receiver on the football team. Speaking of football, I should warn you: You have to get into it at least a little if you're coming to Berkeley. You probably know about the rivalry with Stanford. It's kind of a big deal. Personally I love it. We're 49ers fans in our house even though they can be so unreliable and have broken our hearts too many times to count.

I'm tempted to talk about the 49ers of my childhood and my fondness for Jeff Garcia, but going on a sports tangent this early in our correspondence seems like a risky move.

So do you have a summer job or anything?

Or are you independently wealthy, hangin' at the beach and sending me e-mails from your phone, while I continue to have the dumbest phone in the world and still have to text with the number pad?
Whoa. Bitter. Where'd that come from?

Okay! Have a good day tomorrow. Or whenever you get this!

Lauren

★ ★ ★

When my parents get home, I hang out in the
living room with them a little, talking quietly
so the kids don't wake up. Dad has these
almost comically huge bags under his eyes,
and somehow when he's tired his cheap
clothes and DIY haircut make me sad. Other
days, when his energy is up, I love those
things about him, his self-sacrifice, and his
willingness and ability to work as hard as he
does and still be an awesome dad.

Our family's bigness and its particular
challenges from that bigness can be endearing
sometimes. Or, I can get the kind of thoughts
I had while writing Ebb's e-mail — thoughts
about wishing I really did know people who
owned big companies, or that I had the
mental space to get the *state* of my future
roommate's residence right, or had a better
phone and more time to write to her.

The meltdown hovers.

I distract it by reenacting P.J.'s mystery
food request for my parents.

They look at each other, brows furrowed,

until finally Dad lights up. 'Oh! A dippy egg.'

'Excuse me?'

Mom laughs. 'You know. An over-easy egg. Then you cut the toast into strips and she dips it in the yolk.'

I roll my eyes. 'Wow. Don't know how I missed *that*.'

'You'll catch on one of these days,' Dad says, and Mom makes some kind of a joke, too, but I'm not sure what because I guess I fall asleep, and the next thing I know one of them is squeezing my shoulder and helping me to my room, where I proceed to conk out immediately.

SUNDAY, JUNE 30
NEW JERSEY

There is a leftover dinner plate in the fridge when I get home from a long day of working for Tim — we sometimes work on Sundays — with a note that says, *Don't wait up*. I'm too hungry to even bother to heat it, plus I don't like what happens to chicken in the microwave, the way it seems to absorb some kind of metallic, deathly taste. So I take the plate into the den, plop down on the couch, and turn on the TV. There's a *Housewives* of some kind or another on — like there always is — and I listen to a bottle-blonde braying as I chew. I'm almost afraid to check e-mail because it's been days since I e-mailed Lauren and I know she's not going to have written back yet and that I'll continue to feel freaked out the way I have all weekend, like maybe I somehow pissed her off. Like I should have let the Florida thing go for now. She'd have figured it out on her own soon enough.

Sitting here on the couch alone while my mother is on yet another date with a man I will probably never meet, I think, *This is why I'm looking forward to popcorn popping.* To maybe staying up late talking and watching bad movies. To having a roomie. Most of the time at home these days it's me, myself, and I. I thought my mother would want to try to clock in more hours with her only child this summer — and, in fact, dreaded the prospect — but the shore real estate market is actually doing okay. It seems when people are broke they still take vacations, just cheaper ones, and she's a real estate agent who does a lot of business in rentals. There are signs all over town for her agency, with her picture on them, and a part of me thinks she sees them more as ads for herself than for her professional services. They seem to work really well on both fronts — attracting clients, dates, and clients to date.

My phone is sitting on the couch next to me but I turn it over so that I can't be distracted by any of its blinking lights. I'm not sure why, but tonight I actually *want* to be alone. Just me and the real housewives. But I'm halfway through another episode before it hits me that it *is* another episode and that I somehow missed the scene where the two women who were catfighting made up even though I've been sitting here the whole time. Something must be wrong with my brain because it is thinking about things it shouldn't be. Things like Mark and the frog, neither of whom I've seen in a few days, and for some reason that has me bummed on both counts. Also, my dad and how maybe going to college in the same city where he lives is a bad idea. Because what if I can't walk down the street without checking the face of every man who passes by to see if it's him and whether he even recognizes me? What if I start stalking his art gallery like some crazy person? I close my eyes and try to picture his face and then — *bam* — it's morning.

I wake up on the couch and flip my phone over. It's blinking like crazy. There's an e-mail from Lauren and I open it — before I read Alex's or Justine's or Morgan's texts — and think, *Okay. Good. We've stabilized.*

My mother is actually making breakfast and whistling and when I walk into the kitchen, I feel the need to ask, 'Are we alone?'

'Of course we're alone,' she says. She likes to believe she never brings men home but it's not true. I used to keep count, used to daydream about one of the handsome ones becoming some sort of father figure. Back then my mom was still young enough, having had me right out of college, that I believed we could start all over again with a new father.

I'd imagine us moving out of the condo — with its split-level layout that I always thought was cool until I spent time in houses that had big living areas that seemed to draw families together almost magnetically. I imagined us someplace bright and airy, someplace that wasn't so cut up, so divisive, so annoyingly appropriate for my mother and me, who cannot seem to connect at all.

But I don't fantasize about new dads or new houses anymore. Not when it's easier to fantasize about leaving.

My mom puts a plate of scrambled eggs and some kind of fake bacon in front of me and I pick up a fork with sore hands. I spent my entire shift yesterday digging out rocks for a new garden bed alongside the house, hauling them away to the truck — even pocketing a small one whose weight had surprised me — then digging some more. I enjoyed the work at first, but when Tim said, 'Well, no one's here at the house today so we can make as much noise as we need to,' it all started to feel much more tedious. I *really* wanted to see Mark again, even if I was pretending I didn't.

More proof: I've been looking at that silly rock on my windowsill way too often.

'I don't know if it's going to work out with this one,' my mom says, and for an irrational second I bristle, thinking she's talking about Mark. Then I come to my senses and study her. Something about her body language — loose, sexy, dreamy — makes me not believe her.

I ask, 'Why not?'

She slides into the seat next to me at the table. 'I think he's married.'

'Mom!' I scold. I'm not sure whether I'm angrier that she went out with a married man or that she told me about it.

'What?' She sips her coffee. 'You're not a child anymore.'

I manage a bite. 'Still . . . '

'Well, anyway. It's too bad. I'd love me a nice hedge fund manager.' She shrugs, then says, 'I've got a showing,' and heads down the hall for the bathroom.

I check my phone — there's a new text from Alex confirming plans to meet up on the beach tonight; multiple texts from the girls asking me about a bonfire/fireworks party for the Fourth and do I want to go? — and then go back to reread Lauren's e-mail. I start typing with my thumbs.

Dear Lauren,
Football? Really? Well, I'll give it a try. My father was a big football fan, according to my mother —

52

(What I don't type: who rants, when she's drunk, about how pathetic it was that he thought being a football fan could hide the fact that he was gay, prompting me to roll my eyes and say, 'Mom, gay men can like football!')

— so maybe some appreciation has been passed down. Mostly, when I watch it, I think, Man, that's got to hurt.

I have two jobs, actually. I babysit for this super-rich family when the parents want to go out, which is often. And I work at a landscaping company, where I basically haul rocks out of more super-rich people's yards. But I am learning a lot, which is good because I'm going to be in the landscape architecture department at school. There aren't that many programs nationally. My mother's not entirely thrilled with the fact that it's on the opposite coast but what can you do? Do you know what your major is going to be?

EB

PS My father owns an art gallery in San Francisco, called The Wall. Have you ever heard of it or maybe seen it?

I think about hacking off that PS and filing it away under TMI. But it's not like I wrote, 'And if you have, do you think you could maybe, I don't know, go ask him if he'll cough up a couple grand so I don't have to take out such big loans? Thanks.'

I hit Send. What have I got to lose?

★ ★ ★

When I get to work, Tim is talking to Mark, who is holding a frog. 'We found it!' Mark says to me, grinning ear to ear. The frog — a chubby army-green specimen — pulses in his hands.

'Cool,' I say, and then he thanks Tim and walks off with the frog.

Tim finally shows me the designs for the new garden bed, including a graphed map of what's going where and also a drawing made with colored pencils. He says most people do stuff like this on computers now but he still likes to do it by hand. I've tried and failed to draw plants myself a few times; I guess I'm not artistically inclined, at least not that way. But I look at his plan and I can see how it's all going to come together, with a cool weeping false cypress as the focal point and two neat evergreens that also seem to cry or cascade. More evergreens will crawl on the ground, and they'll eventually work their way toward a brick border and then tumble over. In between, colorful grasses and flowering bushes like rhododendrons guarantee bursts of color.

'What do you think?' Tim asks, and I say, 'I love it.' Then I remember what he's told me, about how it's simply not possible for me to love everything he does. So I add, 'If it were me, I'd probably get rid of one of these and this.' I point to a hydrangea plant that seems lost and to a whole cluster of wild grasses.

'Why?'

'Too much going on. They'll stifle each other in a year or two.'

Tim smiles and says, 'Let's get going. Client's coming plant shopping.'

Great, I think. *Annoying blond mom from the window wants to get her hands dirty.* But then Mark comes out of the house and flashes a credit card in the sun and says, 'Mother's under the weather,' in a fake snooty voice. At least I hope it's fake.

'So you're in charge?' Tim asks.

'I've been given a carte blanche.'

'Fair enough.' Tim nods toward the truck. 'Let's go!'

Mark and I follow and he whispers to me, 'What's a carte blanche?'

I laugh and say, 'It means you can do

anything you want.'

'Really?' he says, all flirty, and I have to look away when I say, 'Yes, really.'

We spend the next hour, Mark and I, catching glimpses of each other between rows of shrubs and racks full of hanging plants. He mimics the poses of some garden gnomes and of statues of boys holding lanterns and I laugh and I know that Tim is sort of onto us, but I decide not to care.

When the stuff Tim has picked out is rung up, it's an awful lot of money but Mark hands over the credit card and signs for it like it's no big deal at all. 'What do your parents do?' I ask before I realize it's probably rude.

'Oh,' Mark says. 'Well, Mother works very hard at not working. She is, in fact, so anti-work that she insisted I quit my usual summer gig painting houses so that I can enjoy being a man of leisure this summer, possibly for the last time in my life.'

'Sounds dramatic,' I say as we follow Tim to the truck.

'Yes,' he says, 'and terribly boring. I've read like twenty novels so far this summer. Not that reading is boring. I mean, I love to read, but you get my point.'

'Sure.'

He looks me right in the eye, as if to confirm that I really got the point.

Noted, I try to say with my eyes. *Loves to read*.

Then he says, 'And Dear Old Dad is a money manager. You know, a Wall Street type.'

Of course he is, I think. Half of Tim's clients are.

'What about yours?' Mark asks me, and I say, 'My mother's a real estate agent — you've no doubt seen her many, many signs around town — and my father owns an art gallery in San Francisco.' I add, 'They're not together.' Then feel like I have to say, 'He's gay.'

For a second it looks like Mark thinks I'm joking but then I guess he sees it in my face that I'm not. He says, 'He's probably *way* more fun to hang out with than my dad.'

I shrug and say, 'Wouldn't know.'

I should have totally deleted that PS.

MONDAY, JULY 8
SAN FRANCISCO

I don't know what a panic attack is, technically, *medically* speaking, but I think I have something like one on Monday night. I'm lying there in my bed listening to P.J. softly breathing, and Gertie not-so-softly snoring, and there's a crushing feeling, a sort of pressing, on my chest and neck. It comes from nowhere. I mean in the sense that when it starts I'm not having consciously anxious thoughts.

About, for instance, moving out. The nights ahead of me during which I will not be kept awake by Gertie's snores. The days of not having to do five thousand dishes. How my clothes won't smell like Francis spit-up.

How I won't be taking my familiar bus to Galileo come fall, or seeing Zoe waiting for me there in the courtyard.

How, considering I'm only going across the Bay, my life is about to change in more ways than I can imagine.

Leaving home for freshman year was never my plan. I thought I'd take care of some

58

gen-eds at State and live with my parents and save money. The scholarship came into the picture so suddenly and now everything is . . .

I get out of bed because I actually feel like I might let out a little scream and I don't want to scare the kids. The living room is lit up by the streetlamps, and I can hear the rumbling of a late L car going by. Sometimes, when I have to get up in the night to pee and I pass by the living room, I'll stand there for a minute. And I'll look at it and have this sensation of: contentment, peace, safety. Home.

That's the feeling I want now. So I stand and look. But pretty soon I have to grab a pillow off the couch and sort of bite it, stuff it in my mouth. I'm not exactly crying, but I'm not exactly *not* crying.

How can I leave?

It's not a question with a rational answer. Because, of course, I have to leave and I'm going to leave. *It's happening, Lauren. Grow up. It's twenty-five miles.* I press my face into the pillow awhile and try to take better breaths. Eventually, I start to calm down, but not enough to sleep.

I creep back to the room to grab my laptop and distract myself online.

There's an e-mail from Keyon. The subject is spud head. The e-mail reads:

You know that Potato Head you got at the GW? I'm sitting here watching channel 9 w/ my ma and someone is on there w/ a potato just like it and it's worth like 65 bucks.

He includes a bunch of links that go to toy collector sites, where Mr. Potato Head, among other things, is highly prized.

I write him back.

Neither Mrs. nor Mr. Potato Head is for sale. Interesting, though. Especially that you watch Antiques Roadshow. 'With your ma.' You know you love it. Don't worry, I won't tell. See you tomorrow.

That feels good. Better, anyway, than pacing the floor with a pillow in my mouth.

Keyon and I have kind of had this e-mail thing going ever since our microwave trip. At first he was trying to text me all the time and finally I was like, look, I'm on the lowest text-per-month plan there is and also I have to text on the number pad and am awful at it, and gave him my e-mail address. He said, 'I can e-mail from my phone, so all the same to me.'

It's weird but also fun. Weird because when we're at work it's like the e-mails don't exist; we're all about sandwiches and salads and maybe some commiserating about difficult customers. Fun because between work and the kids and getting time in the chem lab when I could, I spent my entire senior year with virtually no interesting contact with cute boys. And I have missed it.

Working through my accumulated e-mail has a calming effect. It's a fairly mundane task, given that so few real people write to me.

There is one from Zoe — about some Galileo grads party on Saturday night. She always knows these things I don't, probably through Twitter or whatever she's always checking on her phone. I almost missed the senior trip because the whole event was planned on Facebook and I'm not on it. E-mail, IM, and research are about my limit. Meanwhile, Zoe's made all these short films she puts on YouTube and can text faster than she can type.

I can't help but think our friendship has suffered. When she and her boyfriend from all of junior year, Buck, broke up, I found out two days after the rest of the school. 'Didn't you see my tweet about it?' Zoe asked me, in tears. And I know she's hurt that I don't watch all her videos, which I've heard around school are pretty good. I've known her so long and she's always done creative stuff, and maybe I take it for granted. She says she understands, but, you know, the videos mean a lot to her and I'd be hurt, too. Maybe I can block out some time soon to catch up.

I do hope Ebb isn't one of those people who are constantly attached to their phones, texting from two feet away.

I meant to reply to her last e-mail sooner, but I had to go on a Costco run with my mom, which involved waiting for new tires for the van. While we waited, we played 'Mother May I' with the kids in a deserted office supplies aisle. When that got boring for them, we wandered around. All this summer stuff was out, including swimsuits, and there was one I thought would look great on Mom. I held it out to her.

'Look at this,' I said. 'It's cute, it's your color, *and* it would hide your 'problem areas.''

She laughed, her fingers grasped in Francis's little hands while he looked out from the front-facing baby carrier that was strapped onto her. 'That will be perfect for all the beach vacations I'll be able to take in about twenty years.'

And I don't know, for some reason that made me feel really bad. Like depressed. I love my little brothers and sisters. It's not that. But lately I have this constant awareness of what my parents, what all of us, have given up to have them, and how much more road there is ahead. I mean, Francis isn't even walking yet! Sometimes it feels like it will never end, ever, and though I can see a light at the end of the tunnel for *me*, and it's close, I can't see it for my parents.

I feel sad about them getting old. Imagining them old before Francis even starts high school. Dad never getting to retire. Mom going back to work when Francis starts preschool. It's so . . . relentless. Life, I mean.

Anyway.

I can't think about that right now, not more than I already have.

So after the Costco day, I went into the insurance office at seven in the morning to do some filing before lunch at the sandwich shop, where Keyon excitedly told me about his big Goodwill moneymaking plan. Mikey said he'd try to text Keyon when something good gets put out — or when it comes into the donation room, if he notices. 'Collectibles,' Keyon said. 'You could help me figure out what's worth anything, then we could sell it online.'

'Is that, like, *okay* to do?'

'Yeah,' he said with an emphatic nod. 'I got it all worked out with Mikey so it's straight up. If he notices good shit, he notices it. If we get there in time we get there in time. If not . . . ' He shrugs. 'And we pay the Goodwill price. Not like we get it for free.' He put his palm on his chest. 'Hey, it's me. I'm not about to take from the needy, right?'

He's so cute, I thought.

Then a customer interrupted us, and then it was the weekend.

Because the weekdays are so insane, weekends are sacred in our family. We basically spend the whole thing in some version of togetherness, and there's lots of cooking and eating and being outdoors and watching movies and bending rules about bedtimes and sugar.

No Internet on the weekends. Dad even turns his BlackBerry off and puts it in a drawer.

Zoe would die.

And this is why I don't have a huge circle of friends. Between school, work, and family, when would I see anyone? Never, that's when. If Ebb expects that I'm going to be this fun roommate who's always up for partying and going out to coffee and wandering Telegraph Avenue, she's going to be disappointed.

She's also going to be disappointed about the art gallery thing. Me and art do not mix, and this is what has kept my fingers hovering over the keyboard with no action for the last ten minutes.

Here's me looking at art: 'Oh.' Or 'What's it supposed to be?' or 'Gertie could paint that.' But I don't want to sound like a rube and I can already tell Ebb thinks of me as this hip San Franciscan, while she actually seems more authentically Bay Area-ish than me. Art, landscaping, not into sports. Maybe she's hairy-legged with smelly dreadlocks, and smokes pot. Maybe she'll be protesting at People's Park every weekend while eating organic sprouts. Which is *fine*, but really different from me.

An image of her and her landscaping-major buddies setting up a hydroponic pot-growing system in our dorm closet makes me shudder.

I hate feeling so negative.

This is an exciting time in my life. Right? Why do I sort of want the clock to stop?

I reread her e-mail and I guess I'm relieved to hear that, like me, she has two jobs. It makes me feel slightly less like the Sad Working Poor, or at least that having more than one job at our age isn't completely weird.

I end up writing to her about Zoe, because I need to write *something*, and compared to my family stuff and the whole why-can't-I-breathe thing it's a neutral topic.

EB:

I didn't know landscape architecture was a major. Neat. I'm sure if Berkeley has a program in it, it's good. Congrats on getting in. I'm a biochemistry major, hoping to go into the graduate comparative biochem program. It's really boring to talk about but the main thing is that there aren't very many women in the program, and that helped me get a pretty big scholarship. Berkeley was the opposite of my 'safety school.' More like a wish on a Magic 8 Ball. I assumed I'd be going to SF State and living at home for a while, then my teacher made me promise to apply for the scholarship and trust me, NO ONE was more shocked than me when I got it.

Question in two parts:

A. Do you have a best friend?

B. If yes, do you think your relationship is going to change now that you're leaving each other behind for college?

C. I guess there's a C, too, which is, do you guys TALK about it?

My best friend, Zoe, and I have basically been pretending nothing's going to change. Maybe it won't in ways that matter in the long run. But it does matter, right now. I mean if you were married and you knew you were suddenly going to have a four-year break in your marriage, that would CHANGE THINGS. Then again, she's my friend, not my wife. Also, change doesn't have to = bad. (I have been telling myself that so much lately!)

There's this party on Saturday with kids from our high school and she wants to go, and wants me to go with her. I don't know. I just feel like high school is over, and I'm probably never going to see those people again (other than Zoe), and what's the point?

If the answer to A is no, disregard B and C.

I bet you didn't expect an essay question. Surprise!

You don't have to answer at all if you don't want, obviously.

— Lauren

THURSDAY, JULY 11
NEW JERSEY

I had sort of given up on Lauren, so when her e-mail arrived *eight stinking days* after I last e-mailed her, I read it, closed it, and decided that two could play at that game. *Just watch me!* Why am I always in such a hurry to respond to her e-mails anyway? So now that a couple of days have passed I think about writing back but, ironically, can't figure out how to explain why it's taken me so long. I decide to write later because I need to shower and get dressed and eat breakfast and head to work, where I'll be finishing up the last of the new flower beds in Mark's garden.

The frustrating thing is that this latest e-mail from her is the first one that I actually *really* want to respond to, the only one with any meat on it. Because the best friend stuff heated up with Justine big-time after she got drunk at that July Fourth bonfire party last weekend. We fought and haven't spoken since and it's highlighted everything that has been feeling off about our friendship these past few weeks, maybe even months.

I want to write back my answer to A.

I'm not sure anymore.

And then my answer to B.

For a while I'd been hoping I'd come home from college for holidays and pick up right where I left off with my friends, but now I'm hoping that maybe when I come home it'll feel more like it used to. Like we'll be so excited to see each other after being apart that we'll forget that the end of high school and this summer were both sort of weird between us. But I don't know. Most of my friends are staying local for college so it seems likely they'll still be in touch more than I will be with any of them.

And (C), no, we don't talk about it. Lately my friends and I don't talk about anything I find interesting. I'm not sure when that started. Maybe when we got boyfriends and started spending all our time together with them, too? But my two besties — Justine and Morgan — seem to find each other wildly entertaining and interesting. Not sure when that started, either.

But I should wait. Meaning, I should make *Lauren* wait more than a measly three days.

Shouldn't I?

At the party, everyone but me got annoyingly drunk. And all any of them wanted to talk about (to me, anyway) was sex. Justine was thinking of doing it with Danny that night, and Morgan and Mitch, who've already done it, kept talking about how it wasn't a big deal. ('That's what I've been trying to tell her!' Danny said.) A few times, I pulled Justine aside and told her it wasn't a good idea, since she was drunk and shouldn't be drunk the first time. And she said maybe she'd wait until the night of her birthday party because that would make it even more meaningful and I said not if she was drunk then, too, and she called me a buzz kill. Then Alex and I took a walk down the beach and he started coming on way too strong with his hands and mouth, like in the limo after prom all over again. I pushed him away and he stormed off and then when I told Justine about it, she muttered something about me being a prude.

Nice.

I ended up sitting by the bonfire, holding a beer I wasn't even drinking, and no one even seemed to notice or care that I was all alone. They just kept drinking and talking and shouting and the whole thing made me wonder what the point of parties was anyway.

I started thinking about stuff my mom and I used to do before I was old enough to even go to parties on my own and I suddenly missed those nights when we'd do each other's nails and hair, and watch dumb movies, and the nights when we'd pitch a tent in our pathetic little yard and look at stars and eat nothing but cookies for dinner.

We *did* used to do that. *Didn't we?*

And then I realized the beer I was holding was warm, so I put it down, twisting it into the sand, and got up and walked home.

★ ★ ★

I'm opening a bag of mulch on one side of the yard while Tim works on the other when Mark comes over. He waves a hand in front of his nose and says, 'Excu-use you.'

It takes me a minute to realize he's talking about the mulch, which comes out of the bag moist and ripe and stinky. 'What are you, five years old?' I ask.

He smiles and says, 'So you're done here, huh?'

The mulch is warm in my hands and it feels almost alive. 'Pretty much.'

Today's our last day — and I'm sort of sad about it though I don't want to admit why. Even if Alex and I are broken up — and I'm not sure we are — I wouldn't want to move right on to some other guy.

Not like my mom.

'It looks good.' Mark stands back and nods. 'I think Froggy will be very happy here.'

I crinkle my nose. 'Froggy?'

'You got a problem with that?' He crosses his arms at his chest defiantly.

'Just not especially creative is all.'

He shrugs and says, 'Hey, so listen. These buddies of mine, they have this house on the bay in Toms River and their parents are out of town and I know it sounds really B-movie or something but they're having a party.'

I stiffen, then force myself to relax, and I dump out more mulch without looking up at him.

'The house is actually awesome and they do all the requisite party things — you know, Jell-O shots, skinny-dipping — so that makes for some pretty spectacular people-watching.'

The mulch really does smell bad.

'I was wondering if you'd want to, I don't know, come along?'

I look up at him, totally prepared to say something like 'I have a boyfriend' or 'I don't think that's a good idea' or 'I have to work' — which makes no sense since I don't even know when the party *is* yet. But he's taken off his sunglasses and he has this look in his eyes that's electric and sweet. So I don't say any of those things.

'When is it?' I ask, and he says, 'Tonight.'

'A Thursday night?'

He shrugs. 'That's how they roll.'

Now I get the chance to say 'I have to work,' because it's true. I'm babysitting until nine because the Schroeders are going out on some happy hour boat ride with friends.

Mark looks more puzzled than disappointed. 'You do landscaping at *night*?'

'No,' I say. 'Babysitting. Until nine or so.'

'Well, this doesn't start until like nine, anyway. So I can pick you up and head over then.'

'Okay,' I say. 'If you're sure.'

Because I am not.

'I'm sure,' he says. 'Tell me where to get you and I'll be there.'

I give him the address, and he says, 'Excellent.'

And then he drifts off and we finish his garden and there's no point denying that this invitation takes the edge off the sadness.

I almost e-mail Lauren a million times that day — This cute new guy asked me to a party! I said yes! Even though I totally shouldn't have! — but for some reason I don't. Which I know probably doesn't bode well for our friendship — or roommateship — if I'm already playing games by making her wait, but there you have it.

★ ★ ★

Babysitting is a horror show. Vivian is in the worst mood possible, constantly chewing on her hand, and just looking at her makes my teeth hurt. She won't let me put her down so I don't have any time at all to fix my hair or do my makeup or eat or anything. Finally, she falls asleep on my lap in the glider in her room and I'm able to transfer her into her crib. But her parents come home five minutes later and Mark is already waiting, his car idling in front of the house.

'Your mother know about this?' Mrs. Schroeder asks.

'Yes,' I lie.

My mother is out on another date with the man she thinks is married. I'm not supposed to know that but I do. I figure that makes us a little bit even.

When I get to the car, a guy gets out of the passenger seat. 'Mark told me you've got shotgun,' he says, and then he shakes my hand and adds, 'I'm Vic.'

'Elizabeth,' I say, leaving out EB again; then we both climb in.

Mark says, 'Hey,' and glances in his

rearview mirror. 'That's Emily.'

I turn to the girl in the backseat, with her super-tight purple tank dress and black nail polish, and think I couldn't look more boring in my denim skirt and black tank top if I tried. 'Hey,' I say, and she says, 'We better motor, Mark. We're already way late.'

Whatever, I think. *Bitch*.

Why are so many people so hard to get to know? And what if Lauren dresses like that?

Mark pulls out into the street and we drive for a while — windows down and wind whipping through the car over the sounds of a song I've never heard before. It's one of those songs that's sort of sad but also full of something like promise and I almost feel a lump in my throat. My phone buzzes and I look down and see a text from Justine that says, Sorry about the other night. Hope ur on ur way?

Her birthday party. Which I completely blanked on when agreeing to babysit, and when saying yes to Mark.

There's nothing I can say in a text that will improve this situation and anyway I don't feel like dealing, not with this song playing and doing strange things to my heart.

I look over at Mark and think about Alex's hot breath on my ear, and my mom on her date with some random married guy, and

75

Justine thinking about losing it after her party, and I wish I'd written back to Lauren already so that I'd have an e-mail to look forward to — something that involves the future and not the past — even if it takes weeks or months. Then Mark smiles at me and I wonder if he could've been the future, too, if I weren't leaving.

We wind through some woods after we get off the highway, then pull off onto a gravel road and park. Behind a bunch of cars all facing this one house, the bay is a big black void. Mark gets out of the car and Vic and Emily do, too, but I find my phone and start typing.

> Sorry for not writing back sooner. I had a huge fight with my best friend last weekend, mostly because she seems to be turning into this lush who is hell-bent on losing her virginity. I am out right now with this guy, and we're at this big party with some of his friends and I have no idea what I've gotten myself into. Did you go to that party? Wait. It's this weekend. Are you going? If so, have fun! More soon.
>
> EB

Mark is at my window, knocking with his index finger, and when I look up from my phone he says, 'You coming?'

'Yeah,' I say, opening the door. 'Sorry.' And as I follow him up the front lawn to the house, I hit Send and put my phone away. 'I've been e-mailing with my roommate for fall,' I say.

'Yeah? What's she like?'

'I don't know yet,' I say. 'It's weird. You know. E-mail.'

'Yeah. I think I got an e-mail about mine but I haven't reached out. You know. Guys.'

I smile. 'Yeah.' After a pause I ask, 'Where are you going?'

'Northwestern,' he says. 'In Chicago?'

'Yeah,' I say. 'I know it.' It's a good school; I'm impressed.

'My older brother just graduated from there and he got a job so he's staying in Chicago.' He nods excitedly. 'I think being near him again could be cool.'

'That's awesome,' I say, wishing for a second that I were also moving toward a sibling and not an estranged parent.

He turns and looks at me a little bit like he's afraid to say what he's going to say; then he asks, 'Do you want a beer?'

And the thing is, I do. I want to drink a beer and feel loose and free and not have it go warm in my hands while I sit by a bonfire alone. I nod and say, 'I would love one.'

'Good.' He seems to relax a little around the shoulders. 'Me too.'

Inside, the house is crowded, smoky, loud — everything I usually hate — but it all feels a little exciting. Especially when Mark looks back and takes my hand and says, 'Follow me,' and leads me through the crowd to a cooler full of beer, where he doesn't drop my hand as he grabs two bottles by the neck. He leads me out the other side of the house, and there is something about his pulling me forward that feels so incredible. Because I wish that I were being guided a bit more through life, that I didn't always feel as if I were drifting, like an untied balloon that nobody even realized was slipping away.

We end up on a big deck that overlooks the bay and the dock, where I can see some pasty bodies, clearly naked, doing repeated cannonballs and jackknives and generally whooping it up.

'This isn't my usual scene,' Mark says, 'for the record.' He opens one of the beers and holds it out to me, and my hand is warm from his touch.

'No?' I take the beer. 'What is?'

'Good question,' he says; then he takes a swig of beer and I do the same and already I don't want the night to end.

MONDAY, JULY 15
SAN FRANCISCO

I don't want to go to work.

I really and deeply do *not* want to go to work.

But I have to. I can't avoid Keyon forever.

And of course I need the money and would never leave Key and his dad, Joe, in the lurch with no notice, et cetera whatever, but if I could get away with faking a broken arm and not have it be an obvious avoidance tactic, I would.

It's muggy out, for San Francisco, and the ride downtown on the L Taraval (aka the Hell Taraval) is gross. When I catch a glimpse of my reflection in the window, I feel like I'm gross, too. My hair isn't growing out its last cheap cut very gracefully and is basically a frizz ball. The dark-red polish I put on for the party is already chipping. I didn't have time to shave my legs this morning, or yesterday morning, or the morning before that, and the hairs prickle against my jeans.

Mostly I feel gross inside.

* ★ ★

On the train, I narrate to Ebb in my head . . .

So, yeah, I went to the party. There were way too many people packed into Yasmin Adibi's little Bernal Heights house, music bumping, and within like five minutes of getting there I already had a headache. Zoe drove but immediately peeled off when she saw Melissa Birch, one of her arty friends who graduated last year. 'Mel!' she screamed (when I say 'screamed' I mean it), and that's basically the last I saw of her until we left.

It felt like half an hour before I squeezed through the crowd and made it to the back door so I could escape into the yard. Typical San Francisco summer night weather — cool and foggy, enough to keep the outdoor crowd pretty thin, which, you know, fine by me.

I found a rusty lawn chair away from the cluster of smokers, and sat on that, and looked up to the sky and, I don't know, just felt so lost all of a sudden. Okay, not all of a *sudden* sudden, because I'd felt that way most of the day. We went to Trader Joe's — yes, the whole family at once, it's what we do on Saturdays, and I'm sure it's a frightening sight for the other customers — and P.J. opened a bag of chili-lime pistachios (have you had those? they're yumm-eee) and got them all over the floor. I picked them up while this young, hip couple stepped over the whole scene, looking at each other like 'And this is the problem with our country.' (Do you know that look I'm talking about? It's pretty common around here. I don't know about in NJ.)

And I said to my mom, 'I don't understand why we all have to come. Why can't *you* do it, like a regular mom? Or send me? Or Dad? It's groceries. Why does it have to be this giant ordeal?'

Ebb, do I have to tell you the look on her face? Like: Ouch. 'Ordeal?'

'Yes,' said I. 'It's an ordeal.'

'Funny, I've been thinking of it as a tradition. One you won't be a part of soon.'

And she pushed her cart away from me.

Well, so this was my state of mind at the party. Then I beat myself up about it, you know, like thinking, *What's wrong with you, Lauren, that you can't even have fun at a party?*

And that is the moment Keyon appeared in the yard and sat on a stump next to my chair. (It really did feel like he 'appeared' more than 'arrived.') 'I didn't know you were coming to this thing.'

'I didn't know *you* were.'

He shrugged. Keyon looks very cool when

he shrugs, by the way. Like he can take or leave the whole world. Not like when I shrug and probably look like an indecisive flake. 'I was gonna. Mention it, you know, but then I was like . . . ' He looked at me and shrugged again.

I finished his thought. 'But then you were like, what if Lauren isn't invited and it's all awkward?'

'Right,' he said, putting his finger against the side of his nose, something his dad does all the time. 'You want me to get you a drink? Yas is fully equipped. She's showing Zoe and Mel how to make martinis.'

'Great. I guess I'm driving us home.'

He got up off the stump and said, 'I'm gonna get something. I can bring you a soda?'

'Water would be awesome.'

When he came back with water for me and beer for him, he sat down and asked me if I ever drink.

And Ebb, I'll tell you what I told him and I hope you don't think I'm the boringest person in the world. It's not like I have anything against drinking. But I promised my parents I wouldn't until I was twenty-one. In the interest of being a law-abiding citizen.

Keyon got it. 'And setting a good example for . . . however many you got. Brothers and sisters and whatnot.' He pulled the tab off his beer and threw it into the bushes. Then he stared out at nothing and said, 'That's kinda low class, huh?' and got up and went into the bushes, like *into* them, until all I could see were his legs. When he came back out he said, 'I can't find it.'

And he smiled this sheepish smile that reminded me of Jack, when he's in trouble but not bad trouble, and I'm not sure, but my heart or stomach sort of did something, and I think that was the moment. Which led to the next moment, and the next one, and I'm sorry if I'm being unnecessarily suspenseful but I'm still figuring out what happened and telling it carefully helps.

He came back to the stump and stretched his long legs out in front of him and rubbed a smudge off the side of his sneaker. 'So I'm serious about selling that collectible stuff online.' (*Long story*, I add to my imaginary Ebb letter.) 'Are you in?'

'What exactly would my role be?' I was feigning interest, sort of, to keep him there.

'Same as me. Finding shit. Pricing shit. Selling shit. Mailing shit.'

'Sounds . . . unsanitary.' (This is me, making a joke. I know.) 'Yeah, I'm in.' Why not? More time to hang out with him, and maybe earn some pocket money.

'Keyon!' someone yelled from behind us,

from the smoker crowd. 'Key, come over here and light it up.'

He lifted his beer. 'Nah, I'm good.'

'It's okay,' I said, shoving my hands deeper into my jacket pockets. 'You don't have to sit here and keep me company. I fully realize I'm no fun right now.'

'Yeah, what's up with that?'

The way he said it was nice, though. It's hard to describe. Caring, I guess.

I shook my head. 'Change.' Then before I could stop myself, I was crying. Like the quivering chin and tears spilling over and my nose filling so I had to keep sniffling. 'It's just . . . hard.'

'Oh, yeah, well. Change.' I wasn't looking at him right then, but I sensed him swig his beer and heard him clear his throat. 'Who needs that shit.'

I wanted to be able to laugh, Ebb. I wanted to shrug it off, cool like him, and then go in and watch Zoe shake up a martini. But the weight of it was on me. The more I cried, the sadder I felt about leaving. I kept picturing Jack and his sly little smile. That made me cry harder, and pretty soon, there I am, holding my jacket sleeves up to my face like the kind of drama-at-party girl I can't stand, and rocking back and forth and wishing to hell I were home in bed.

And I *know* it's not like I'm going to the other side of the world. I *know* that. So what's wrong with me? If I can't handle this, what's going to happen if I leave the state for grad school? Or get married or join the circus or whatever?

'Hey,' Keyon said softly. 'It's okay. I mean, don't, like, lose it.'

He wasn't saying it in a guy-freaking-out-in-the-face-of-emotions way. 'You do this now and all these nosy punks are going to come over and ask what's wrong, and you don't want that, do you?'

No, I didn't.

Still, I cried harder.

'For real, Lo. Keep it together.'

He was being so *nice*, the way he was saying it. Truly looking out for me. Truly knowing me and that I would hate that kind of attention. His voice was tender. And he came around and knelt in front of me and put one big hand on each of my knees and kept saying, 'Keep it together. There you go. Take a breath now.'

The way it worked was: My arm sort of reached out to his shoulder and rested there. Then my other arm did the same. On their own they did this. And my hands came together on the back of his neck. So he couldn't get away if he wanted to. The angle kind of forced us to lean closer so he wouldn't fall over. Our faces were like half an inch apart.

What can you do, Ebb, once you're in that position, but kiss?

It's a law of physics or something.

Here's the thing, though. It wasn't what I would call romantic. It was more kind of . . . lusty. Which is fine, I don't judge it. Sometimes you want to make out with someone, anyone, the way you crave a salty snack. But your salty-snack category of kissers should definitely not be your friends and/or coworkers . . .

The L lurches to a stop at Montgomery Street, interrupting my fantasy e-mail. I come up out of the Muni station and nearly get run over by a bike messenger, then am promptly told by a homeless guy that I have a nice ass and can I spare some change? I give him two quarters and feel dirty doing it, like I rewarded someone for sexual harassment.

This day is really shaping up.

And now, I have to face the music that is my injudicious kiss.

Keyon is pouring mustard into the sandwich station tray when I walk in. 'Hey,' he says, barely looking up.

'Hey.' I pass him, go to the back, put my messenger bag in my cubby, and grab my apron. When I get to the counter I ask how we are on tomatoes.

'We could probably slice another case before rush.'

'On it.' I give him a super-dorky thumbs-up and imagine him having the same regretful thoughts I am.

Except I'm not really that regretful.

★ ★ ★

Late that night, with two fresh paper cuts incurred during the hour of filing I did at the insurance company after closing the sandwich shop, I type out a slightly condensed version of the party story to Ebb. I even write a little bit about Keyon being black and how this city is pretty diverse but he was my first nonwhite kiss. Not that I have a zillion kisses to compare it to. Only seven. Maybe eight? And that's counting all the fifth- and sixth-grade mashed-lip quickies. Zero in recent memory.

Rankings-wise, Keyon's was pretty good, I have to say. Pretty damn good. Maybe that's reflective of my poor control group but . . . no. Scientifically and objectively, Keyon knows how to kiss a girl. Me.

Then I read it all over and think I sound like an overdramatic idiot, and possibly racist. What if she's not white and something I say offends her and she opens some kind of discrimination case against me and I become the most hated student in Berkeley?

So I delete and start over.

Hey EB,

Fighting with friends is the worst. I'd rather put up with almost anything than fight. Suffer in silence, that's my motto!

Kidding. Sort of. Zoe and I don't really fight. We bicker and annoy each other and give each other 'space.' Then it's cool.

I did go to the party. Too many people and I'm not a fan of huge crowds. Nothing really to report except Zoe overdid the martinis and I had to drive us home and I'm not great with a stick shift. Maybe we can get my best friend and your best friend together to drink (or go to rehab).

So the party. I probably should have stayed home and gotten some sleep. I can always use more sleep. Wow, I sound old. Sorry! I guess I'm feeling kinda . . . ugh-ish. Sorry again. Downerville! Depression Central! Haha! Okay, sorrrrrry. Sorry for saying sorry over and over.

Attached with this is a link to a song that sort of cheers me up when I'm feeling this way.

The video is stupid. (I mean why does it have to be a video inside a video? Why can't it just be a video?) But the song is pretty good. Zoe likes this band ever since seeing some documentary about them and she thinks the singer guy is hot. Or he was whenever they recorded this. He's probably like a hundred now.

Anyway it's a good song if you're in a fight with your friend. But I hope it's over soon. Your fight, I mean.

Hope work is going well and all that.

— Lauren

TUESDAY, JULY 16
NEW JERSEY

Something about Lauren's e-mail, which I wake up to, makes me wish there were no time difference and that we already knew each other so that I could pick up the phone and call her. Because I click the link and see that it's a video for 'We Used to Be Friends' by the Dandy Warhols — which was the *Veronica Mars* theme song — and I suddenly want to know if she ever saw the show, which my mom and I once watched like crazy people over the course of a long, rainy weekend. Also, Lauren's starting to sound sort of, I don't know, nice? And thoughtful. Not like do-nice-things-for-you thoughtful — I don't see her baking me cookies or anything — but meaning, she is *full of thought*. I like people who think. Who examine things from all the angles. That's probably why she's so good at science.

My mother is clearly not a great thinker, as evidenced by the fact that there is a man in the kitchen with her. He is having 'a quick one' — and thankfully he's referring to a cup of coffee — before catching his 'flight home . . . *if you know what I mean.*'

I'm overhearing this all from my perch at the top of the stairs, where I have so far been unsuccessful at getting a look at him, this married man who says 'I hope to' when my mother flirtily says, 'And do you travel for work a lot?'

I try to picture his wife, his family if he has one, and imagine them thinking that he is on an airplane, or in some dreary Marriott somewhere, when really he is here. In my house. Having spent the night. With my pathetic mother, who is *charmed* by the fact that he's running around with her behind another woman's back. I get to wondering what kind of clueless wife wouldn't know that her husband was having an affair. Maybe one who had something of her own going on? Would that make what my mother was doing any less morally reprehensible? And am I doomed to be some kind of cheating soul, too, because I was spawned from two cheaters? (Yes, supposedly my dad cheated on my mom. 'With a man!' she always says, like that makes it worse, but I don't really think it does. Betrayal is betrayal.)

I get the sense that these are questions that someone like Lauren might actually understand, might even ponder along with me.

I go back to my room to hide until he's gone. Her, too.

★ ★ ★

I spend most of the week hiding, really. From my mother. From Justine, and Alex, and the rest of the six-pack. Even from Tim, who has me doing a bunch of nursery runs and solo check-ins on gardens we did last summer. I like seeing how a garden has started to grow into itself after a full cycle of seasons, seeing the way plants start to find their own way toward the sun and to mingle with each other, or not.

Friday I have no choice but to go back to Mark's house, on Tim's orders, to see how the gardens are faring, and whether the mulch borders got muddied at all by a big rain we had. I've been avoiding Mark, too. Which is all tied up in why I'm also avoiding answering Lauren's e-mail. It's not like she even asked how the party was; I just feel like I should tell her about it, and I don't want to lie by omission. But what is she going to think of me if I tell her that I kissed a guy I barely know even though I already have a boyfriend? Did I even tell her I have a boyfriend? What does it mean if I didn't?

And I mean, I *really* kissed him. And it was

92

so lovely and intense that just thinking about it again makes me a little woozy.

He's home, of course. And when I'm pulling dead leaves off a few annuals on the border of the garden — mostly pansies, with their weirdly sad sort of smiley faces — he comes right over and says, 'Hey.'

I look up and then stand and my knees feel weak.

'Where've you been?' He has sunglasses on so I can't really read him. 'I texted you. Multiple times this week.'

'Oh.' I push some hair out of my face and say, 'Yeah, I saw those.'

I haven't stopped looking at them, in fact. One said, That was nice. Another said, Better than nice. The last two were Can I see you again? and If so, when?

He laughs. 'Oh, you did, did you?'

I laugh, too, because it's honestly kind of funny how bad I am at this.

'So you saw them.' He nods fake-seriously. 'That's good. 'Cause you know it's not like you're supposed to, I don't know, text back or anything. That would be crazy.' He waves his hands in a gesture to mean crazy, palms out and shaking. Then he's smiling and waiting.

'I'm sorry,' I say, and I'm about to add, 'I have a boyfriend.' But then a car pulls into the driveway, the same sort of car that was parked in my driveway earlier that morning, and Mark's dad gets out and Mark says, 'I thought your flight got in later,' and the dad says, 'Caught an earlier one but have to drive down to Philly for an overnight,' and it all clicks.

His voice in my kitchen that morning.

Money manager. Hedge fund manager. Wall Street type.

Then his father says, 'Hi, are you a friend of Mark's?' and I nod and he gives me a small wave. I can't be sure I'm breathing.

Mark turns back to me when his father goes inside and says, 'I had fun the other night and I think you did, too.'

He's right. I did. I had more fun with him than maybe I've ever had with anyone. And it didn't have anything to do with the party or even the kissing. After realizing we weren't mingling or trying to, we went down to the bay and found two Adirondack chairs and talked about who our friends were, maybe trying to find people in common but not coming up with any, then moved on to things like the dumbest movies we'd ever seen or the world's most overrated songs. For what felt like hours, we played this game where we thought up funny last words, like 'These wild berries are absolutely delicious' or 'I can totally jump over to that building.' Then after that, we were quiet together, skipping stones on the bay. That was when he turned to me out of nowhere and put his arms around me and kissed me and I felt, for once, like everything was going to be okay. More than okay, even. Maybe actually good. But none of that matters anymore. His dad and my mom made sure of that.

'I want to see you again.' Mark's smile is so easy and real that it hurts to look at. 'I mean, I know I'm seeing you right now, but I mean, I want to *see* you, see you.'

'I have a boyfriend,' I say.

He jolts like I've kicked him in the gut and then he tilts his head and says, 'I don't understand.'

And I say, 'My life is sort of a mess right now. I had *too much* fun the other night. I'm sorry,' and walk toward my car.

'Elizabeth,' he calls out after me, and, for a second, I regret not making him call me EB because it all sounds so dramatic and serious now. Then even though I shouldn't — because what's the point — I turn.

He says, 'I can wait.'

'For what?' I'm definitely going to cry.

'For you.' He starts to back away and he still looks sort of confused and wounded and like he's trying to shake the feeling off. His voice is softer, more tentative, when he says, 'For you to sort out the mess.'

★ ★ ★

I only drive a block before I pull over and have a good cry. I want to call my mother and scream at her. I want to call Justine and apologize about missing her birthday and tell her the whole messy story, but we still haven't talked and, well, I'm still miffed about the prude comment. I wish, again, that I could call Lauren and let it all out but what would she think of *this*? Mostly, I want to turn around and drive back to Mark's house and tell *him* about the mess — tell him he's in it, too — but then he wouldn't ever want to be with me anyway, and how could he? And all of this thinking about who to tell what, makes me wish there were *one person* I could share everything — all of me, all my shit — with and that I weren't stuck trying to cobble together some kind of (groan) 'support system' out of this bunch of random people in my life. Sometimes, when I feel so adrift, so like that balloon slipping away, I wonder if it's my father's fault. If his leaving *did this*. Did this to me.

My phone buzzes and I reach for it and hope it's a text from Mark but it's an alert from my calendar, something I've set up to notify me of how many days I've got left: forty. I wonder, if I told Lauren everything that was going on, whether I could go out there early, maybe stay with her and her five sibs. They'd hardly even notice if there was someone else bunking in their house.

Or, I don't know, would it be crazy to ask my dad? Doesn't he owe me that much? A place to crash for a few weeks before college? Because I can't possibly be around my mother *or* Mark now that I know what's going on.

Alex calls right then and I pick up. I can't avoid everybody forever.

'We need to talk,' he says, and I say, 'You're right. We do.'

I shoot off an e-mail before heading to meet him on the beach.

Dear Lauren,
Things are crazy here. So crazy I don't even think you'd believe me if I told you. I will suffer in silence like you, at least until we meet, and then I will inevitably bore you with all the gory details. Right now I'm going to meet my boyfriend to 'talk.' Did I even mention I had a boyfriend? I do. Sort of. For about six months. Or did. I have a feeling he's breaking up with me. He's the one who wants to 'talk.' I'm not sure I care. Ugh. Do you have a boyfriend? Wish me luck.

— EB

PS Almost forgot! Love that video. LOVED
Veronica Mars. Do you know it?

PPS Also good job on the scholarship! Been
meaning to say that!

I think about e-mailing my father then,
too. But here's the kicker. I don't even have
his e-mail address. I Google the gallery and
there's an info@ address that might go to him
but what if it goes to someone else? And am I
really going to ask him if I can . . . how to
even say it . . . 'crash' at his 'pad'? After all
this time?

Just imagining his face when he reads that
e-mail is reason enough not to send it. But
what else am I supposed to do? Forty days.
Forty.

I start to count forty seconds, real slow,
with the Mississippis and all, out loud in my
car. And though it seems nutty — like
something only a crazy person would do — I
force myself, even when I want to quit at
nineteen and again at thirty-one, to count the
whole way up to forty. Like that will
somehow help. Like that will make the rest of
this day — and the rest of summer — more
bearable.

Then I head to the beach. Alex is waiting. He's waiting to end it, waiting for it to end. In that way, at least, he's an awful lot like me.

FRIDAY, JULY 19
SAN FRANCISCO

Mom and Dad decide, kind of at the last minute, to go on a Friday-night date. Leaving me with all five of the kids.

'Seriously?' I'm leaning in the bathroom doorway, watching Dad smooth his hair down while he checks himself out in the mirror. Marcus stands on the toilet, patting his own hair the same way. It's somewhat adorable. Still. 'I couldn't get a little more warning?'

'You've got plans?' Dad asks the mirror.

No. But I could maybe make some. Get out of the house, get together with Zoe and tell her what happened with Keyon.

'Honey.' He turns and gives me his full attention. 'If you've got plans, you need to write them on the family calendar. We checked and didn't see anything.'

'Because I don't have any.' *Hugely surprising, I know.*

'Well, Mom found this coupon for Villa d'Este at the bottom of a pile of mail and it expires tomorrow so we thought we'd better jump on it.'

I picture them laughing, having a glass of wine, speaking entire sentences without interruption. Zoe probably wouldn't be free, anyway. 'Bring me home some garlic bread. Mom can sneak it into her purse.'

'Daddy, shave my face,' Marcus says. My dad does this thing where he puts shaving cream on Marcus's face and then pretends to shave it off with the edge of his finger.

'No time, kiddo. You'll have to live with your five o'clock shadow.' Dad says to me, 'Francis and P.J. are already asleep. All you need to do is get some food into the rest of them and get them off to bed.'

'No baths?'

He makes a fake-serious face, then suddenly picks up Marcus and turns him upside down, holding him by the ankles. Marcus screams with delight. 'Lemme take a sniff,' Dad says, burying his nose in Marcus's bare feet. 'Stinky toes! This one definitely needs a bath.'

'Gross, Dad.'

After I turn to go back down the hall, I smile, Marcus's giggles floating after me.

★ ★ ★

Keyon calls during dinner, while Gertie and Marcus and Jack are eating their franks and beans in a relatively civilized fashion.

101

When I see it's his number, I consider dodging. We've gotten through the week all right so far, but neither of us has said more than two unnecessary words and I still feel awkward.

On the other hand, it could be nice to talk to someone who presumably doesn't have beans mashed onto his chin like my siblings. 'Hey,' I answer, standing to take the call.

'Lauren. Yeah, so, um.'

Uh-oh.

'What's up?' Chipper!

'Huh? Oh, right. My dad said I should call you.'

His dad? Am I about to get fired or something?

Of course the second I can't give Jack my full attention, he starts singing the 'beans, beans, good for your heart' song, causing me to rue the day I taught it to him. 'Jack,' I say sharply. To Keyon, 'Does he need me to . . . change my schedule?'

Keyon pauses. 'No. I mean he said I should call you. To talk.'

Jack's about to sing another stanza. I get to him in one lunge and put my hand over his mouth as what Key says sinks in. 'You told your dad? About what happened at the party?' So fired. The last thing Joe probably wants in his place of business is me groping his son.

'Yeah, I needed advice.'

I'll never be able to look Joe in the eye again. 'And he said to call me.'

Then Jack sticks his bean-goo-covered tongue through my fingers. I yank it away. 'Eww!' I walk to the sink to rinse my hand. 'Sorry. It's my stupid little brother.'

'Mama says you can't say stupid,' Gertie says.

'Um, is this a bad time?'

When is there a good time? 'No, go ahead.' I motion for the kids to settle down and eat, making what I hope is an extremely threatening expression.

'Anyway, he said, my dad said, like, you should never make a . . . ' He clears his throat. 'A woman . . . think that when something like that happens it doesn't matter. It's disrespectful.'

'Your dad called me a woman?' I laugh nervously.

'Basically.'

Had he told Keyon that he had to *date* me now or something? 'It's okay, I don't feel disrespected.'

'Oh. Yeah, good.'

'I mean I kind of came at *you*.' I'm the one who got myself into the kissing position that the law of physics demanded lead to his lips.

Keyon laughs.

'What?'

'Lo, I planned that whole thing from the minute I saw you sittin' there alone in the yard, so don't even.'

My stomach does a little stutter. 'You did not.'

'What can I say? I love me a sad white girl.'

I chuckle, because his delivery is funny, then wonder: What if he actually sees me that way? Pasty and pathetic? 'I'm not always sad,' I say, trying to sound not-sad.

'Oh yeah no I know, sorry, I don't mean . . .' He does another little throat-clearing thing.

Great. Now I've made him feel all weird. My flirting skills are so undeveloped. I take a breath to say something to smooth it over or show I have a sense of humor. Maybe: *But I am always white! Hahaha!*

Thankfully, he speaks before I have the chance to. 'You feeling better about that stuff we were talking about?'

Now *that* is sweet. 'I think so. I — '

Then I catch Jack mashing a bean onto Gertie's arm, which in itself is fairly tame given other violations I've seen go down at this table, but Gertie's reaction is to flick it back at him; then he picks up an entire handful of beans and — 'Key, I gotta go, my brother is being *so bad* and he's going to be in *so much trouble* when I tell my dad.' Jack freezes.

'E-mail me later. Or call. Or something.'
'I will.'

★ ★ ★

Later, when everyone is in bed and I'm hanging out in the living room, I want to call him, but for some reason that seems daunting and impossible. I run through it in my head: He answers and says hi. I say hi back. Then he says . . . what? That the Rule of Joe now demands nightly phone calls? During which we'll talk about . . . what? Why is the idea of two humans talking voice to voice sometimes so troublesome? I kissed the dude. We work together every day. I should be able to maintain a five-minute conversation.

I chicken out and retrieve my laptop from the bedroom — quietly, so I don't wake P.J. and Gertie. E-mail: the coward's solution to everything. You control the conversation and can turn it off and on at will. You can edit and revise and shape your words and use a thesaurus if you want, to avoid sounding dumb.

Key,
Sorry about before. Jack was being a total criminal.

It's really sweet what your dad said. Really.
And what you said. But please don't worry
about it, okay? I was glad you were there to
talk to me and everything. It was really nice. I
don't expect whatever your dad might think I
do. See you on Monday!!!

Lo

There. He's off the hook. So am I, I guess,
though it's not exactly a relief.

I've got an e-mail from Ebb. The timing of
this girl is sometimes spooky. Do I have a
boyfriend? Good question. I check the time
and know that whatever 'talk' she had with
hers must be long over and she's either crying
herself to sleep over a breakup, or maybe
getting it on with him in her room, or his
room, or I don't really know where people my
age actually go to have sex. I mean, I have
an idea. Zoe tells me things, but I sort of
block it out of my mental landscape. It all just
seems like a logistical nightmare, among
other things. Who has the time or energy to
figure all that out? I'm sure I'll eventually
understand the big deal and it will be lovely
and fireworks and deep soul connection or
whatever. Until then, I can keep taking care
of my own needs the few times I have the
interest and some privacy.

Like now, for example, the memory of Keyon's voice in my ear . . .

Having those thoughts while Ebb's e-mail is open feels a little bit like she's watching me or something. There's also the possibility of one of my parents getting up for a glass of water. Not that they've *ever before* gotten up for a glass of water after they've gone to bed, but that would be my luck. Then I start wondering how your sex life works with a roommate. It's got to be as bad as, or worse than, living at home. What if Ebb is hooking up like crazy while I'm writing research papers three feet away?

Now my thoughts are so fixated on her, I have to write back.

EB,
I'm sitting here wondering if you've 'talked' with your boyfriend yet. I'm figuring it's all done by now. Hopefully it was nothing bad, although usually when you put 'talk' in quotes it's nothing good.

This is going to be a long one.

Also it's going to be of the gory details variety if that's okay. (Hey, it's a whole new Lauren!)

Remember how I said nothing really happened at the party I went to? The truth is I sort of wound up making out with Keyon. Not sort of. Definitely. And I feel all weird about it because we're friends but not really tight friends, and we work together, and we were never in the same social world at school. Maybe I think he's a tiny bit 'out of my league,' to use everyone's favorite terrible sports analogy. Also I haven't had a lot of crush-like feelings for him before this. I always thought he was really cute/hot but I didn't think of him as someone something could potentially happen with. With whom something could potentially happen. Whatever.

Now I don't know!

He didn't say anything about it at work all week, then he calls me tonight to say . . . well he didn't get a chance to say anything because I was on child care duty. He called because HIS DAD, Joe (who is also my boss), told him he should call so I didn't feel disrespected. As in he told HIS DAD. Which is in itself a sign of something? And kind of sweet?

The thing is I thought it was one of those accidental kisses, where you're like, 'I don't know what happened, Officer, one minute I was sitting there thinking about how I'm not going to be part of my family anymore and the next minute I had my tongue in his mouth.'

Keyon claims all this was no surprise, that he actually planned it. Or wanted to or something, implying: Maybe he's been thinking about this for a while? I'm making too big a deal, I know, because it was a party and he's cute and I'm not a troll or anything and I don't have a boyfriend and I doubt he has a girlfriend so why shouldn't we? Only now I'm confused and I sent him this ENTIRELY LAME e-mail making it sound like I don't really care either way. Because I don't know how I feel. I hope it doesn't hurt his feelings or anything.

I hate it when you click Send before you've really thought it through.

(But I was too wimpy to call. I get phone-phobic.)

I don't want to get all tangled up in something right now. I've never really had a boyfriend . . . not the kind you have. There've been guys I've hung out with in a semi-not-platonic way for a few weeks at a time but I can't imagine dating someone for 6 months. On the other hand I like Keyon. I just don't know if I like him like him.

Sorry to dump this on you! Zoe isn't the ideal person to tell because she'll probably put something on Twitter that she thinks is cleverly cryptic and everyone will figure it out in 3 seconds. Not that I would care that much if people knew but I need time to THINK about what happened and SORT through it. Something about the way Zoe is makes it hard for me to THINK and SORT. Writing it to you feels helpful. Maybe that's a little use-y, though, if you're not in the mood. But feel free to use me back if you are. I mean I guess what I'm saying is that if you WANT to bore me with all the gory details anytime, instead of waiting for August, be my guest. Or not. I'm easy breezy, like Covergirl.

Lauren

It's too much. I know. But what the hell. I hit Send and go to my room, where I collapse into bed, too tired to conjure up pleasant need-meeting thoughts of Keyon or anything else.

SATURDAY, JULY 20
NEW JERSEY

I bolt up in bed at the sound of my mother's voice. There is a man's voice mingling with hers and for a second I think I've woken up mid-home invasion but then there's some laughing and the sound of ice cubes, low music, my mother shushing her companion with a shush that is louder than anything she's supposedly shushing. I reach for my phone and check the time — 2 AM — and then open my bedroom door, listen more closely, and recognize the man's voice.

Mark's dad is spending the night here in Philadelphia.

With my phone in my hand, I see I've got an e-mail from Lauren — sent last night after I was already asleep; the time difference is sometimes a plus, sometimes not — but there's no text, no nothing, from Mark. Not that I was expecting one. Not exactly. He'd be crazy to bother any more with a nutcase like me, but still . . .

It turns out that Lauren's e-mail is really long — I scroll down to see how long before actually reading — so I decide to read it on my laptop because I messed up my phone last night. The screen has a weird dark digital slash across it from when I dropped it when Alex and I were breaking up, and I'm pissed because I really don't want to have to spend money on a new one. Even though I did the dropping I can't help but feel like it was all Alex's fault.

I grab my laptop, crawl back into bed, and try to block out the ice cubes and talking and fake-naughty laughter. If this is what my mother's life is like now, I can't even imagine what it will be like when I don't live here anymore. I get up again to find some head-phones, then plug them into my laptop, put on my 'Most Frequently Played' songs, and turn up the volume.

Finally, I read Lauren's e-mail and wonder what it means that she and Keyon were never in the same worlds at school. If her school is anything like mine, my guess is that it means she's white and he's black. I confess that I'm a little disappointed by this theory. I've never had a friend of a different race and I guess I think it'd be cool. And I sort of feel like unless I'm pushed together with someone really different from me, it'll never happen. But maybe that's just small-town Jersey thinking?

Black or white, I think maybe Lauren and I

will get along okay after all. I also can't help but think that Keyon's dad sounds like a good dad. A *really good* dad. Because isn't that what parents are supposed to do? Teach you the hard bits? The rules? The morals? The *way to be?*

Keyon's dad would never be having drinks at this hour with a woman who wasn't his wife.

Keyon's dad wouldn't bring a stranger into his home when his son was sleeping.

Keyon's dad wouldn't stand for any of it.

And I shouldn't have to, either.

I close the computer and walk downstairs and stand at the entrance to the living room, rubbing my eyes — to make it clear that they have woken me up. 'Hi,' I say, but not to my mom, to Mark's dad.

My mother was laughing a second ago but now she's not. She comes over to me and pulls me into a hug and says, 'Oh, did we wake you? I'm sorry, sweetie.' She presents me to him, holding me awkwardly by the shoulders. 'This is Elizabeth.'

I look right into his eyes and try to decipher if he recognizes me or not. But I don't even care. I only have one goal and it is to make it clear that I know who he is and where he lives and that he is not welcome here. That he is not, and never will be, the sort of man that Keyon's dad is. I don't care that I don't even *know* Keyon's dad — or Keyon. Or Lauren. They suddenly seem like better people than everyone in this room — I make no exception for myself — and so I say, 'I did some work on your garden.'

He looks a little bit shocked, and maybe he has a vague memory of seeing me that day, judging by the expression on his face. He looks at my mom, then back at me, and says, 'You must be thinking of someone else.'

And for a second I think maybe I've got it all wrong. Like maybe Mark's dad has a twin brother or something, and this is just going to be a crazy misunderstanding that Mark and I will laugh and laugh and laugh about — but no. I am sure. So I say, 'The house on Honeysuckle Drive. Your son is my age.'

Then his eyebrows arch up and he reaches for his keys, which are on the table near the couch, and he says, 'I should really head out.'

'Ohhhh,' my mother whines. 'Don't.' She turns to me and says, 'EB was just going back up to bed, weren't you, EB?'

But he has already decided to leave and so he does. Mission accomplished.

When the door closes behind him my mother turns and leans against it and I can't believe she still looks dreamy. I feel the fists forming at the ends of my arms when I say,

114

'He has a house. And a wife. And two sons. Tim and I redid their whole yard.'

She doesn't look dreamy anymore, that's for sure. She looks old and weary and sad but also a little bit mad. So I say, 'You can do better, Mom,' even though that's not how I feel. What I want to say is that she should *be* better.

'Yes, Elizabeth,' she says as she pushes off the door and heads for the stairs. 'I'll be sure to do that.'

★ ★ ★

Another person who is not like Keyon's dad: Alex.

It turns out he wanted to 'talk' so that he could make this earnest, last-ditch plea for me to sleep with him in order to 'deepen' and 'solidify' our relationship. No puns intended! When I was able to combat my stunned silence and say, 'It's never going to happen,' he actually asked me if I was into girls. Can you believe the nerve? Asking *me* that?

So I guess I didn't drop my phone; I threw it at him. Then he started to walk away and I said, 'This is us breaking up. This is me breaking up with you.'

He said, 'No argument here,' without looking back.

It takes me a while to get to sleep again but then I do and then I wake up for real and it is Saturday — and a day off. I wish I had a better way to spend it than hanging around feeling cut off from all my friends but at least my mother is gone and will stay at work all day. I take a bath, which I hardly ever do anymore, but I figure in college I won't have the option, so why not? After the water has cooled too much and I can no longer deny how uncomfortable I am in there — who decided the standard size of a bathtub, anyway? — I get out and sit down on the bath mat with a towel around my shoulders, trying to cover every inch of my wet self. I used to do this all the time when I was younger. Back then I pretended the mat was some kind of doomed raft and I was its lone passenger on stormy seas. The memory makes me sort of sad for myself, even though the act of doing it again — silly as it must look now that I'm grown — is oddly comforting.

Down in the kitchen, I fix a bowl of cereal and look at the calendar hanging on the side of the fridge. Still five and a half weeks to go. It feels like college is never going to get here so I take one of my mom's yellow legal pads off the counter by the phone and start to

116

make a list of what I'm going to pack. I've already made a number of similar lists on my phone and my laptop but doing it like this, on paper, makes college — escape — feel real.

The doorbell rings when I'm on number thirteen — *gray hoodie* — and I look down at the skimpy tank and shorts I threw on after my bath and decide to ignore the bell. I'm not expecting anybody and UPS always leaves stuff on the porch without a signature anyway so what's the point of opening the door so they can *hand* the package to you? But then a minute later my phone dings — a text from Mark. I have to hold the phone at strange angles to read through the slash. The message says I know you're in there.

For a second I get that horror-movie sort of panic. I'm alone. Scantily clad. A creepy guy is at the door. But it's Mark. He's the opposite of creepy. I text back That's not creepy at all.

There is a text from Morgan, too: This sucks. Make up with her already.

I walk to the front door and open it right as Mark is reading my text. He smiles and says, 'I should've crept over to the kitchen window, right? So you'd look up from your cereal and see maybe one of my eyes peering in at you.'

'That would've been better, yes.'

We just stand there, then, and I know I

should've thrown on a robe or hoodie or something because my tank is sort of loose and I'm not wearing a bra and he seems incapable of not noticing. I'm not sure if I'm supposed to invite him in or what he's doing here at all. Which reminds me.

'How did you know where I live?'

'I didn't want to ask Tim and get you in trouble, so I asked your mom.'

'What?' This can't be good. I'm imagining some kind of scene in which the crazy mistress shows up at the cheating man's house, maybe throws rocks at the windows until the wife comes over and pushes aside the curtain just in time for the mistress to shout, 'I thought you should know your husband is screwing around on you.'

Mark says, 'I found one of her signs and went by her office. I introduced myself and told her I wanted to bring you flowers.' He smiles. 'She seemed quite taken by the idea.'

'Did you tell her, like, your last name?'

'Uh, no.'

'Did you mention where you live? Like the street?'

'Uh, no. Why?'

So she can't know it's her lover's son. 'Never mind,' I say. 'Well, where are they? The flowers?'

He looks away for a minute, then says,

'Well, once I was actually at the flower shop I decided it would be inappropriate to give a girl who has a boyfriend flowers.'

I deflate a bit. But he is here, so that means something. 'So then why did you come?'

'Because I feel like you owe me an explanation. Because you shouldn't have let things go, well, as far as they did. I know I said I'd wait for you to figure it out, but I guess that's not really working for me.'

I can't be sure but I think Keyon's dad would approve of this. Of Mark.

I step back and say, 'Will you come in?' So he joins me in the foyer and I close the door behind him.

I am too quiet for too long, figuring out how to explain.

'Take your time.' He stretches exaggeratedly, then leans back against the wall, crosses his arms, and tries hard not to crack a smile. 'I have all day.'

I laugh a little and he does, too, and I say, 'I'm really sorry. I should have told you. I shouldn't have gone to the party with you.'

'That's an apology,' he says. 'Not an explanation. But, for the record, apology accepted.'

'Things were bad with my boyfriend so I —'

'Well, then you break up with him. You

119

don't drag me into it.'

I nod. It's all so sensible I want to cry.

'I *really* don't want things to be weird,' he says.

Oh, but they are, I think. *You have no idea!*

Still, I cannot bring myself to tell him about my mother and his father.

'So I guess we should, you know, just be friends,' he says.

'I broke up with him,' I blurt. Then I chastise myself for not saying, 'Yes. Friends would be best.'

'You did?' His eyebrows shoot up.

'I did.'

There's a smile sneaking onto his lips when he says, 'So I guess if I were to ask you out, that would be okay. Unlike that last time, which was really totally not okay.'

'I know. I'm sorry. But yes, it would be okay.'

'And if I were to try to kiss you?'

'Also okay.'

'Like right now?'

I nod.

And then we're kissing and our arms are entangled and we're moving toward the wall and we knock a picture crooked and then I feel the strap of my tank top fall off my shoulder. The kissing is super-sweet but not without . . . *intent?* . . . and I think there is no way I am leaving early to crash at my dad's or Lauren's if this sort of kissing is what I would be leaving behind. Then we stop and Mark pulls back a few inches and then he takes his finger and puts my strap back up on my shoulder and it tickles there and everywhere.

I am allowed this. I deserve this. And if my mother never sees Mark's father again we can absolutely pretend it never happened. I can pretend I never knew. I am prepared, if I must, to carry that secret to my grave if it means Mark will spend the next five and a half weeks kissing me like that, whenever possible. I will suffer through a lifetime of awkward Sunday dinners and holidays at his house, me and his dad complicit in our secret, if it ends up we are meant to be and we get married. I do not have to tell him. Because why hurt him if I don't have to? Surely Keyon's dad would understand that?

'So what are you doing later?' Mark says. 'Tonight, I mean.'

'I don't know.' I lean back into him. 'Maybe this?'

* * *

We make plans to meet up that night and he leaves and suddenly the day seems wide open again, but in a good way. I take my list upstairs and look around my room and add a few more things — my favorite boots, my most comfortable baseball hat, my jewelry box — and then decide to write back to Lauren.

Hey,

I don't even know where to begin with what's going on with me so I'll start with you. Keyon really sounds like a great guy. His dad does, too. And I'm starting to think that what people's parents are like is HUGELY important. Because you either turn out like them or you go so far in the opposite direction for whatever reason that you end up being totally unlike them. Where this will leave ME further down the line, I don't know. But I digress. I'm sure your e-mail to Keyon wasn't as lame as you think it was. I bet you've probably already heard back from him. I don't always know the difference between liking someone and LIKING liking them but hmmmn, do you want to kiss him again?

That's as good of a segue into what's going on with me as I am likely to get. Alex and I are broken up now and I saw Mark today — that's the guy I went to that party with — and even though there's parental weirdness that really is too complicated to explain I'm going out with him later tonight. I've already kissed him. Twice. I'm sure this makes me sound like some kind of tramp or something but I'm really not! A tramp would've stayed with Alex, who always wanted sex, which was a problem since I wasn't giving it to him. It may sound silly but with Mark, well, my tank top strap fell off my shoulder when I saw him this morning and he put it back up. It's a silly little thing but it seemed ridiculously sweet and I feel like maybe it says something about who he is. And it's probably dumb to even bother trying to get to know him since I'm leaving for California in five and a half weeks, but not trying seems even dumber. I hope I don't end up regretting it.

I think about ending it there but then I reread her e-mail, mostly to see if there was anything else I should mention, and I reread the invitation to use her, to give her all the gory details. So I get down to it.

Okay. Full disclosure. Because, like you, I feel like there's all this stuff I need to talk about. Justine is pretty much the only person I talk to about anything real here and we still haven't made up.

So here goes: My mother went on a date with Mark's dad. No, several dates. And they were here last night and WOKE ME UP. Not doing the nasty or anything but, well, the WHOLE THING is nasty, isn't it? So I can't believe I did this but I let his dad know I knew who he was and where he lived and that he had a wife and two sons. My mom seemed more pissed at me even though I was helping her. Wasn't I helping her?

Anyway, so when Mark came over and we kissed, I decided that I will take the secret of his dad and my mom to my grave. Because I will not ruin everything. I can keep a secret for five and a half weeks, can't I?

I'm sure if you do some Googling or make a few calls you can get a 'Roommate Reassignment Request Form' from the housing office at Berkeley. Tell them that living with a soap opera star will not be conducive to your studies.

EB

Before I hit Send, I glance over at the yellow legal pad.

PS Been thinking about what to bring with me.

Yes: Flip-flops (for nasty shared showers; read this in a magazine)

No: Stuffed animals. Not even my beloved brown bear, Bud. Sniff. Sniff. (Right?)

Maybe so: Do people wear black leather boots in California?

WEDNESDAY, JULY 24
SAN FRANCISCO

Keyon hasn't abandoned his idea about getting rich reselling other people's junk on eBay. It's way too early to be up, but he got a text from Mikey last night saying that a whole bunch of stuff would be put on the floor this morning. Keyon picked me up in his dad's car and we stopped for coffee, and I thrust my money at the barista before Keyon could pay for mine because, well, I don't know why. I guess I didn't want him to think that *I* think we're on a date.

Keyon brought a couple of small empty boxes from the sandwich shop into Goodwill. 'Here,' he says, handing me one. 'If you see any good DVDs put them in this.'

'This *is* totally ethical, right?'

He gives me a puzzled look and points to an older lady aggressively rifling through the shelves. An old cookie tin clatters to the floor in her wake. 'At least *we're* not making a mess. Seriously, though, probably half of Goodwill's business comes from people like us.'

'People like us?'

'You and me. Antiques dealers.'

I laugh.

'Plus, it's *recycling*, Lo.'

I walk slowly down the aisle with my box, scanning for anything of value.

Keyon follows me. 'Are you okay?' he asks. 'I mean, are you for real worried that this isn't cool?'

'No. Sorry if I'm being weird.'

My state of weirdness has nothing to do with this Goodwill thing, I know. It's that ethics and morals and, frankly, the Ten Commandments have been on my mind since Ebb's last e-mail. Her mom's affair seems pretty delinquent and appalling, and I don't really know what to say about it. I sort of want to drop the whole subject and file it under TMI, but I'm the one who was all 'hey, tell me your deep dark secrets!' in the first place and I can't leave her e-mail unanswered for another day after it's already been so long. It's a big deal, though. It's adultery, right? Or is only Mark's dad the adulterer? But Ebb's mom *knows* he's married. I admit I'm not exactly a theologian. We go to Mass maybe three times a year. Even so, Catholic must be in my blood because I feel sort of judge-y about the whole thing and a tiny bit of vicarious guilt from merely *knowing*.

'Don't space out on me,' Keyon says. 'Let's focus.'

'Right.' I survey the room. 'I don't think the real money is in DVDs. We should be looking for rare stuff.'

'I know, but we need cash flow to get into the higher-ticket shit.'

Maybe I can lighten the tone of my e-mail to Ebb by describing Keyon's vocab: *Keyon's favorite word is 'shit.' It can be used as a replacement for 'stuff,' 'crap,' 'things,' as well as for circumstances and feelings. I'm afraid if I spend too much time with him I'm going to say it all the time, too, and wind up dropping the s-bomb in front of my sibs.*

'Aw, Lo! Check it!' Keyon stumbles over some boxes and bags on his way to me. In his hands is a CD of the soundtrack to *The Lion King*.

'Are you serious? That movie is a total cheeseball.'

'No, man, this is my whole childhood right here.'

'Live in a house full of children under the age of seven who want to watch it every day and you might change your mind.'

He starts singing 'The Circle of Life' and doesn't stop until he gets to the end of the first verse.

And yet he continues to grow on me and I

am spending more and more time with him. And staring a lot. His body is really . . .

Oh, nice, I'm all morally outraged by Ebb's mom but I treat Keyon like a slab of meat! I've been somewhat obsessed, especially since he's made no move to kiss me again when he's had the chance. Maybe Joe told him there's a ten-day waiting period after random party hookups.

Or maybe he's playing hard to get, or doesn't want to be got.

I wish there were an algorithm to help with this stuff. Something by which I could analyze his metabolic pathways as related to his desires in this particular situation.

When we've moved on to the household goods section he catches me, again not filling my box, and staring at his hips. 'That money ain't gonna make itself.'

I'm sure I'm blushing like mad. 'Oh, right, I'm not the one dancing down memory lane on my cloven hooves.' Then I feel extra-dorky because that joke is so obscure.

He's right on it, though: 'Do not dis the mighty warthog.'

After searching several more aisles and finding mostly kitchen stuff — pots and pans with the nonstick coating scratched off, tacky casserole dishes, and mug after mug after mug after mug — I spy something that's definitely different shoved behind a stack of plates. It's smooth and blocky and when I pull it out I see that it's a sea-green plastic old radio.

'Keyon.' I hold it up. 'This might be something.'

He sets down his box and comes over to take the radio from me, turning it over to examine every angle. 'I think this is that Bakelite shit. This stuff always gets good money.'

'You really do watch *Antiques Roadshow*.'

'I'm telling you I happen to be in the room when my mom's watching.' He fiddles with the knobs until one clicks on and we hear static. He tunes in KMEL.

'It works!' I'm surprised how delighted I feel at the miracle of battery power.

Keyon points to the price sticker and grins. Eight bucks. 'Our first big find, Lo.'

I do a geeky little dance and we high-five.

★ ★ ★

He drives me to my filing job so I can get in a quick hour or so there, and talks enthusiastically the whole way about our future as Bakelite experts. 'This is the Bay freaking Area, Lo. I bet that shit is in every crack and crevice of every thrift store from here to Walnut Creek.'

130

'You do understand there are limits to our prospects. This is going to be good for some pocket money but that's all.' Despite being proud of my find, I've become cranky and on edge, the Voice of Lauren's Judgment loud again in my head. Adultery! That's the word I can't shake. I once heard my grandma and my mom talking about some couple they knew breaking up over the husband 'cheating,' as my mom put it. 'Cheating is what you do on tests,' Grandma said.

I guess statistics show half of married people do it. And I mean I know Ebb's mom isn't married, but she's doing it with a guy who *is*, so she's half responsible for his statistic. How can Ebb even live with her mom after that? If I caught either of my parents at that I'd be too distraught to function, let alone type up the whole thing in an e-mail to a practical stranger. I never thought of myself as morally superior to anyone, but . . .

'Are you *sure* you're okay?' Keyon asks.

Oh, God, I think. *I am a sad white girl. And a complete drag.*

'Totally fine.' I smile at him and feel like a fake. 'Actually,' I say, my smile drooping, 'I'm distracted by some stuff going on with . . . a friend.'

He waits, like he's inviting me to say more. When I don't he doesn't press it and goes back to the subject of our status as antiques dealers. 'Okay, so we're not going to be million-aires. But money in my pocket is money in my pocket, and I didn't have to make sandwiches to get it. Also,' he says, and points at me, 'finding that radio made you *dance*. So that's worth it right there.'

'Yeah, I am a pretty amazing dancer now that you mention it.'

He laughs, then makes his face serious. 'Wasn't laughing at you.'

'Uh-huh.'

Near the insurance office, he says, 'My dad said to invite you over for dinner, by the way.'

By the way? He says it all casual, like it's not a huge deal.

My immediate response is 'Oh. Okay!' Then I have a terrifying thought: that everything Keyon has been doing since the party is because his dad is telling him to. Calling me, e-mailing every day, inviting me for dinner. He feels guilty and is trying to be the kind of good guy his dad wants him to; then he will oh-so-gently lower my expecta-tions down to nothing and cut me loose. 'I mean, if *you* want me to come over,' I add.

'Hell yeah,' he says. He puts his hand on my thigh, which immediately bursts into flames, and my fears about Keyon being his dad's puppet evaporate in an instant. 'If I

132

didn't want you to come I'd make up some shit to my dad about how you don't date the brothers.'

An excruciatingly awkward pause befalls the car. It's the second time he's said something to point out that we're different colors, something I don't really know how or whether to talk about.

'You do, though, right?' he asks, with a quick glance.

'Oh, yeah. I totally do. I date the brothers. Like nobody's business. Yes.'

We both burst out laughing.

'I thought so,' he says.

'Just promise me you won't start singing 'Can You Feel the Love Tonight' at the dinner table.' As soon as it's out of my mouth I'm mortified I said the l-word even though it's in a totally neutral context.

He doesn't seem to notice, and takes his hand off my leg, shaking his head. 'Can't promise that.'

★ ★ ★

There are three unanswered e-mails from Zoe in my in-box at the end of the day. I'm scared to read the most recent one because I know I'm in trouble for not replying. The message preview shows me the first line. Did you get my last two e-mails? Or my texts? Are you dead? Because if you are it would be nice — I can imagine the rest. Something in me won't click on the message. Like the specter of Ebb's e-mail and its contents sitting there has spooked me away from the whole idea of e-mail.

Dad appears in the doorway of my room, holding a limp Gertie in his arms. 'She finally conked out in front of the TV,' he whispers.

I get up to help peel Gertie's sweaty self off him and get her tucked into bed. We work silently and deftly, like accomplished jewel thieves. How many times have we done this before, with each kid? How many times is it going to happen now without me? Dad crooks his finger at me to beckon me into the hall. We pull the door behind us.

'What?' I ask.

'Nothing.' He puts his arms around me for a hug. 'How are you doing? I feel like we haven't talked in ages.'

'We haven't.'

Of course we had our family times over the weekend but that was like a thousand percent absorbed with child management. Dad releases the hug and takes my hand, pulling me into the living room, where Mom lies on the couch with her eyes closed.

'I'm taking Lauren out for gelato. Want us to bring you anything?'

134

Mom moves her head about a quarter of an inch back and forth in a no, then lifts one index finger. We know from experience it means 'See you later, have fun, don't talk to me anymore because I am getting some precious rest.'

We walk up the hill to Marco Polo, where Dad gets spumoni and I get half mocha chip and half cinnamon. And we sit at an outside table, even though it's typical chilly Sunset summer weather, and talk. It's not like we have this deep father-daughter discussion or anything; he shares what's going on at work and I talk about what I still need to wrap up before moving across the Bay.

And I ask, 'When you were in college, were you friends with your roommate?'

He shrugs. 'Not particularly. Well, wait. There was one, sophomore year. Dale Greenwald. He was a good guy.'

'Are you in touch anymore?'

'Oh, gosh. Haven't heard from Dale since graduation.'

I lick cinnamon-mocha off the little plastic spoon. 'Did you guys, like, *agree* about everything?'

He laughs. 'No. He was more into the Grateful Dead than any thinking person should be.'

'I don't mean about that stuff. I mean

important stuff. The meaning of life. Ethics and morals and sh . . . stuff.'

'To be honest, it's hard to remember. We got along. I don't remember us fighting about anything.' He stretches his legs out in front of him, resting the heels of his sneakers on the cement. 'Ethics and morals, huh? Do you have some deep thoughts about that?'

I shrug. I'm not going to be talking about Ebb's mom with my dad, thanks. 'Not really. Just kind of wondering what it would be like to live with someone who thinks about things in a totally different way than you do, you know? I've never exactly had a roommate who was capable of opinions much stronger than favorite color, or thoughts more profound than fairness in toy sharing.'

'True, that.'

Also I wonder about Dale Greenwald, and how he and my dad never talk. Is that the destiny of all friendships, no matter how good they are? To die out or fade away? To end? 'Maybe if you'd had e-mail and stuff when you were in school you'd still be friends with Dale. I bet if you went on Facebook you'd find him in about two minutes.'

Dad grimaces. 'That could be fun for nostalgia purposes. But I've got your mom, and one or two good buddies. A person doesn't need much more than that. As you get older you tighten up that circle pretty well, I think.'

One or two good buddies. And hopefully a partner or spouse. Zoe, whose self-esteem sometimes seems governed by how many friends and followers she has online, wouldn't like that. But then maybe it doesn't matter that much how Zoe and I are different, or how Ebb and I may be.

'Zoe is my Dale, I guess.'

He laughs. 'Zoe is *not* your Dale, hon. Zoe is your Thelma.'

'Who?'

'*Thelma and Louise?* Don't tell me Mom and I haven't made you watch that yet. Great movie. The ending, though . . . I'm not saying that should be a *model* of friendship for you. I only mean — '

I interrupt him before he goes on a whole big tangent. 'Okay, maybe Zoe isn't my Dale. But I think I'm probably going to be friends with my roommate this fall and then *she'll* be my Dale. That's totally depressing.'

'Forget about Dale,' Dad says. 'Live in the present. Take care of the relationships in front of you now. Most friendships have a natural life, and when they've lived that out, you'll know.'

'It's still depressing.'

He lifts his spoon to me in acquiescence as the L train rattles down the hill.

EB,

I'm completely wiped and brain dead but I know I've slacked on answering, and I'm sorry! Also, sorry that my replies here are going to sound memo-like. Brain. Dead.

Parents: I have to admit, I have pretty good ones. Their biggest flaw is their relentless desire to procreate. So. Many. Kids. And also: gross.

According to your theory this means I will either have zero kids or a dozen. I vote for zero.

Soap opera lives: Unless you have faked your own death, had plastic surgery to look like someone else, built a prison in your basement where you're holding an ex who always has his shirt off, or caused someone else's miscarriage by pushing them down a flight of stairs, I think you're okay. (I went through a soap phase in ninth grade. I'm not proud.)

Not to minimize the weirdness of your mom kind of cheating —

Adulterating?

— with your kind of boyfriend's dad. It's actually . . . well, I mean how do you feel about that? I sort of can't believe she'd do that with you in the next room. I don't know if I could keep that a secret from someone I cared about. I get that you wouldn't want to mess things up with Mark, but. Hopefully he's not like his dad. Based on your parental theory, again, he'll either be a cheater himself or a monk. Scary. On the other hand, he moved your tank top strap up. I don't know.

Do I sound like a self-righteous a-hole, or like a supportive friend? I can't tell. Whichever, it's an opinion I can't seem to hold in. I leave it.

Keyon: The question of like vs like like doesn't seem that important anymore. Maybe it's all more fluid than that. His parents invited me over for dinner, and he put his hand on my thigh. Otherwise, no new news.

Sex: Really? You were with Alex all that time and never did it? What DID you do? Something, right? Maybe this is too personal or I'm too curious. Naturally having all these kids in the house makes me terrified of getting pregnant, but it's more than that. I'm not sure what. Also I still feel like I just met Keyon.

Also I think I should do about a thousand more sit-ups and push-ups before anyone sees me naked.

Good night.

Lauren

About ten minutes after getting in bed I realize I didn't play Ebb's Yes/No/Maybe So game about what to bring to school. To leave that hanging seems as bad as my semijudgmental thoughts on her mom. I climb out and send a separate PS.

Yes: A variety of confusing crayon art my little brothers and sisters have made for me. I won't hang it on the wall, but I like to have it with me.

No: Anything with a 49ers logo on it. I'll have to become a Cal Bears fan.

Maybe so:

My sense of right and wrong?
I can't put that.

Maybe so: Thinking about stuffing my sister

P.J. into my backpack. She's a little bit my favorite.

Oh by the way, yes to black boots in CA. Big yes.

THURSDAY, JULY 25
NEW JERSEY

Must. Be. Nice.

Must be *really, really* nice to have two super-duper parents.

Good for you, Lauren!

Well done!

You picked the right vagina to pop out of so let me give you a round of applause.

Clap.

Clap.

Clap.

Oh! And how do I *feel* about my mother gallivanting around town like a desperate whore?

I feel shitty about it if that wasn't clear, thanks for asking.

And no, Mark's *not like his dad*. Don't you think I'd have copped on if he were an asshole? He was the one who confronted me and demanded an explanation for kissing him when I was otherwise entangled!

(In fact, Mark made several references when we were out on Tuesday — bowling, of all things — to his dad sort of being 'a dick.'

142

Each time I wondered whether that was an opening I should leap through but each time I kept my mouth shut and then changed the subject, which seemed to suit him fine.)

Suffice it to say, I will not be asking Lauren if I can go crash with her picture-perfect clan, but since my mother has been ignoring me ever since my confrontation with Mark's dad, it's becoming harder to imagine staying at home for another five weeks. At first, when I realized I was getting the cold shoulder, I was sort of okay with it because, like Lauren, I was feeling pretty morally superior. Besides, being estranged from my mother felt like good practice for next month, when we won't be together anyway. But then the shoulder seemed to get colder and the frozen dinners and leftover plates stopped appearing, and I realized I was basically living on my own — but without the real freedom of being alone — and I stopped liking it and starting hatching my escape plan, otherwise known as Operation Deadbeat Dad. Much as I don't want to leave Mark's kissing behind, I cannot hack it here.

The days started to feel really long, especially the ones without a peep from Lauren, who I guess was too busy feeling holier-than-thou to write. I started wondering, *Is this what life will be like in college, if me and my roomie don't hit it off in the flesh?* Suddenly I could see it going that way — a whole freshman year of fights about who ate whose last package of ramen noodles or who never picks their dirty clothes up off the floor, a whole year of sharing a room with a hostile.

Surely there is something fundamentally flawed about the idea of the freshman-year roommate. Because on the one hand, yes, you've got this sort of friend forced on you when you most need one, so you don't have to walk into the dining hall or orientation meeting alone, but on the other, when has forcing friends on people ever worked?

It was probably loneliness — and a few more texts from Morgan — that drove me to pick up the phone and call Justine. I'd been thinking about her a lot — and actually *missing* her, too — and I'd been wondering what Keyon's dad would tell me to do about the situation. I had a feeling he'd tell me to call her, to be the better person.

And so here we are, at a local coffee shop in the middle of the day on a Thursday. Already it feels wrong because we've never gone out for coffee or tea or any kind of beverage before, but we go through the whole routine of ordering and getting a table and then sitting and sipping. We're quiet, and I think about telling her about Lauren, whose e-mail I've just gotten, or about my mom and Mark's dad — or just about Mark — but there's so much catching up to be done before I can get to anything of substance that the mere thought of it makes me tired.

After another long minute of silence she says, 'This is weird.'

I say, 'Let's get the hell out of here,' and we both laugh.

We put lids on our drinks and decide to take my car, and leave hers, and go to the beach because it's sunny and hot in town and it's always cooler by the water. We don't talk at all in the car. It feels like maybe we both know that we're on our way to a better place to talk about the stuff we need to talk about — because it's big stuff, or maybe because it feels like there's an ocean between us.

After we park I grab a blanket out of the trunk and think of all the times Alex and I sat on this same blanket on the sand, and I figure he is as good a topic as any to start with. After I spread the blanket out beyond the dunes that separate the beach from the board-walk I say, 'I guess you heard about me and Alex.'

'Yeah.' Justine sits down and wipes some sand off her hands, brushing them together. 'Are you okay?'

145

I nod and study a big group of people sitting near us as the sun starts to fade. Judging by the coolers, chairs, and umbrellas, it looks like they've been there for hours — or plan to be. They're mostly older, not quite as old as my mom, but way older than me, and there are some kids who are maybe around six and twelve and everything in between, coming and going with boogie boards and paddle games. I can't imagine I'll ever have a vacation like that. Not unless I marry into some massive clan.

I say, 'It always sounds like a lie but it was totally mutual.'

She kicks off her sandals and buries her toes in the sand but I can still see a slice of silver from her toe ring. 'You guys never seemed like that great of a fit to me.'

'Why didn't you say so?' I say.

She shoots me a look. 'Yeah, you would have loved that.'

I shake my head. 'It's true, I guess.' I think about Alex in detail for a minute — his love for at least two sitcoms I can't stand and the way he wore that baseball cap all the time — and already I can't imagine how we were ever together.

'I was mostly bummed for myself,' Justine says, nudging me. 'No more six-pack.'

I am about to say, 'I always hated when you

called us that,' but she says, 'Anyway, Karen's okay.'

I feel my whole body tense.

'Karen?' I say, raising my voice even though I don't want to.

'I figured you knew.' Justine wiggles her toes free, then starts to burrow again. 'He's been hooking up with Karen Lord.'

I sort of know her from school. She's on the soccer team and has a party girl reputation.

'Are you jealous?' Justine asks, and it annoys me because it almost sounds like the answer she wants is yes.

I shake my head. 'I met somebody, too. So no. Not really. Not at all.'

And in saying it, I realize it's true. I'm over him. Over it. Between Alex and Mark there's simply no comparison.

'Oh,' Justine says. 'Well, that's cool. Who is he?'

'I want to tell you about him,' I say, 'I really do. But I don't even know what to say. I mean, I'm going away in a few weeks anyway so it'll probably end. It hardly seems worth talking about.'

'EB,' she says seriously. 'Everything used to be worth talking about. With us. Everything and anything. Farts, even. Or the best way to shave your legs. Or shrubbery.'

'I know!' I say. 'I want that again!'

'Me too!'

What I don't know is whether I want it again with her — if that's even possible — or if I want it with someone else. For a while I was hoping Lauren was going to be that for me but now I'm not so sure. It's one thing for me to get all judgmental about my mother; it's another thing for someone else to.

'I've been thinking about e-mailing my dad,' I say then. 'Maybe seeing if I can go out west a few weeks early. You know, get the feel of the place before classes start and stuff.'

Justine raises her eyebrows.

'What?' I say. 'He told me I could come visit. The last time he wrote.'

'He *did*?'

'He did!'

Her eyebrows only move higher.

'It's complicated.' I sigh. 'My mom seems to want me gone, though. In a big way.'

'Your mom doesn't *want you gone*.' Justine lies back and pushes her sunglasses up to the top of her head. 'Your mom is just having a hard time dealing with the fact that you're leaving and she's going to be alone.'

I'm not sure why I'm so surprised to hear Justine's precise assessment of the situation — even without her knowing all the messy details — but I am. It's like I'd forgotten why we were ever friends in the first place and for a moment, at least, I've been reminded. Then she says, 'The woman needs therapy,' and I've sort of had it.

'Why is everyone suddenly picking on my mom?'

She holds a hand up to her eyes to block the sun and says, 'Who's everyone?'

I don't feel like explaining. 'I just mean she's not all bad. She got dealt sort of a crappy hand with my dad.'

'Everybody has a crappy hand.' Justine closes her eyes again.

'You don't believe that,' I say, and I watch as one of the kids of that big group starts putting together a kite shaped like a dragon. It has a long double tail made of gold-and-red fabric.

'Maybe not, but anyway, it's not about the hand all the time. It's about how you play it, whether you can bluff or not. And your mom has no poker face. You get that from her.'

'I have a poker face,' I say, and the kite is up — the kid did it all alone — and whipping in the wind but way too close to the sand.

'You do not.'

'I'm hiding all sorts of aces from people these days, trust me.' The dragon dips and dives and then plummets nose-first onto the beach.

149

'Doesn't sound like you,' Justine says.

'I don't even *feel* like me. Everything is changing so fast. And I'm about to leave everyone and every place I've ever known . . .'

'You chose that, you may recall. You don't have to go. You could stay.' She is propped on her elbows now, watching as the kid tries to get the kite up again. Why isn't anyone helping him? They're all just *sitting there*.

'I don't know.' I stand. 'That doesn't feel right, either.'

I walk over to the boy and say, 'Need a hand?'

He says, 'Sure,' so I take the kite and walk a few paces away from him and turn and say, 'Ready?'

'Yeah!' He smiles.

I run a bit with the kite and hoist it high and let go and it catches and my work is done.

Back at the blanket, Justine lets her head fall a little to the right, and half smiles. 'Morgan's on her way,' she says, and I'm sort of irritated. I mean, I like Morgan a lot but I get tired of all the posse togetherness sometimes. Then Justine says, 'You could come stay with me. I mean, if you want.'

'Thanks,' I say, taking a seat again. 'You're the best.' I look out at the ocean and wonder how different the color will be of the water on the opposite coast: More blue? More green? More what? 'But you're right about my mom having a rough time. I should probably stick it out.'

'I'm telling you. Therapy.'

I decide not to get irritated, because it's true that my mom could use some help, and also, the kite is still up and really soaring high now and for some dopey reason that makes me happy. I say, 'My mother needs therapy to figure out why she won't go to therapy.'

We both laugh then, and it feels like old times for a minute. But then Justine says, 'We should hang out more. I guess beach mornings are weird, though. 'Cause, you know, the boys.'

'Yeah,' I say.

'What about Saturday? Danny has some family thing and I'm not going. Are you around?'

'I'm supposed to go to that water park in Seaside with this new guy.' This was Mark's idea — his friend Vic is a lifeguard there — and it sounds like fun but also involves bathing suits. For some reason picturing the scene — me in my suit and him in his, shirtless — makes me sort of tingle with fear. Or something. We've been kissing a lot but always with clothes on. Lifted and pushed aside some but still *on*.

'And the next day?'

'Working. But I have Monday off!'

She wrinkles her nose. 'Great Adventure with . . . some friends.'

I shake my head as I picture Justine and Danny, Morgan and Mitch, and Alex and Karen Lord riding roller coasters all day. 'How easily I've been replaced.'

'It's not like that.'

'No? Then what's it like?'

She gets up. 'Good luck in California, EB. Maybe I'll see you around Thanksgiving or Christmas if you're not too busy.'

'Justine, come on!' I grab the blanket and follow her. 'Let's figure something out.'

'The whole thing sucks,' she says. 'You guys breaking up.'

'But I was miserable!'

'But I wasn't!' As soon as she says it, she laughs at herself. 'It just sucks.'

'We'll do something fun together. I promise. And I'm sorry about missing your birthday.'

'I'm sorry, too,' she says with a sigh. 'About the stuff I said to you. Really sorry.'

'So did you . . . you know?' I ask, sort of sheepishly, looking over my shoulder to see if Morgan's appeared on the beach yet. 'After your party?'

'Nah,' she says. 'I chickened out. Him, too.'

'Well, when it's right it'll feel right.' I know it's a cliché but I believe it. I don't necessarily think I'll wait until marriage or 'the one' — just the right time.

Justine shrugs. 'I think it's more likely to feel right in a dorm room than on the back porch of his parents' house, you know?'

'Totally,' I say.

Morgan's voice calls out, 'Hurray! My two besties are besties again.'

*   *   *

The house is quiet when I get home and my mother has left a note on the kitchen table that says *Hope you ate!* The fridge is so empty it's like she might have actually dumped stuff just so I couldn't eat it.

I fix myself a bowl of cereal and take it up to my room. Then I start looking through the drawer in my desk where I keep important things because there is a letter from my father in there. It's the one in which he told me he had bought the gallery in San Francisco and was moving. It's not like we'd been in touch or had seen each other in years, even when he'd been living in New York — a measly two-hour drive away — and I was pretty sure I got that letter because he had a legal obligation before moving clear across the country, but I'd saved it out of some kind of misguided sentiment. After sifting through a lot of junk that I end up tossing into a recycling bag, I find it and read it again and, sure enough, at the end he says *PS You can come visit!*

So maybe it's not the *craziest* idea.

I lie down on my bed, wondering whether Mark would be a good person to talk to about this kind of stuff, and I send him a text that says Hey and he writes back Hey yourself.

A minute later, he texts Psyched for Saturday and I write back Ditto.

Then I reread Lauren's e-mail.

I sort of can't believe she'd do that with you in the next room.

Well, me neither!

I don't know if I could keep that a secret from someone I cared about.

If you don't *know*, then don't judge!

I actually type Dear Miss High and Mighty before deleting and trying very hard to give her the benefit of the doubt.

Dear Lauren,
Nope. No sex in six months. Shocking, I

know. Especially when you consider that I'm already thinking that having sex with Mark is something I might actually want. Even though we haven't known each other a long time it feels like we have. Totally scared of getting pregnant, however. Alex and I made out a lot, and there was some touching and, um, targeted rolling around (for lack of a better way of saying it?) but that was pretty much it.

I guess I am not a hot date. Or haven't been yet!

On that note: Any more thigh touching?

I took Keyon's dad's (imagined) advice and called Justine and we talked and it was good. We're going to try to do something fun soon. Hopefully just the two of us, but probably with Morgan, too. I think I told you I had two besties but in reality Justine and I go way back and Morgan's great but also sort of new. I guess it's dumb to get possessive about your friend. Especially now?

Anyway, I am actually not sure I can keep a secret from Mark and I feel SICK about what my mother did, which means I feel sick about the thought of telling Mark. He has alluded a few times to the fact that he's less than impressed with his dad but it is still, you know, his DAD. I so wish my mother knew how to handle all this better. Right now she is pretty much ignoring me. I half expect I'll wake up tomorrow with an eviction notice taped to my door. So I dug out this letter my dad wrote me, in which he said I could come visit him. It was years ago (I mean, it was a letter! Like, on PAPER) but I've been thinking maybe it wouldn't be that crazy to e-mail him or call the gallery and see if I COULD come out to San Francisco before school starts. I know I'm going to be living there and could possibly see him anytime or all the time but I'm going to be in school by then and I'm sure it'll be busy. Am I delusional? I think I probably am. Maybe I'll just change my ticket and get on a plane and stroll in like I'm going to buy some art and see if he even recognizes me. Good plan, right?

— EB

I look around my room, wishing I had a little sister to pack.

Yes: Super-comfy slipper socks with nonstick bottoms. (I live in these, you should know.)

No: Slips. (My mother is obsessed with them but I have never met a slip that didn't show under my skirt or ride up to my waist.)

Maybe so: All new underwear and bras?

SATURDAY, JULY 27
SAN FRANCISCO

This nasty flu that's been going around the city strikes our household. Gertie and P.J. are up all Friday night blowing chunks, Jack has a fever, and Marcus says his throat hurts. Mom has Francis sort of quarantined and suggests to me on Saturday morning that I get out of the house and *stay* out until whatever this is has passed. She says I can go either to Grandma's or to Zoe's, if it's okay with her parents; it's up to me.

'I know you're trying to make as much money as you can this summer,' she says. She's talking to me from the hallway, keeping a safe distance, holding a tissue over her mouth. Right now all the sick kids are in the boys' room. 'I'd hate for you to miss a week of work.'

Yeah, me too. Not only because of the money, either. I like being with Keyon at the deli. Even though the work itself is generally a grind, being near him isn't. It's something both chemical and emotional, a kind of excited calmness I feel as long as I stay within a few feet of him. *Excited calmness* may not make sense but it's the best way I can think of it and I've been feeling it all week.

So, no, I don't want to miss work. Still, I feel obligated to ask, 'Don't you need me to stay and help?' even as I'm stuffing a handful of underwear into my backpack and thinking about T-shirts and jeans.

'I think Dad and I have it covered. Thankfully it's the weekend — maybe by Monday no one will be contagious and then you can come back and take care of them *and* us.'

Yay.

We hear a pathetic, weak 'Mommy?' cry coming from the boys' room. Mom trudges off to answer. I call my boss from the insurance company to see if anyone's there today, thinking I could go in and do some filing to kill some of my time. But the office is getting carpet-cleaned and de-mildewed over the weekend. Zoe or Grandma. Grandma or Zoe. I wonder if I could sleep in the van . . .

Not that I don't love Grandma, but she's a total worrier and never goes anywhere and still treats me like a kid. Her idea of a good time is playing Crazy Eights for hours and making ice cream sundaes, which of course was my idea of a good time, too, ten years ago. It's basically impossible for her to see me as an independent, capable near-adult. Last time I spent the night over there, I offered to go out and get us a pizza. She pulled back the living room curtain, noted the dark, and said, 'Do you think that's safe?'

Zoe, though, is also problematic, and that's mostly my own fault — there's the matter of her unanswered e-mails between us. But then I think about what my dad said: Take care of the relationships that are in front of you. There's no way my friendship with Zoe has lived out its natural life. And Ebb's last e-mail (also unanswered) worried me a little. If she comes to San Francisco to stay with her dad, is she going to expect me to hang out with her all the time and show her around or whatever? Like I need one more thing to be responsible for.

It all gives me the feeling I should do a better job of maintaining things with Zoe. I should have been more cautious with Ebb before jumping into this 'you're my second-string BFF' stuff.

I hit good old number 5 on the speed dial, right in the middle of the keypad. It's been a while. 'Zo?' I say to her voice mail. 'The kids have the plague. My mom is kicking me out for the weekend. Can I stay with you? If it's no trouble? Call me. Don't text! You know I'm so bad at texting. Bye.'

160

It's not ideal that the first time I've called in a week is to ask a favor, but there it is. You sort of earn the right to do that when you've been friends with someone for a decade.

I finish loading up my backpack, and Mom shoos me out of the house, thrusting the keys to Dad's old Saturn at me. 'It's not like we're going to go anywhere,' she says. 'I sanitized the keys but keep washing your hands.' I head over to Simple Pleasures Cafe to wait for Zoe to get back to me. It's a great little run-down hole-in-the-wall, in the middle of the fog bank that is the Outer Richmond in summer, furnished with dirty, saggy old couches, and funky art on the walls.

As I sit with my coffee, I have a lively conversation with myself, in my head, about whether or not to call Keyon and see what he's up to. We haven't actually set a date for me coming over for dinner, but I don't want to be one of those girls who's always, like, 'Look at me, look at me, look at me,' afraid that if you don't remind a guy every five minutes that you exist, he'll forget about you. Even if I feel that way a tiny, tiny bit.

The thing is, I don't know how seriously to take his flirting. From what I remember about him at school, he always had some girlfriend or other. Never the same one for long, like he was always looking for the next thing. Which isn't a crime. It's high school, after all. Was Joe advising him about *those* girls? Does Keyon flirt with me mostly because I'm *there?* Or is there something specific about *me* he likes? And if he finds out I'm a virgin, as in if *I tell him* I am, will he drop me like a hot potato or make it his goal in life to be my first, for the conquest of it? Neither scenario is fantastic.

What I want to know is: Am I special?

It does occur to me that I only feel insecure when I'm not around him. When we're together, or talking on the phone, or e-mailing, I feel completely at home and these questions don't torment me.

As I stare at the café wall measuring out the pros and cons, my eyes land on a flyer for a new exhibit at a gallery called The Wall. After racking my brain for a full half-cup's worth of coffee sips, I realize why it's familiar. That's Ebb's dad's place.

The pictures on the flyer are exactly the kind of 'art' I don't get: big blocks of color with, like, one black dot randomly applied. I'm intrigued, though, by the idea that Ebb's dad is right here in the city. Maybe getting a glimpse of him will help me know something about *her*, and trigger some intuitive sense of whether or not we should go forward with the whole being roommates thing.

A little stalkery, I admit.

But really, what else do I have to do today? I tear the flyer off the wall and stuff it in my messenger bag, getting a refill of my coffee to go.

★ ★ ★

'Remind me again why we're doing this?' Zoe asks while I drive in circles around SoMa in search of parking. She called me right as I was pulling away from the coffee shop and after shrieking at me a few minutes for being out of touch said yeah, of course I could stay with her. Then I talked her into coming with me on my art adventure.

'I want to get myself cultured before I start at UC. You know how those East Bay hipsters love their art. I saw this flyer and thought — '

'There's one!' she shouts, sticking her arm right in front of my face and pointing to the other side of the street. I flip a U-turn and jerk into the space, earning several wrathful honks from other drivers. Zoe's always had the magic when it comes to finding parking.

We lock up and embark on the seven-block walk to The Wall. In traditional San Francisco microclimate fashion, it's as sunny and warm here as it was cold and foggy in the Richmond. As we walk, I peel off layers of clothes and Zoe stares at her phone, thumbs busy.

I compose imaginary tweets and status updates and say them aloud. It's my favorite way to harass Zoe about her phone addiction.

'*I'm walking down Eighth Street to go see art a child could paint.*'

'*There are a lot of pigeons out today.*'

'*About to cross Folsom. Hope I don't get run over.*'

She finally fires one back. '*Lauren is bugging the shit out of me.*' But she does put her phone into her pocket before we cross. 'When's the last time we got together on a weekend?' she asks, fingering the ends of her recently highlighted hair.

'Never. And like I said, I'm sorry for being out of touch. My family — '

'I know. Your family needs you.' She sounds bored. 'Always such a handy excuse.'

'There's a difference between a reason and an excuse.'

'Yes,' she says. 'I know.'

Before I can answer, she stops and walks backward a couple of feet. 'Is this it?' We stare at a nondescript storefront with the name THE WALL stenciled on the glass door in modern-looking block letters.

'Yep.'

We step in. It's small; a few bare, narrow

rooms, little but the art on the white walls. There are a few other people here. It's hard to tell who's working and who's like us, looking. 'So what do you do in an art gallery?' I whisper to Zoe.

'Stroll around. Look thoughtful. Nod.'

We do, and spend some time staring at a single huge canvas painted green, with three small white squares in one corner. 'This one's only five thousand seven hundred dollars, Zo.'

She nods. She looks thoughtful. 'Would be great for your dorm room.'

'Did you have any questions?' a voice behind us asks, and I turn around and I just know from how he's dressed and the whole effect of him that he's the owner. Ebb's dad, I assume. He's super-good-looking, like one of those middle-aged guys in a Ralph Lauren ad, on a yacht, tan and windblown and slightly squinty.

'No, thank you.'

But Zoe says, 'Actually, I wondered, what's this painting supposed to be . . . saying?'

'Did you read the artist's statement?'

I detect a slight New York-y kind of accent. It has to be Mr. Ebb. I mean I guess he could have a partner or a *partner*, also from back east, but I have this feeling.

'Oh,' Zoe says. 'No?' She glances around the room.

He goes over to a small wooden stand and picks up a trifold brochure thing and hands it to Zoe with a smile. His teeth are very straight. I try to construct a face for Ebb made up of some of his features. Does she have the blue eyes? The narrow nose? I'm suddenly filled with an urgent need to see her, as if this will answer all my uncertainties about her as a person, roommate, and potential friend.

And I could send a picture of me. Maybe with Keyon. I'd like to have a picture with him and me together before I go to school.

Zoe reads the artist's statement, then hands it back, unimpressed. 'Hm.'

'Not for you?' Mr. Ebb says.

'Not really.'

'I've got a new artist coming in next week. A local, Edward Sherman. You should come back. He's more accessible. More representational.'

He reaches into his chest pocket, withdraws two business cards, and gives one to each of us. I look at the name. Neil Logan. That's him. 'Thanks,' I say.

'Thank you for coming in.' He bends from the waist slightly, with his hands behind his back, then moves on to a hipster couple examining the green painting.

Out on the street, Zoe asks, 'Do you feel cultured now?'

'I feel . . . hungry.'

If Zoe knew the real reason for my wanting to be here . . . well, she'd love it. But I don't know, I guess I do already feel some loyalty to Ebb and don't want to turn her into a story for Zoe. From her last e-mail, it was obvious she *does* find the affair issue totally upsetting, and life with her mom seems generally not awesome.

We head to Blondie's for a slice, and when I've wiped the pizza grease off my hands, I ask Zoe, 'Can you show me how to e-mail from my phone?'

'Oh my hell, Lauren. You are so pathetic! You probably don't even have a data plan.'

'Data plan?'

'E-mail from my account if it's that urgent.' She sets it up for me and I'm not even sure I remember Ebb's address right, but I try.

Hi it's Lauren. A sickness has befallen my house and I'm exiled. Long story I can explain better later. Is it weird we haven't sent each other pics yet? I know, I should be on Facebook. But I'm not, so . . . send me one? I'll send one too when back to my computer after safe from plague. Sorry so short on Zoe's phone.

I hit Send.

SUNDAY, JULY 28
NEW JERSEY

The words — *one* and *month* — keep colliding in my head like bumper cars and I'm almost jumping out of my seat with nerves and excitement and something else as Mark and I drive through town.

One month.

One month from today is August 28th. (I actually pulled out my plane tickets this morning, to be sure I had the date right.)

The big day.

I'm entirely preoccupied by one question: Can I survive a month or do I really need to get out of here sooner than that? Lauren hasn't written back to give me advice or to judge me — only to alert me to the plague — so I've realized I need to come to my own decision about whether to reach out to my father. I am not making it up when I say that Mark is hitting his radio presets in the car and *the freaking Clash* comes on with 'Should I Stay or Should I Go?' and, of course, he stops there and turns up the volume.

168

'What's going on with you today?' he asks. 'You seem . . . on edge?'

'Just thinking about how I leave in exactly one month.'

Or sooner?

'No fair,' he says. 'I leave in a month and a day or two, so you get to go first.'

He's driving. We're on our way to the beach after stopping to finally buy me a new phone and I feel okay about the bikini under my clothes since I survived the water park yesterday intact. I didn't end up feeling that self-conscious at all in my swimsuit — at least not after the first few minutes, not when I got the sense that Mark liked what he saw. Is it weird that I found that exhilarating? Whenever Alex used to look at me that way, I felt all nervous and somehow put-upon. With Mark it's different. It's not that he's a total look-but-don't-touch sort of guy. He definitely likes to touch. But there doesn't seem to be any pressure behind it; it's like he enjoys it for what it is without the annoyance of wanting more. And there was something about going down crazy water slides and shooting at each other with big water cannons and laughing so hard that my stomach still hurts that made me feel like a kid again, and I liked it. I hadn't had fun — good old-fashioned fun — in the longest time, too long, and it was almost like my body had chemically changed by the time we'd turned in our tubes and dried off and headed for the car, holding hands, all achy and giddy. It was as if we'd stepped through a kind of magic mirror when we'd entered that park and had somehow relived a moment from a childhood we'd never even shared.

I am in complete denial about the secret I am keeping from him. And that secret is multiplying now that I am considering skipping town early but haven't told him.

'Okay,' Mark says. 'So let's talk about this.'

I push some hair out of my face — we've got the windows down. 'What's there to talk about?'

'You're serious?' He looks over at me.

I shrug a shoulder and don't know why I'm acting this way, why I don't tell him that I've already gone online to see how much plane tickets between California and Chicago cost. (His going to Northwestern gets him closer to me but not by much.) Why I don't unload about my mom and his dad. Why I don't tell him everything.

'Us,' he says. 'That's what there is to talk about.'

'But what *about* us?' I just want him to say it, whatever he's thinking — whether it's that we should give the long-distance thing a try or absolutely plan on breaking up. 'I mean, what do you want to do?'

I can't look over at him while I wait so I watch this woman crossing the street in front of us. She has a baby strapped to her chest in some kind of fancy harness and another kid, like three years old, in a stroller. The baby is clawing at her neck and she's holding her head at an awkward angle to try to avoid getting mauled and he's bouncing against her chest, like he really doesn't want to be strapped in. It looks painful for both parties involved.

'What do I want to do?' Mark says. 'I want to pull over and kiss some sense into you is what I want to do.'

I smile as he pulls into the beach parking lot and parks as far away from other cars as possible. He turns off the engine and leans over and kisses me and I feel calmer, but not by much.

When he pulls away he says, 'If you go by anecdotal evidence, we're doomed. Most relationships that start in high school — and probably right after, like us — don't survive the transition to college. There's too much in the way of temptation.'

For a second I can't imagine myself being tempted by anyone else more than I'm tempted by Mark but I also know that a part

171

of me doesn't want to go away to school — to freedom — wearing any kind of shackles at all. Also, ending things makes the whole Keeping of the Secret easier. If we never get serious, I'll never have to tell.

'So I think we need to make the most of this month,' he says. 'Try to pack as much relationship stuff in as possible and then go off to school and just see. But with no hard feelings or pressure, you know? We'll give it the ol' college try, as they say.'

We get out of the car and grab the beach bags from the trunk.

I say, 'That all sounds highly reasonable.' Which is good. Because I know that I am not feeling particularly reasonable about anything these days, and if this is what a reasonable person thinks is wise, then that's okay by me.

'Who knows?' he says as we head down onto the sand. 'Maybe we'll have a fiery breakup before then anyway and then it won't even be an issue.'

'Do you have a lot of fiery breakups, in general?' We haven't talked about previous relationships or experience at all. The fact that he likely has some serious ex-girlfriends — girls out there in the world whose breasts, and more, he has touched — actually makes me sort of ill.

'A few,' he says, 'but I bet a fiery breakup

172

with you would be a lot better.' He puts an arm around my shoulders as we walk toward a blinding ocean, and says, 'Everything with you is better.'

This prompts me, for no good reason I can think of, to ask, 'Do you want to have kids?'

He looks at me funny as he spreads out a blanket.

'I mean, not *now*,' I clarify. 'I mean, like someday.'

'Yeah, definitely.' He nods. 'Why do you ask?'

'I don't know.' I guess it was the woman crossing the street but I've also been thinking about my theory about our parents determining who we are, and how Lauren entertains the idea of never having kids and how I just always *assumed* I would. It's not like I look at people like that mom crossing the street or the Schroeders and think, *I want that*, in some lovey-dovey urgent way, but I like the idea of having a family. 'You know how I've been e-mailing with my roommate for this year?'

He nods.

'Well, she has five brothers and sisters and she said she'd rather have zero kids than six. And I've always thought I wanted kids, but maybe I don't really. Maybe I want a family but not kids. Like I sort of wish I could pop out a couple of siblings for myself right now.'

He laughs and I laugh.

It's funny because it's true.

'I want a big family.' Mark plops down on the blanket and I do the same. '*Huge*, in fact.'

'Really?' I laugh.

'Well, I don't know. I mean, even three kids would seem huge to me, since there's just me and my brother and he's never around anymore. But of course I want to make sure I have those kids with the right person.'

I am only seventeen, I say to myself. Eighteen in October, but still. I will not take the bait. I will not ask him if he thinks it might be me. I will not imagine that scenario for us at all, will not ask myself whether *he* is the right person for me.

'My parents sort of screwed that one up big-time,' I say.

He finds my hand and squeezes it. 'Mine, too, I think, though they are too blind to see it.'

I watch a wave crash on the shore and imagine it washing my secret out to sea like so much seaweed.

We go bodysurfing for a while and when we're drying off we make a list of things we think we should do in the next month in the spirit of packing in as much relationship stuff as possible. Highlights include 'have a fight,'

174

'make up,' 'pick 'our song,'' 'slow-dance,' and 'buy each other a present.'

I put 'tell him the truth' on the list in my head, sort of like I'm skywriting it in there, then cross it out.

I lie down on our blanket when we're done with the list and close my eyes and see a kaleidoscope of yellows and reds and greens behind my lids. I think about the present Alex gave me for Valentine's Day — a super-tacky, super-Jersey gold necklace with my name written in curly script. I only ever wore it when you couldn't really see it because of the cut of my top. I honestly have no idea what I'll get Mark.

I feel his arm sneak across my belly as he curls up on his side next to me. He says, 'I'm falling for you really hard.'

'Me too,' I say, and I can't imagine a better gift he could give me than this moment.

'Oh,' he says then. 'One more thing. For the list.'

'What is it?'

I'm half expecting him to say 'make love' because even in this sweet moment I feel like our bodies are connecting to each other, relaying some kind of heat back and forth.

'Meet the parents,' he says.

'Nooooo,' I say, and it comes out like a funny sort of moan, even though I'm not trying to be funny, or at least didn't *plan on* trying to be funny.

'Parents ruin everything,' I say, all too aware of how perilously close I am to the edge of the Cliff of Secrets. 'And anyway, I met your dad that one time.' It's seriously like rocks and earth are falling away by my feet.

'I mean, I want you to meet my mom,' he says. 'She seems sort of down lately with my dad traveling so much and I think she'd like you.'

I teeter there on that cliff for a minute, as if knocked off-balance by some gust of wind; then I pull back. 'We'll see,' I say. 'We've got a lot of other stuff on that list.'

★ ★ ★

I've been waiting for another e-mail from Lauren — one of substance, with a picture attached — for more than twenty-four hours but it hasn't come yet so I decide to just send her mine when I get home around dinner-time. When I'm on Facebook looking for a good shot, I decide to search for her friend Zoe, because Zoe's e-mail is her name @gmail and her name isn't that common and sure enough she's got a Facebook page — at least I think it's her since it says San Francisco, CA, under her name. She's

176

cool-looking — and white, which seems to maybe confirm my hunch about Lauren. I can't see anything else on her page because it's blocked unless you're her friend, and anyway this is stalkery. I click away.

I hear my mother come home, and for a second I'm tempted to hide in my closet, another weird thing I used to do when I was younger. I'd climb in there with a book and a blanket and a flashlight and pretend I was like Anne Frank, hiding from evil forces. And now that I'm thinking about that — *and* the bath mat fantasies — I'm even sadder about leaving this condo, and my childhood, even if it all suddenly seems even more sucky than I thought. Surely you can't hide in your dorm room closet when you're a college freshman, at least not without your roommate calling an RA and probably putting you on suicide watch, so I had best come up with some new coping skills.

I hear cabinets being opened and dishes being taken out and decide that I need to make my presence known if only because it might score me some kitchen scraps, so I walk downstairs. She doesn't turn to look at me, so I say, 'Hi, Mom.'

'Oh!' She startles. 'I didn't think you'd be here.'

I'm sure she's faking her surprise — the

stairs of our house are pretty squeaky — but I don't call her out on it.

She says, 'It's hard to keep track of your comings and goings these days.'

I want to say 'Right back at you,' but I don't.

'Sorry about that,' I say.

'It's what you're supposed to be doing,' she says. 'I know that.' She puts down the butter knife she's using to spread peanut butter and jelly onto bread and presses her hands on the countertop. When I hear her exhale hard, it all has the combined effect of signaling to me that she's about to cry. 'I guess I'm not sure what to do with myself.'

'Oh, Mom.' I slide into a kitchen chair. 'You're plenty busy. You'll be fine. You really will.'

She turns and presents the sandwich to me and she doesn't look like she's going to cry anymore. 'I don't know why I even made this,' she says. 'I've got a date.'

I study the sandwich and I'm suddenly not hungry. 'Please tell me it's not with the married guy.' I actually close my eyes.

'Elizabeth,' she says. 'I'm a grown-up.'

'Well, then, act like one!' My voice goes up as my eyes open. It had, honestly, never occurred to me that she might continue to see him.

'He's *leaving* her,' she says. 'They're going to *get* a *divorce*.'

'Mom! Are you really that gullible?' But I wonder, is this what Mark was talking about, when he said his mom was feeling down? I sincerely hope not. Because if his dad leaves his mom and then introduces his new girlfriend to Mark and it's my mom, I am in some serious trouble.

'How do you know it's not true?' My mother's voice is shaky. 'It could happen! Someone could love me.'

'*I* love you, Mom. Me. *I* do. And I'm telling you, this is a bad situation and you need to walk away.'

'Well, we're going to have to agree to disagree on this one,' she says. Then she drifts out of the room, saying simply, 'I've got to go get ready.'

★ ★ ★

Upstairs, after forcing down half the sandwich, I attach a picture to an e-mail file; it's one that Tim took of me the week we were working in Mark's parents' garden, with the weeping false cypress behind me — and enter Lauren's address. Then I delete her address and put in the info@ e-mail of the gallery and the subject heading I come up with is this:

179

FOR NEIL — PERSONAL.

As much as I hate to cut things off with Mark, as much as I hate to not get to half the stuff on that list, I need to get out of this town.

Hi there,
It's me, Elizabeth, and I've got exciting news. I'm going to college at UC Berkeley, starting at the end of August. So I was thinking of maybe changing my ticket and coming out a few weeks early, to get the lay of the land, and I was wondering if I could crash at your place or something. You said ages ago that I should visit and this way I don't have to buy extra plane tickets or anything because I'm already coming and the fee to change is no biggie. Let me know what you think. Would be great to catch up before things get hectic with classes. Recent pic attached, since, you know, it's been a while.

— Elizabeth

When I hit Send, I feel like something's wrong with my head, like I'm having some kind of aneurysm. I can't believe I did it. I have to tell Lauren. So I click on her e-mail and hit Reply and attach my photo before I forget.

How are you feeling? I am not good with puke. You should know that.

I am attaching a photo of myself with my favorite tree — yes, I have a favorite tree. BOTANY NERD ALERT!

So, call me young and restless, but I did it. Just now. I e-mailed my dad and asked him if I could come out early. Keep your fingers crossed for me because things here seem to be deteriorating rapidly. No need to get into details.

Meanwhile, as the world turns, Mark and I made a list of things to do together before we leave so I'm bummed that I may leave early and not get to do it all but I think it's for the best. We decided we wouldn't officially end things before we left — at least we said those words — but now that I'm sitting here and writing that it sounds ridiculous. Because if one of us DOES meet someone else at school, then we're left with some horrible phone — or worse, e-mail! Text! — breakup and will probably hate each other forever. And anyway, I'll have to end it when I tell him I'm leaving early, won't I? Maybe come clean about the whole sordid affair on my way out of town? He's going to Northwestern, which is pretty far. Where's Keyon going? Will you guys try to still be together?

Like sands through the hourglass, these are the days of our lives.

(And yes, I am done with my soap opera references. Or almost done:)

Bold and beautiful,

EB

Yes: A bath mat. (Long story.)

No: My mother.

Maybe so: A broken heart.

I know it's not the best e-mail, but I send it anyway because she hasn't even properly responded to my last e-mail. Then I go back and reread the e-mail I sent my dad, which I decide is pretty much the dumbest thing I've ever written. That doesn't make me want him to say yes any less, though. And while I'm hanging out in my sent box, I realize I've sent the e-mail I meant for Lauren to Zoe's address. Could I be more stupid? I dash off another quick e-mail.

Hi Zoe,

You don't know me. Please disregard the e-mail I sent you in error.

Thanks.

No more need to explain, right? I feel ill. I forward the e-mail to Lauren's actual address.

Dear Lauren,
I just sent the e-mail below to Zoe by accident. So sorry but I don't think I said anything that will jam you up!

EB

Really, really ill.
Mark sends me a text that says Thinking about you. Missing you. I write back Me too and now all I want to do is cry.

SUNDAY, JULY 28
SAN FRANCISCO

On Sunday Zoe and I go to Target and do some shopping for her dorm room. All summer she's seemed about a hundred times less nervous about going off to college than I am, and *she's* actually leaving the state, like a real grown-up.

She's puzzling over which of two sheet sets to get. 'If I stick with a neutral color, it won't clash with whatever my suitemates bring. On the other hand, neutral is boring so maybe I should go ahead and get the crazy pattern . . .'

Her setup is going to be totally different from mine and Ebb's, with four or six — I don't remember — sharing an apartmentlike space. She hasn't expressed any worry about it or said if they've communicated, and I consider asking if she *is* worried and if they *have* communicated. But then I'd have to tell her about Ebb and I don't want to get into it right now. I like keeping Ebb inside my computer and Zoe out here in the 3-D world.

'Get the crazy pattern,' I say. 'Live your dream!'

'You're such a dork.' But it makes her laugh and she puts the patterned set into her cart.

* * *

We stay up late, drowsily watching old *Buffy* episodes on Zoe's iPad, both of us under piles of blankets on her queen bed, and as I drift off I think of the sleepovers we've had over the years, the hundreds of accumulated hours I've spent in this house. Sliding down her carpeted staircase in slick nylon sleeping bags, setting up stacks of pillows in the long hallway and hurdling them like Olympians, daring each other to go outside after dark in our pajamas.

I snuggle against Zoe and start to say, 'Remember when . . . ' but an e-mail notification pops up on the display and she does some fancy hand gesture to switch screens. I close my eyes, used to this. Zoe hasn't had an uninterruptable moment since she got the iPad for graduation.

After a few seconds of quiet, she mutters, 'Are you and Keyon Smith, like, a thing?'

Suddenly, I'm very awake. 'What?' I sit up and pull the blanket to my chin. The only light in the room is the glow of the iPad, which I try to see, but she's holding it almost against her chest now.

'I mean, some people said they thought they saw you guys kissing at Yasmin's party but I know if that were true you would have told me.'

'Let me see that.'

'*Right?*'

I flop back down. 'I was going to.'

She then proceeds to read me Ebb's latest e-mail, which Ebb accidentally sent to Zoe's account, of course, because I'm so technologically impaired that I didn't bother to bring my laptop to Zoe's, and so impatient that I couldn't even wait to use hers to e-mail.

'Who is this chick?' Zoe asks when she's done reading. I'm simultaneously processing the information in Ebb's letter — that she probably *will* be coming out early because of course her dad will say yes — and trying to think how to explain all this to Zoe.

'My Berkeley roommate. We've been e-mailing a little.'

'A little? You sound like soul mates.' She waits for more but I don't know what to say or where to begin. 'So wait, though, first of all, Keyon. He's so . . . '

Hot. Awesome. Popular. Nice. Smart. 'I know.'

'And *you*! I'm trying to remember if he

ever went out with a white girl before.'

She stares past my head, recalling Keyon's social life at Galileo. 'Asian, I think, and black, and then I guess for like five minutes there was that exchange student from Colombia . . . '

'You can stop,' I say, and think, *He's mine now, bitches! Did Joe invite you for dinner? Oh, no? Then shut up.* The imaginary girls in my head look back at me like I'm crazy.

Zoe is still in shock. 'I never would have imagined Keyon Smith and Lauren Cole. Ever. Are you guys trying to keep it a secret or something?'

'No, but — '

'Then why didn't you tell me?' She's hurt. I hurt her.

'Zoe,' I say, rolling toward her on the bed. 'I really like him. I guess I didn't want to, like, put it out there.' I wave my fingers in the dark — *out there* is meant to indicate Twitter, Facebook, the universe. I didn't want to make it real in that way. Because once it's real it can become unreal. 'Ebb's just some girl in New Jersey. She doesn't know him or anyone we know. It seemed easier.'

Zoe studies the screen again. 'She looks pretty normal.'

'There's a picture?' I sit back up.

'Well, yeah, you asked for one.' She finally

hands the iPad over to me and I get to see the face that belongs to the name I've been telling all my secrets to, the person who's been telling me hers.

It's weird. I wish I were alone while looking at this, so I could study it and match it up to the idea I've had of Ebb, but I'm self-conscious about looking too long with Zoe watching me. Ebb's got her dad's eyes, is all I can notice before I give Zoe her iPad back.

'Do you want me to delete this from my e-mail?' she asks.

'Can you forward it to me first?'

'Obvs. We could look her up on . . . you know, everything. I'm fast at this.'

'No,' I say, but can't explain why. To Zoe or to myself.

Zoe, awesome Zoe, doesn't question. She taps the screen a few times and then sets the thing down on the floor and the room goes totally dark. 'Okay,' she whispers. 'Tell me all about you and Keyon.'

* * *

Monday morning I do something I never do: I call the insurance company and leave a voice mail saying I can't come in. I hate that place, to be honest. After turning off my phone, I get back in bed and we sleep for what seems to me like hours compared to my usual 6 AM Gertie-breath wake-up call. Then Zoe sets me up on her laptop. 'I can't believe you left yours at home, especially when you're away for an indeterminate amount of time.'

'I didn't think about it.'

'Well, you're a freak.'

I check my own e-mail to make sure I have Ebb's message and picture. Yes, now I have them twice. And a message from Keyon dated yesterday, saying he knows it's late notice, but can I make dinner on Monday? Tonight. I call my mom to find out what's going on in the TB ward. Three out of five people still have a fever, she tells me, and says not to come home yet, not even to pick up more clothes.

So I'm borrowing some of Zoe's, which sort of sag at the boobal area, where Zoe is abundantly blessed, and are tight in the butt, where most of my 'development' happened at fourteen.

She's lying on her bed and aiming her little digital video camera at me while I walk around the room getting ready to head to the sandwich shop. 'How are you feeling in this transitional moment?' she asks.

'Between being here and going to work?'

'No, smart-ass. Between high school and college.'

'Who wants to know?' I experiment with one of her cool, crafty hairpins, but my fine hair slips right out.

'I'm doing a vlog series asking all my friends what it feels like to be finally growing up. Answer,' she commands.

I look into the mirror so that she's filming me talking more or less to myself. 'I'm moving across the Bay. Is that growing up? Or is it just leaving?'

'Ooh, deep. That's good,' she says, before putting the camera down and wriggling back under the covers. She has no summer job or responsibilities and sort of lounges around like a princess until she decides what she wants to do with her day. It's charming, in its way.

Other than her video camera in my face and the constant chirps and beeps and dings and whooshes coming from her various devices, it's been so quiet here. Zoe's parents are cool but busy and have left us to ourselves. I actually wouldn't mind a screaming toddler running through now and again.

'I'm going to be late tonight,' I say, pulling on Zoe's 49ers sweatshirt. 'Keyon's dad invited me for dinner.' No big deal. Easy breezy.

It's hard to interpret her silent stare. If

she's still hurt that I didn't tell her about him, I don't blame her. I come sit on the bed. 'I'm sorry.'

'You *are* sorry. If you think you're wearing that sweatshirt to dinner at Keyon Smith's house, you are sad *and* sorry.' She throws back the covers and walks to the closet, studying its contents. 'Here,' she says, shoving a midnight-blue flowy tee with elbow-length sleeves at me. 'Change into this after work. This is your color.'

'Thank you, Z.'

She waves her hand like it's no big deal. 'Promise you'll tell me everything when you get home.'

'If *you* promise me you're not going to tell the Internet about this before I even figure out if it's anything.'

She returns to her bed and leans back on her elbows. 'The fact that you're all protective of this alleged nonrelationship means it's something already.'

Good point.

★ ★ ★

Keyon and I hang out late after work while Joe does the money stuff, then we drive together to Glen Park, where they live. Keyon sits in the backseat with me, and Joe jokes around about having left his chauffer's cap at home. We all smell like mustard and pickles and I realize I didn't change into the nicer shirt Zoe lent me. It's quiet in the car; we've been talking all day at work so it's not like it's awkward. Lunch rush at the sandwich shop can tire you out.

When we get to their house, Joe excuses himself to change and Keyon's mom — 'Call me Sue' — gives me the tour while Keyon takes a shower. I've met her before, in the shop, but this is the first time we've really talked. 'We try to keep Joe Junior's room nice in case out-of-town family comes in,' she's saying, swinging open a door off the hallway. 'Of course normally he's here with us on summer break but this year he had to go off to Europe to prove something so I'm borrowing one corner of his room for my craft table . . . '

I want to ask what Joe Junior had to prove and why he had to go to Europe to do it, but there aren't what you'd call a lot of gaps in Sue's commentary as we continue down the hall.

' . . . five years ago we went ahead and took a second mortgage so that we could redo and I finally got the master suite I always wanted when he took out the wood paneling, what an eyesore that was . . . '

A small, paranoid part of me wonders if she's keeping up the constant chatter to avoid any awkward 'you're just so white' moments. Or that maybe she's barreling through it so fast because she does it all the time — it's her spiel, the one all of Keyon's ladies get, and she's had lots of practice. I don't know where I get this idea he's such a player. A guy having a bunch of girlfriends doesn't mean he's *playing* them, necessarily.

Another door in the hallway opens up and we both turn to see Keyon, from the back, walking away from us wearing nothing but a dark-blue towel around his waist. 'Keyon James Smith,' Sue yells after him, 'I didn't buy you a robe so that you could go walking around the house half-naked in front of your guest!'

I stare at a frame full of family pictures before Keyon can turn around and see me taking in his muscular back and calves.

'Sorry, guest!' he shouts. It makes me smile.

'I'm good,' I say, now looking at the pictures for real. Keyon and Joe Junior were adorable kids. I've always thought black babies are the cutest, and I almost say that to Sue before realizing there's no way to say it without being totally offensive or making Sue think I'm an idiot. Race. It's so tricky, even though we're all supposedly enlightened and color-blind. I don't want it to be a Thing. But it kind of is a Thing, isn't it?

When the tour is over, I go to the bathroom to change my shirt and wash as much of the deli smell off my hands as I can. It's steamy and soapy and Keyon-y in there and I wish I could take a quick shower, too. There's a bottle of lotion on the sink. I pump some out and sniff; flowery and not my style. But it's better than eau de Grey Poupon so I rub a blob into my neck and arms hoping it will help.

Dinner is nice. Sue talks nonstop so there's no chance to get uncomfortable, and she makes an awesome pot roast.

'It's the easiest thing in the world,' she says. 'You just spend five minutes in the morning putting it in your slow cooker and it always comes out perfect. Do you cook? Keyon can't cook to save his life and I don't know what he expects to happen when he gets out into the real world.'

'I can cook!' Keyon protests.

'I don't count sandwiches.'

'I do,' Joe Senior says.

After dinner, Joe needs his car for something but makes Keyon ride the Muni with me all the way out to West Portal, which is walking distance from Zoe's house. He walks me there, too, in the dark, in the fog, and at some point he takes my hand and at some point after that his hand pulls me to him as he stops and leans me up against a random car.

He gets close. Very, very close. Then pulls his head back a second. 'Sorry. You smell a little bit like my mom.'

The lotion. Oops. 'I'm not, though,' I reassure him, laughing, and he kisses me like I've never been kissed before. I mean, really, he puts a lot into it. He applies himself to the task. It's like he's been saving it up for me since the party, maybe seeing a personal kissing trainer in preparation for the big event.

It's that good.

Dear EB,
Writing from Zoe's laptop, but my own account this time, obviously!

So, yeah. No big deal about the e-mail thing. I hadn't aaaactually told her about Keyon yet so that sort of came up but I'm glad she knows now.

My tone in this e-mail is different than it has been. I can tell, and Ebb will be able to feel it, too. But I don't feel so close to her right now. She's not my best friend. *Zoe* is my best friend. She took me in after I ignored a bunch of her e-mails, she forgave me superfast for not telling her about Keyon, and when I got home tonight and told her how it went she gave me some kissing tips for next time. Like breathing in Keyon's ear. 'Don't, like, *blow* into it,' she said. 'You don't want to give him an ear infection. Just sort of . . . exhale. Warmly. It will be good, trust me.' She leaned over and showed me, and I jumped back and squealed, laughing. 'Eww.'

I don't want to worry about what to say that will make Ebb feel better, or write about whether or not I have hopes that Keyon and I will stay together. I only want to think about the next time I'm going to kiss him. But I feel kind of sorry for Ebb. I thought my life was complicated, but hers is no picnic. At least the people in my life behave like the adults they mostly are. At the same time, being sorry for a person isn't the best basis for a friendship. It's gone all out of balance somehow.

'Hurry up with Jersey Girl over there,' Zoe says from the bed. 'I want to edit my vlog.'

Come on, Lauren, I think. *Step up here and make an effort.* I would hate it if my desire to escape the chaos of my life turned me into one of those . . . I don't know

196

. . . people who runs away, I guess, from stuff that's complicated. Like trying to be a friend to this girl who's going to live in the same small space as me for the next year. And might be coming out here sooner than later.

I reread her last couple of e-mails and look at her picture some more. She may be 99 percent words on a screen to me, but she's a real person. There is no 'inside my computer' vs 3-D. It's *all* real life, and I can't pretend like it isn't. I inhale and type fast.

I had dinner with Keyon's parents tonight. You probably already guessed this, since there aren't any white Keyons that I know of, but he's black. And I felt slightly awkward about it and hope to God it didn't show. In San Francisco you aren't supposed to notice these things.

More importantly, Keyon is an amazing kisser. He rode the train home with me (Joe made him!) and walked me to Zoe's and it happened. So the situation is no longer ambiguous. Not that I know what it is, but it is not like gee I don't know if he likes me. He likes me. That kiss couldn't lie.

Sounds like you and Mark have done some good talking. You just, like, TALK about all this stuff? Is it awkward? I don't know how to do that with Keyon. He's going to Chico State, which is well within visiting distance but not close close. Like three hours. But we're not even near that discussion yet, I don't think. Maybe it's a summer fling.

So that's cool you might be coming out early to hang with your dad. Let me know when you get here and I'll show you around.

I know I owe you lots more replies. Like I wanted to say about that thing with your mom: yes, you were helping her.

Thanks for sending the picture. I like your hair. I've tried to get mine to do that beachy wavy thing. Not happening. Here's one of me from Zoe's computer. I'm the one on the left, with the darker hair and smaller boobs.

Lo (that's what Keyon's been calling me and I sort of like it as my new college name — Zoe sometimes calls me LoCo, partly because of my last name but also partly to imply I'm crazy)

Yes: A new phone. Something that can e-mail and all that. Zoe keeps telling me I'm living like it's 2006, in the pre-iPhone epoch. (She didn't actually say 'epoch.' That's more a

Lauren word.) I don't want to be married to my phone but I guess I should join the future.

No: The six pounds I've gained, all in my ass, since starting at the deli. Chicken salad is not our friend.

Maybe so: The microscope my dad gave me for my tenth birthday. I mean, it's a cheap kid's thing with no real power but it's symbolic of . . . something. Do we have room in our room for symbolic knickknacks?

WEDNESDAY, JULY 31
NEW JERSEY

Tim has a new job and I'm back at it, though work definitely feels less exciting now that there's not a chance to see Mark. As I prune some existing plants Tim wants to work around, I slip into a daydream and imagine Mark driving by randomly, like on his way to a friend's or to the beach, and seeing me. I picture him beeping his horn, me turning, then getting up and walking over while he watches me, waiting and wanting. But then Tim shouts something over at me and I snap back to reality and, really, when I'm like this, with dirt under my fingernails even though they're inside my gloves, I have a hard time thinking of myself as sexy. As someone that anyone — but more specifically Mark — would want to have sex with. I sense that he does, though — at least in theory. But there's a big difference between wanting and doing. Either way, I think I want to with him, too. Which feels so strange considering how long I spent trying to keep Alex at bay.

But anyway, it's all too complicated with

the secret I'm holding and also, I recognize that it seems ... fast. It's like there's this grandfather clock of college chiming whenever we're together and I don't want that to influence the timing of things.

Or do I?

Because maybe that's how life works. Maybe having sex with him is the decision I'm supposed to make and it doesn't matter that I'm making it in a sort of pressure cooker.

But I'm scared.

That I'll regret it.

That it's all too random.

That I really have no idea what I'm doing or feeling at any given moment of the day.

Which is part of why it's taking me longer than usual to write back to Lauren. I guess I am still waiting for my father to respond, so that I know what kind of limbo I'm actually in. Two-week limbo? Or one-month limbo? If he takes much longer to reply there won't be any point in changing my ticket and leaving early since it won't really be early. Nothing is going according to plan.

Another reason I haven't written yet: I don't actually know what to say about Keyon's being black. Because I can't be like 'Oh, that's funny 'cause I don't associate San Francisco with black people at all — only gay people LOL' or 'Yeah, I sort of guessed that — I mean, duh!' I think maybe I won't say anything about it at all. Because I'm slowly figuring out that you never know who you're going to connect with in life, or why, and I like to think I'm the kind of person who could be roommates with, or fall head over heels in love with, someone from another heritage or country if that's what the universe had in store for me.

And though it's true that I've studied that picture of Lauren and Zoe for way too long and have pulled it up on my phone way too often, it's only because I'm *fascinated*. One of them is the person I'm going to be living with for an entire year. This is what she *looks like*, the person on the receiving end of all these e-mails I've been sending.

I'm starting to dig a hole in which to plant a small ornamental tree, and I look at its roots and think about how this tree will never leave this spot. I will put it in the ground here, and this is where it will stay. And it seems sort of sad to me but also safe — in a good way. I'm about to uproot myself, and because of that, I'm spending the next few weeks in a state where I'm afraid to make any real choices. Because what if everything I know is wrong? What if I get to Berkeley and take one look around and think, *Why did I lose my virginity in* New Jersey? *With Mark?*

My phone rings right then and I know it'll be him. I slide my gloves off, pull the phone out of my back pocket, and answer the call without bothering to confirm it's him. 'Hey.'

'Is that considered an acceptable way to answer the phone these days?'

It's my mother.

'I thought you were someone else.'

'Who?'

Tim is giving me the evil eye so I cradle my phone at my shoulder and keep digging. I snap, 'Mom, I'm at work.'

'Well, I want you home for dinner tonight,' she says.

I have plans with Mark, to go to a dopey swing band concert at a gazebo by the bay. So that we can cross 'slow-dance' off our list. My mother won't get it.

'Okay,' I say. 'What time?'

When we hang up I see that I've got an e-mail from The Wall. I don't care about Tim's dirty looks, I read it.

Dear Elizabeth,
This has to be a quick one. As much as I would love for you to stay here for a few days, I'm actually in Italy at a friend's villa and won't be back until late in the month. But if

203

you want, I can help you move into your dorm room when you arrive? Let's be in touch.

Best,

Neil

His cell phone number is there but that's the end of it. So all sorts of stuff is wrong with this picture and I feel a little like I've caught some sudden flu. I go back to my work, preparing the hole, so that Tim will stop watching me. When I think I might cry, I pull my sunglasses down over my eyes.

First off, I didn't ask him if I could come for a 'few days.' I distinctly remember saying 'weeks.'

And I hate the fact that he's the sort of person who takes these fabulous vacations and my mom is, well, my mom. Not that it's his fault that she's the way she is. But maybe it is, at least a little bit? My *mom* deserves a vacation in Italy. For that matter, so do I. This house we're working on right now is ridiculous — a total dream mansion on the beach — and it makes me angry to think of Neil in a similarly swanky villa in Europe for weeks upon weeks.

And I know he's not exactly 'Dad' and probably doesn't really think of himself as my father but still. *Neil?*

I won't even get started on 'Best' as a sign-off. Best *what?*

I'd be lying if I didn't say I'm excited about the offer to help me move in, though — even if I am only bringing two suitcases. The thought of turning up on campus that first day alone is still pretty terrifying to me, even if — or maybe because? — Lauren'll be waiting. I try to imagine for the first time what that moment's going to be like. Will we hug each other? Or start giggling? Lauren doesn't exactly seem the giggling type but you never know. Are her parents and all her siblings going to be standing there weeping? Will Keyon give her this massive kiss good-bye? Should I call her Lauren or Lo?

I can't go to California early.

I have to tell Mark what's going on. In more ways than one.

I text him and say: Mom requiring my presence at home for dinner. Not sure I can make the concert.

He writes back with a frown face and I think, *If you only knew.*

★ ★ ★

Our dinner that night is one of the three meals my mother can make with her eyes closed. Breaded and fried chicken cutlets.

Orzo with butter and Parmesan. And asparagus, from a can. It's hardly a special dinner and I'm sort of annoyed. She made such a big deal out of making sure I would be home to eat that I expected something better. Maybe a steak. Or a 'surprise, we're going out!' Or maybe, I don't know, an apology.

'I got a very upsetting e-mail from your father,' she says as soon as we've finished our meal, and I catch on the phrase *your father*. It's not like I had any say in the matter. It's not like he's *mine* in any real way. It feels like it would be more right for her to say that she got an upsetting e-mail from her ex-husband. Or from the man she had a child with. Or from Neil.

She is refilling her wineglass. 'Trying to plot an early escape, are we?'

'It was just an idea.'

'Well, he told me he offered to help you move in. But then he wanted to check with me to be sure I wasn't going to be there. Or if I was, if I minded.'

I brace myself.

'So I'm wondering if maybe I should go, you know? Help you get settled.' Her phone buzzes and she looks at it, then smiles and sends a text. She puts it back down on the table, takes a deep, happy breath. She is still seeing him.

Hi, Mr. and Mrs. Awesome Parents to Lauren. This is my mother, the adulteress, and my father, the gay deadbeat.

'It's sort of a long way to go, just to come back,' I say.

In theory, I would want my mother there, but this is my *actual* mother we're talking about. Not some perfect idealized mother who'd handle the whole thing with charm and grace and make it awesome.

'Yes, it's far,' she says, 'but it's San Francisco. There's plenty of stuff to see and do. We could kick around for a few days.'

'I don't know, Mom.' Will I regret it if I don't take her up on this?

'I think you do know.' She puts her plate in the dishwasher with a bang. 'You don't want me to come.'

Two can play at this game. It is our favorite game, in fact.

I put my plate next to hers and say, 'Do whatever you want, Mom,' as she leaves the room. When she's gone, I mutter, 'You always do.'

'You're one to talk,' she calls out from the stairs.

★ ★ ★

It's not too late for the concert so I text Mark and un-cancel our plans. I can walk to the

207

gazebo by the bay from my house so I set out on foot after I leave my mom a note. *Going to concert at gazebo*, it says. *Don't wait up.*

The night is hot and sticky and makes me a little angry, because I've got to suffer exactly four more weeks of this brutal summer weather before I can leave. I've started checking the San Francisco weather forecasts and they make me want to go out and buy sweaters and dark blue jeans but then all I have to do is step outside and bam — still eighty-plus degrees at eight o'clock at night.

Still my life.

My father doesn't want me. He'd rather be in Italy.

My mother doesn't value my opinion. She'd rather go about her deluded existence, if it means she doesn't have to face being alone.

I hear a car slow on the road beside me and I turn and see Mark's smile through the open passenger-side window. 'I'd offer you a lift,' he says as the car inches forward, 'but it seems kind of silly.'

We can see the gazebo. If I keep walking, I'll be there before he will because he'll have to go past it, to the parking lot, and then walk back. I hear a trumpet or trombone play a sharp note then, and realize I have no interest in this concert at all.

I say, 'Well, it's not silly if you're giving me

a lift somewhere other than this dopey concert.'

He stops the car and I get in.

'Where to?' he asks.

I dare him with my eyes. 'Maybe one of those motels in Seaside?'

'Elizabeth,' he says, all serious. Then he raises his eyebrows. 'You mean it?'

I nod. 'I think I do.' The trumpets are warming up in earnest now and it sounds sort of jazzy and fun, which is not at all how I am feeling. 'But I have to tell you something first and I cannot do it with this music playing.'

He puts the car in gear and drives toward Seaside, where he pulls into one of the parking spaces in the shadow of the water park — now closed for the night and dimly lit. He turns off the engine and sits and waits and I watch a bunch of inner tubes bobbing ever so faintly in one of the pools. I am thinking about how we rode tubes around the park's lazy river while holding hands when I say, 'My mother has been seeing your father.'

His exhale is loud and he just sits there for a minute, shaking his head. I feel like I'm about to start crying but I need to get some more words out, so that he doesn't hate me forever. I say, 'I really wanted to tell you but I thought she would end it because I told her he was married and I'm so sorry that I — '

'Stop talking,' he says, so I do that and

wait. But I can't wait long.

I say, 'I'm *so sorry.*'

'It's not your fault.' He has both hands on the steering wheel and I want to reach over and take one of them.

'I should've told you sooner.'

'It really doesn't matter who it is,' he says. 'Now or later. It's not the first time. They're getting divorced. I think. I don't know. I mean, I sort of want them to get divorced.'

I am not sure he is making sense but I let him talk.

He takes a deep breath and says, 'The main point is that he can't keep seeing your mom, for the obvious reason.'

I'm looking straight ahead at one of the slides we went down together, the one where I nearly lost my bikini top. 'What's the obvious reason?'

'Us.' He starts up the car and the AC kicks in again. '*We're* the obvious reason.'

We sit silently for a minute and then he says, 'I should probably just take you home.'

'I really wish you wouldn't,' I say, so we sit and he reaches over and squeezes my hand and then, after a minute, he lets go and starts driving and I don't ask where to.

'I haven't told her,' I say. 'I mean, I haven't told her that he's your dad.'

He accelerates through a yellow light. 'I'm

going to tell him that he has to end it. It's nonnegotiable.'

I watch the water park get smaller in the side mirror of the car. 'She's going to be a mess.'

He says, 'But it's the only way.'

I know he's right, and I love him for taking the responsibility of destroying this, of breaking my mother's heart, out of my hands.

And then he pulls into the parking lot of a U-shaped motel called the Moonlight, with a lit-up scripty sign like something out of an old Hollywood movie. There is a VACANCY light flashing red, but with the second C burned out. He turns the engine off and looks over and our eyes meet.

'Cable TV and everything.' He nods at the sign.

'For us, only the best,' I say, but he looks a little shaken so I double-check. 'You're sure about this?'

'It's the only thing I'm sure of right now.' I hear in his voice that it's the truth.

'I broke up with my boyfriend because of this,' I say. 'I mean, there were other things but it was mostly because he was pressuring me. Isn't that weird?'

'Not to me.' He shrugs a shoulder.

I look out the window, at that burned-out C, when I ask, 'Have you ever . . . before?'

'Once.' He takes my hand. 'For the wrong

reasons. And it was pretty bad and I didn't handle it all especially well so I decided to wait for the right reasons.'

'What if it's bad again?' I ask, looking at him.

'Well, we'll be bad together.' He smiles and I don't hesitate when I reach for the door handle.

Dear Lo, (I like it! Though in an ironic twist, I am thinking of dropping MY nickname and starting college as Elizabeth for real.)

My father said no, to make a long story short, BUT he said he'd help me move into the dorm. So I won't seem like Little Orphan Annie when I show up. And you'll get to meet my gay dad if I take him up on his offer. Which would be weird since I feel like I'd pretty much be meeting him for the first time, too? Oh, and my mom is now threatening to come, too, so help me God. Anyway, I let the cat out of the bag and Mark is going to tell his dad to end it. So the you-know-what is about to hit the fan here.

I want to write about the Moonlight but I want to do it justice and I'm so *sleepy*. Mark didn't bring me home until about 4 AM, and I'm exhausted so I write the easy stuff first.

Thanks for the photo. It's fun to see you
— are you wearing mascara, because your eye-
lashes really pop — and also to see Zoe.
How's the extended sleepover? Are your brothers and sisters better yet? I still feel bad about
the missent e-mail. Won't happen again!!!

Very cool about Keyon and the kissing.

When I get to this, I think maybe it'd be
rude to not at least acknowledge what she
told me? So I go for it.

This may make me sound naïve but I don't
know many black people. I have no idea why
that is, except that I don't seem to cross paths
with any. There are a bunch of black kids in
school but somehow we don't end up talking
much. That's sort of screwed up, isn't it? So
much for the great melting pot.

Way too tired to tackle the Moonlight so I
wrap it up.

And yes, totally room for symbolic knickknacks.

EB

I'm trying to think of a symbolic
knickknack of my own to bring with me but

213

I'm already in bed and the lights are off and I can't be bothered to get up and look around. The only thing that comes to mind right now is the matchbox I swiped from the lobby of the Moonlight, which is sitting on my night table right now. And somehow not at least telling Lo a tiny bit about the Moonlight feels like some kind of lie by omission. So I add:

Yes: A matchbox from the Moonlight Motel.

No: My virginity.

Maybe so: Birth control?

SATURDAY, AUGUST 3
SAN FRANCISCO

My bedroom feels like a foreign country. During the Illness, every inch of my — *our* — space got covered with Gertie's and P.J.'s toys, clothes, books, applesauce containers, and Dora sippy cups. Not sexy. I cross it off my mental list of Places to Spend Special Time with Keyon. Because I guess Ebb's e-mail has made me ponder that. Since dinner at his house Monday, we've made out seven more times. Seven times in four days. Twice in his car, once at his house, once at Goodwill, and three times at the sandwich shop. We have to knock that off at work, to eliminate the possibility of Joe Senior catching us.

The point is, I need the entirety of the scoop from Ebb: where, when, how, what, why.

I mean, I have mixed feelings about the whole thing. I liked the idea of us both being virgins, the sort of equality it would give us to start out the school year. Now if I want things equal I have to —

'Sorry for the mess,' Mom says, coming in with a laundry basket. 'We've been too wiped out to deal with it. This was way more brutal than I could have imagined.'

It's been nearly an entire week. Finally, everyone is better, and Dad is out with Gertie and Marcus and Jack, and Grandma has P.J. and Francis. All so that Mom and I can clean up in peace.

'It's okay.' She still sort of looks like she should be in bed. I take the basket from her and start heaping clothes and blankets into it. 'Sit down,' I say, pointing to my desk chair. She does.

'Did you have fun at Zoe's?' she asks.

'Yeah, actually. It was weird at first to not have a hundred people running around screaming, but I got used to it.' And got used to sleeping till ten every day, and used to staying up till one every morning, and used to her parents leaving us almost totally alone so we could talk and talk and talk and make videos and zone out with *Buffy* marathons and share clothes. It was, I guess, a taste of what college life will be like. Only without Zoe.

Mom laughs. 'A hundred. Is that how it feels to you?'

'Sometimes.' I pick up a pajama top and quickly drop it again. 'Is it possible that I just touched vomit?'

'Very.'

I fold my sweatshirt sleeve over my hand, pick up the rest of the stuff, then add my sweatshirt to it before washing up in the bathroom, with steaming hot water. When I come back into my room, my mom is crying. Not hard. More leaking and sniffling.

'Mom? Are you okay?' Crying, for her, is not uncommon. The woman has taken more than her share of rides on the hormonal roller coaster. 'You'll feel better after you catch up on sleep.'

'It's not because of the flu,' she says, brushing tears away with the back of her hand. 'Well, it's partly because of the flu. But I was thinking about how much you do for us. How your life isn't how I pictured it. What you've had to take on because of . . . ' She waves her hand toward the general vicinity of my sisters' beds.

'Mom, don't, please, don't worry about it.' I lie back on Gertie's stripped mattress. 'I'm used to it.'

'Sometimes I think back to when it was only you and me and Dad,' she says, searching fruitlessly for a box of tissue.

I return to the bathroom for a roll of toilet paper to bring to her. 'Here.'

'It was so . . . Lauren, it was so wonderful. We were so happy, you can't even imagine.'

I've heard this story many times. They were so happy, so happy about me, and they thought if one kid was great, more would be even better, and they tried and tried and tried forever, it seemed, until they were magically fertile again and Jack came along, followed by the rest of them. A vicious cycle of happiness.

'You're happy now,' I remind her, sitting on the floor by her feet. 'This is what you guys wanted.'

'Do I look happy, Lauren?' She points to her splotchy face, then blows her nose. We laugh.

'Well, not right *now*. But epic family flu is not a normal day.'

'True. But days like this make me think about the road not taken. The what-ifs. What if we'd gone on being a family of three? Or what if we'd stopped with Jack? I think about what kind of life we could have had, what we could have given you . . . ' The tears start up again.

I fold my arms on her knees and rest my chin on them, eyes turned up to her. I can't think about Gertie and Peej and Marcus and Francis not existing, or us being different than we are. And I know she can't, either. Despite what she just said, I *know* she loves being their mom as much as she loves being mine. 'Mom. You're exhausted. Why don't you go take a nap. I can handle all this.'

She doesn't move, except to keep unraveling more toilet paper. 'It's been hard on you.'

'It's fine, Mom!'

'Dad and I can't go back in time and change everything . . . '

'I don't want to change *anything*.' Now I am starting to tear up, seeing her so upset and talking as if my life has been this disaster. I blot each of my eyes on the knees of her jeans. She rests her hand on my shoulder.

'Lauren. Honey. These aren't the rantings of a worn-out mommy. I'm trying to make a point.'

I sit back so I can see her face. 'What.'

'Dad and I decided that . . . we . . . we want you to know that you're free. For the rest of the summer and when school starts, we're really going to let you go.' She straightens up and blows her nose one more time. 'We want you to really. Feel. Free.' Her fist pounds her knee with each word.

'Um, okay.'

My head spins for a second. I'd better not be catching this flu.

'We want to give you back some of what you haven't had for a long time. No responsibilities as far as the kids. No having to check your schedule with ours. No ties, no — '

Whoa. I hold up my hands, stopping her. 'Mom. Mom. I get it.' My heart pounds. I want her to go nap and stop talking. I add, 'Thank you,' so I don't sound ungrateful. I get up and start putting clean sheets on Gertie's bed.

'Do you really get it?' She stands, comes over, and takes my wrist. 'We don't want to hold you back. We want you to fly out of the nest and . . . soar, Lauren.'

She's serious. She and Dad have probably been talking about it all week while I was at Zoe's. Plotting my free, soaring future, which is somehow here, now. They've been discussing how great and unburdened I would feel to get this news that the role I've played in my family since Jack was born is so very over.

I don't feel soary and unburdened.

I concentrate on smoothing out Gertie's top sheet. She likes it tight around her body. She likes it when I put her in bed and tuck everything in so that it's a struggle for her to even move her arms. '*Now you're my prisoner*,' I always tell her, with an evil laugh, and she loves it.

'You rest, Mom. Let me get the house in shape, and then I'll embark on my . . . freedom.'

She finally agrees to take a nap. I get the laundry started, do the dishes, disinfect the bathrooms, and run the vacuum.

Obviously they need my help, and they're kidding themselves if they think otherwise. They want me to 'soar'? Ha! Good luck keeping things around here in order while I'm off soaring. What does that even mean? I'll have a huge class load, and a campus job, hopefully, and maybe a boyfriend, and I have to make all these decisions about that boyfriend and I won't even be able to escape to Zoe's house, or have her around to demonstrate how to breathe into a boy's ear or teach me how to use the smart phone I'm going to get, and, honestly, my parents *need* me. They need me! They would be better off if I didn't go to college at *all*, is the actual truth. I could put it off. I could . . .

. . . stop everything from changing.

I wind the vacuum cord back around its holster.

Yeah. Good luck with that.

When the house is in order and there are clean blankets on my bed, I close my bedroom door and pull those blankets over my head and have a good cry.

EB —

Wow. Just, wow, if I read your yes/no/maybe so right. I'm eagerly awaiting more. I mean, as much as you want to tell me. So I guess we won't put a VIRGIN CENTRAL sign on our dorm door now?

Things with Keyon are holding steady. I don't think we're really like boyfriend/girlfriend, though. (BTW it's kind of the same here re: black people, only here we pretend it's not like that.) I think we're friends with benefits. Limited benefits. Though I feel like a floozy saying it ('floozy' is one of my grandma's favorite words), that could possibly be a good arrangement? Something that would not lead to heartbreak. Isn't it enough to like and have affection and warm feelings and trust, and not have to 'be in love'? Or even really date? Are you in love with Mark?

I'm also justwowing about your dad. He said NO? Why??

Quite possibly this is more questioning than is really polite.

By the way, you've sort of mentioned more than once the weirdness of having a gay dad, but honestly, it's not that weird. Not here, anyway. I can see how it would be weird for you as his daughter, but as a SITUATION it is not weird at all. When is the last time you saw him? Did you already tell me that?

Here, I imagine writing, If you want to talk weird, weird is that I already met your dad when I went to his gallery last Saturday. It was sort of an accident. Now THAT'S weird!! But I don't want her to feel hurt or mad or whatever about that and there's no reason to tell her, and it's not like me and her dad had this long talk. It was like hi-bye and there's no chance he'll remember me. Why stir things up?

I'm back home. My family is more or less recovered. My mom had this big talk with me today about how they want me to 'be free' and 'soar' and apparently this means I'm no longer needed in the family. That's not what they mean but that's a tiny bit how it feels. Less like 'Fly, little birdie!' and more like 'Don't let the door hit you on the way out of the nest.' I don't know. Thinking about it sort of makes me want to cry. Okay, I did cry. Before. And maybe a little right now!

Good time to sign off . . .

Lo

I got nothing for yes/no/maybe so right now.

SATURDAY, AUGUST 3
NEW JERSEY

I'm babysitting for Vivian when I get Lauren's e-mail and it makes me want to cry, too. I wish I could drop everything to write back but Vivian is teething or something and clinging to me like crazy and she's red-faced and awful and screaming 'Mama.' I wish I could cry like a baby — really let it rip. Maybe Lauren and I will have to put down our bags, shake hands, send away anyone who drops us off, and have a good full-on bawl before starting college for real.

'Please please please, Viv,' I say, in my best soothing tones. 'Stop crying, sweetie. Please stop.'

The straight-up wailing I can almost handle; it's the 'mamas' that really get me.

I'm seriously going to lose it.

And won't that freak Vivian out? Surely, babysitters are not supposed to completely lose it. It's not like Viv and I can have this good sort of cathartic moment and then both feel better after it. She expects me to be in control. She expects me to be the grown-up. I grab one of her favorite toys, a phone that says 'Hello!' and beeps when you open it. I hold it to my ear and say, 'Oh, you want to talk to Vivian?' and hold it out to her but she's not listening. She's still wailing. So I go to the freezer — a big drawer under the double-doored fridge — and open it and pull out one of her frozen teethers — this one bright pink and shaped like a foot. I hand that to her and she shoves it in her mouth and I sit down on the recliner in the den and she calms down and sits on my nap and gnaws on that foot.

Crisis averted.

Hers, at least.

I could seriously cry at the drop of a hat these days. And people would probably think it was because of the whole Losing of the Virginity — if people actually knew about that — and anyway, that's not it.

As far as first times go, in all the possible scenarios I have imagined over the years, the Moonlight surpassed all expectations by being really *right* feeling. Even now, three days later, I keep seeing vivid flashes of the time we spent there. Just an image of his hand here or there, a certain faraway look on his face, the bones of his hip, the painting on the wall next to the bed, of a girl wearing a bonnet collecting seashells in a bucket. When

I snapped a picture of it with my phone he said, 'That's what you want to take a picture of? To commemorate our night together? Because I'm happy to pose.'

'Yeah,' I laughed. 'That'd be great for when Vivian plays with my phone.'

So he's going to talk to his dad today and I am going to brace for impact. And hope that I get my period, like, right this second, even though I'm not due for another week. We used protection, of course, but wouldn't it be just my luck?

What's making me a little bit sad about the whole thing is that, apart from Lauren, there's no one I really want to tell about it. And as I picture her and her gaggle of siblings while I am holding Vivian — an only child whose parents are out at some fancy restaurant where people probably give babies dirty looks — I feel so alone that for a second I contemplate packing up some of Viv's things and kidnapping her, raising her in some far-off state as my own.

Something about the closeness I feel with Mark makes me *really* wish I had a brother or a sister, all joking about birthing them myself aside. Which may sound totally screwed up because I definitely don't see him as a brother, but there's an ease with him, a sort of acceptance, that I imagine comes with the territory when you have siblings. No one but my mother has to love me just because I am here and I am me and am their daughter/sister/whatever, and obviously even my mother seems to forget that loving me is supposed to be her first job on this planet. But then I decide maybe I'm being melodramatic and Justine and I have been meaning to get together anyway, so I call her but she doesn't pick up.

Vivian has finally snapped out of her funk and is getting into all sorts of trouble in one of the kitchen cabinets, so I go sit on the kitchen floor and we make music with pots and pans and wooden spoons. I say things in a high-pitched singsong, like 'Oh, Vivian, if you only knew what I just did!' and she's happy again and I let her glee rub off on me, at least until it's time to go home.

★ ★ ★

If my mother senses a change in me, she doesn't let on. She's up when I get home from babysitting and tells me there's leftover KFC in the fridge. I fix a plate and join her in the living room, where she's watching a reality show about one of those über-nannies. There is a lot of screaming and crying and judging going on. I've never asked my mother why she and my dad didn't have any more kids after me. It's the sort of question that answers itself, doesn't it?

Because he was gay.

Because they were too young.

Because I was a mistake.

Because the whole marriage was a sham, even if it took them a long time to realize it, longer than any rational person, myself included, can understand.

Sometimes, when I'm wondering if my family situation has permanently screwed me up, I'm surprised by how sane I feel. And having the courage to trust my own feelings actually makes me feel even saner, even more grown-up. But I really wish things weren't so complicated.

I answer Lauren's e-mail in my head:

Yes, I am in love with him.

The show ends and my mother tosses the remote at me and says, 'I'm hitting the hay.'

'Me too,' I say. 'In a few minutes. Once my chicken digests a little.'

'TMI,' my mother says, and that pretty much sums it up.

Mark sends me a text a few minutes later: Miss you.

I'm about to write back when another text says Go outside right now.

I get up and pad to the door and open it

and there's a small box on the doormat. It's blue. Like turquoise blue. With a white satin ribbon tied around it. And even *I* know what that means, probably because my mother once dated a guy who bought her a necklace from Tiffany and she wouldn't throw the box out for years. In fact, she might still have it.

'Mark?' I whisper, not wanting my mom to hear, and then he steps out from behind a tree by the sidewalk and walks toward me.

'Aren't you going to open it?' he says.

And so I sit on the top step and he sits next to me, his knee touching mine, and I stare at the box for a minute. I know he's rich. Or at least his parents are. Richer than I may ever be. 'It's too much,' I say. 'Whatever it is, it's too much.'

'Elizabeth,' he says. 'Please let me do this. Let me do things right.'

I want that, too. But I am putting together a puzzle in my head, connecting a piece of what he has just said with one from our conversation in the parking lot of the Moonlight. 'The last time,' I say. 'That other girl. You didn't do things right.'

He shakes his head.

'So you think this is somehow going to make up for that?'

He grabs my hand. 'No, it's not like that. I just want you to know how I feel. That's all.'

So I undo the silky white ribbon that's tied in a bow around the box and then take off the top. Inside, a small turquoise sack that says TIFFANY and has a white silky drawstring sits perched on a bed of cotton.

'I haven't gotten you anything yet,' I say, and he shrugs and says, 'Doesn't matter if you did or didn't.'

I open the little bag and slide out a silver necklace. There are two charms on the chain, one a heart and the other a circle that says LOVE in engraved script.

'I totally don't want this to freak you out,' Mark says. 'But I mean it.'

I open the clasp and put the necklace on and say, 'I mean it, too,' and then I lean over and kiss him full on the mouth and find myself wanting to cry again. Because it's almost as if I can see into the future, and see a time when the necklace won't fill me with warm feelings but will sit in my jewelry box collecting tarnish and getting tangled after this whole thing has run its course, whatever that course may be.

'So not to spoil the mood or anything,' he says then. 'But I talked to my dad.'

'And?'

'And . . . ' He shakes his head.

'What? He said he won't break it off?' I'm talking as softly as I can.

'No,' Mark says. He is still shaking that head. 'My dad is such a class act that he said, 'Good, I was looking for an out anyway.''

I think I actually feel my stomach churn. 'Wow.'

'Yeah,' Mark says. 'Wow.'

'Well, my dad's no prize, either,' I say; then I spit it out. 'I asked him if I could come stay with him for a few weeks, since things with my mom are so weird, but he's in Italy on vacation.' It all sounds so dumb now. 'Not that he should fly home or anything, but I don't know. I just . . . ' I feel myself getting choked up again. 'I just wanted him to be there for me. You know, in my hour of need or whatever.'

A tear breaks free from my eye, runs down my cheek.

'Well, it was a terrible idea,' Mark says, and he slides his arm around me. 'Leaving me? Before you absolutely have to? I mean, duh.' He nudges me and I love him for trying to make me laugh. 'Plus, *I'm* here in your time of need.'

'How'd you get to be so' — I wipe away my tears and some stuff at my nose, too — 'normal?'

'Who? Me? Normal?' He laughs and I laugh. He says, 'Trust me, I'm all sorts of weird. I just hide it really well.'

Then he kisses me quickly and we sit

quietly in the night as the wind rustles the leaves in the trees. I think about that noise, about trying to record it — the way it sounds sort of like paper brushing together — because the sound of trees in San Francisco will be different. I know this because I know about the US Department of Agriculture Plant Hardiness Zones, which help categorize what kinds of plants and trees will flourish in a particular location. What if I myself, like some of the trees here, am really an East Coast specimen? What if I thrive here, in Zone 6, but will die out in California, in Zone 10?

Then again, is this really thriving?

I reach for my necklace, touch both charms. 'So what do we do now?'

'I guess we wait for it to all go down?' He doesn't sound convinced. 'But how will we even know?'

'Trust me,' I say. 'I'll know.'

After Mark leaves, I go inside and up to my room and it strikes me for the first time how weird my bedroom is, because there are two twin beds in it. One is almost always covered in clothes and books and magazines and whatever and it's almost like I forgot it was a bed for a long time and only now remembered. My mother told me years ago it was so I could have friends sleep over and I've done that a few times but not many. Maybe that's why I feel so lonely all the time and have such longing for a sibling . . . for a roomie. Because of that ghost bed that has been living in my room all these years.

Which reminds me . . .

Lo,
I don't think you're a floozy, for the record. Friends with benefits isn't a bad situation to be in at this point in our lives, is it? Then again, maybe it takes a floozy to know one. I mean, I lost it with a guy I've barely known a month! Who am I to talk? Would you WANT Keyon to be your boyfriend?

So. The loss of the Big V. It was actually sort of great. We went to a motel that was hilariously lowbrow but not in a skeevy way. More like . . . old-school? Old Hollywood? Anyway, it was sweet and intense. I know there are probably a lot of people who would think I'm too young to know that it was the right time or whatever but what do they know? I am a little bit freaked out in an 'I can't believe I did it!' way but not that much. And yes, I think I am in love with him.

And that sounds crazy.

It feels crazy!

I consider writing more, like about how it only hurt a little bit at first and then felt right and a tiny bit funny. Or about how I feel like I know him in this different way now and also know myself in this new way. Even about the painting, and how for a second when I saw it I thought I was going to cry, I don't even know why. But that all feels like a potentially serious overshare. Part of me wants to write Just do it! So we can talk about it after we've both crossed to the other side. But of course I can't. I opt to move on.

As for soaring, well, sign me up. Because I, too, am getting pushed out of the nest. Unfortunately, my nest never really felt like a home to begin with. And I am the only bird in my flock. Which means that if I soar I'm going to ultimately end up feeling guilty about leaving Mother Bird all alone, unsoaring, but soar I must. Okay, enough with my bad analogy. I'm sure your family still needs you. But I'm sure they'll survive without you, too. Isn't that sort of the way it works?

Oh, and as for my dad. He's vacationing in Italy! Who can give shelter to their long-lost daughter when there is wine to be drunk and villas to visit? Must be nice is all I can say. Must be nice. I'm relieved that you don't think it's weird. The gay part of the situation, anyway. They split when I was five and the last time I saw him I was like seven? I guess that's the weird part, right?

Floozily yours,

EB

Yes: The engraved 'love' necklace that Mark gave me.

SUNDAY, AUGUST 4
SAN FRANCISCO

I'm at a *restaurant*. Eating *brunch*. On a *Sunday morning*.

Apparently, this is what people do. Or, this is what certain kinds of people do and have been doing on Sunday mornings all this time while I've been cleaning pancake batter off the kitchen floor and walls, and out of P.J.'s hair.

My parents are deadly serious about 'freeing' me, and my dad practically snatched Francis out of my arms to push me out the door to meet Zoe. But not before remarking, 'You've been spending a lot of time with Zoe. That's nice.'

'Uh-huh,' I said, and pocketed the Saturn keys. 'Since our talk about friends and stuff, yeah.' Half the time he thinks I've been spending with Zoe, I've actually been with Keyon. For some reason I haven't told my parents about him.

Dad held Francis out airplane-style and made him 'kiss' me, aka put his open fish-lips on my cheek. 'Kiss sissy! Sissy takes Daddy's advice! Kiss kiss kiss!'

'*Okay*, Dad. You're getting his drool on my shirt.' But of course I couldn't resist taking a fake bite out of Francis's little cheek before leaving.

Now I'm with both Zoe *and* Keyon, so they can get to know each other a little bit better. Which may be pointless as we're all going our separate ways in a few weeks, but it doesn't feel pointless. They already knew each other, slightly, because of Zoe being generally more social than me at school. She seems intimidated by his cuteness and undeniable charm, though, and swerves between chattering away and staring into her crepes as if they are asking the Riddle of the Sphinx.

In one of her staring moments, I ask what we should do after brunch.

Zoe shrugs and moves to withdraw her phone from her pocket. I hold her arm. 'Let's see if we can think of something without asking the Internet.'

'We could scout for some Bakelite,' Keyon suggests.

'Some what?' Zoe asks.

I ignore her question. The little antiques business Keyon and I are plotting is more fun as a secret. 'What do normal people do on the weekend? Like, after brunch? Walk in the park? Go to a movie?'

'Usually I meet some guys at the gym for ball,' Keyon says.

'Oh. Do you . . . want to do that?' I shouldn't have assumed we'd be spending the whole day together.

But he shakes his head, reaching over to my plate to help himself to my last piece of bacon. I grab it, too, and it tears in half. We crack up and each cram half a bacon slice into our mouths. Zoe's eyes flick from me to him and back to me. 'You guys don't have to hang out with me all day.' *If you want to be alone,* her face says.

I hold her arm. 'Yes, we do.'

Spending all that time with her at her house hasn't made me sick of Zoe. On the contrary, I feel more attached than ever, hyper-aware of what we're soon about to lose. Even if the loss is temporary, it's still loss.

'I was thinking about shooting some footage for my next vlog. It's sort of a diary of my last few weeks in San Francisco,' she explains to Keyon. 'Before college. Do you like art?'

I bite my lip. Is Zoe calling her vlogs art?

But she continues, to me: 'Because I was thinking that gallery we went to last weekend would give me some cool background shots and stuff.'

'I like art,' Keyon says, nodding gamely.

'There are lots of places to see art,' I say. 'Museums, for example.' It's one thing to go spy on Ebb's dad's gallery out of curiosity when it seemed like no big deal. Another thing to go back and do it again before I even confess to her about the first time, if I do.

'Galleries are free,' Keyon points out.

'And I want to check out that local artist dude,' Zoe adds. 'The guy said we should come back. We can pretend we're going to buy something and make it part of my video.'

The guy, meaning Ebb's dad.

'It's probably not open on Sundays. Anyway, the owner isn't — ' I'm about to say the owner isn't there, he's in Italy, but explaining how I know that is way too complicated. 'The owner isn't about to believe *we're* going to buy a painting.'

'We could call, to see if they're open. I still have the card.' She produces it after a second of digging around in her bag, and punches the number into her cell.

Something bumps my foot under the table. Keyon's foot. I bump it back. Do friends with benefits play footsie? That seems distinctly romantic to me. Playful. Boyfriendy. And when I pull some cash out of my pocket and lay it on the table for the bill, he pushes it back.

'I got it.'

'I can pay for mine,' I say.

'I'm good.'

'But — '

Zoe, now off the phone, interrupts. 'Let him pay! Gallery is open. We're going.'

Keyon settles the bill and we head out.

★ ★ ★

Ebb's dad was right about the new stuff he has up. They're paintings by this guy named Edward Sherman — a lot of cityscapes that are recognizable parts of San Francisco but not the same stuff you always see, like the Golden Gate Bridge or the Victorian houses on Steiner Street. There's one of the Financial District at twilight. A line of traffic at sunset. There's also a series of portraits of jazz musicians. Well, not really portraits, because it's like the music is a part of the paintings of these musicians playing their instruments.

'My dad would like this,' Keyon says, standing in front of one called *Jammin'*.

I stand next to him and he snakes his arm around my waist. It's a total boyfriend move, the arm around the waist. There is no question. Zoe takes a few seconds of footage with her digital video cam; I make a face.

'I want this!' Zoe exclaims, putting her

finger on the wall next to one of the cityscapes. I untangle from Keyon, walking over to check it out; the sign reads *Marina, After Rain*.

'Yeah,' I say. 'I love the wet pavement and the way those clouds are breaking up.'

'It's great, isn't it?'

It's Ebb's dad, behind us. I stare at him, blinking. Because as far as I know, we're still in San Francisco, not Italy.

'Unfortunately it's already in someone's private collection,' he adds.

'Not that I could afford it, anyway,' Zoe says.

'So I was right?' Mr. Ebb asks. 'You do like this artist better than what you saw last time?'

'You remember us!'

Sure I do, he might say. *I have a daughter your age.*

No, Mr. Ebb tells us more stuff about the artist. He went to high school in the suburbs around here, and then the Academy of Art right in the city. I nod, watching his face. Maybe it's not her dad. Maybe he hasn't left for Italy yet. Maybe I misunderstood Ebb's e-mail. 'Um,' I ask, 'will you have this stuff up next weekend, too?'

'All this week and next weekend. Then I'm curating something different. Video art, actually,' he says to Zoe, giving her video

241

camera a little tap. 'You should come. We're getting a new Bill Viola piece. Do you know his work?'

'No . . . '

'Is that going to be *here*?' I ask, sounding incredulous. I point my finger to the floor on which I now stand, so that he knows I mean *here* here. Not Italy here.

'Yes.' He gives me an odd look. And so do Keyon and Zoe.

'Just double-checking,' I explain to them both. 'Is there a bathroom I could use?' I ask Ebb's dad.

He points me to it, and once inside I lean against the door. I feel queasy. Like I know too many things I shouldn't know. I know this guy's daughter lost her virginity and I know he has no idea. I know he's lying to her and I can't imagine why. Or she's lying to me. And now I'm lying to her, or that's how it feels, knowing something that's none of my business like this.

Why did I feel it necessary to come here last weekend? Everything was fine. *And it still is*, I tell myself. Forget this whole thing and carry on. It's summer. The last summer. Nothing needs to be serious — not my friendship with Ebb, not things with Keyon, not even the weeks I have left with Zoe.

I pee and wash my hands and attempt,

alternately, to smooth and fluff my hair, and reapply my tinted lip balm. 'No responsibilities,' I say to my reflection, repeating my mother's words. 'No ties. Be. Free.'

When I open the door, Keyon is standing there. 'You all right?'

I nod. Then shrug. Then nod.

One corner of his smile twitches and he leans close, saying low in his sexy voice, 'Who were you talking to in there?'

'Myself,' I whisper back.

He kisses me. It feels different. I mean, every kiss has been amazing, but this has something behind it. A feeling. This kiss communicates. It communicates *I hope you're all right, and you being all right is my business, and yes, we can talk about it later and I'll be listening, I'll be whatever you need me to be.*

I back away, dizzied from hearing all that through his unspeaking lips.

We return to the main gallery, where Zoe is now interviewing Ebb's dad on video, asking, 'Do you have to be totally rich to own a place like this?'

'Zoe!' I exclaim. 'Rude.'

Mr. Ebb laughs, the tan skin around his eyes crinkling. 'You have to have some cash flow, I will admit.'

'I have to go,' I say to Zoe.

'Why?' she asks, still shooting.

'I just do.'

'There's a reception for the artist next weekend if you'd like to come,' Mr. Ebb says, giving me a postcard. 'I can introduce you both.'

Keyon rests his hand behind my neck.

What's *happening?* Why is everything so serious, so suddenly?

I make his hand go away by walking toward the door.

Outside, the air cools my face and I try to sort through the last twenty minutes. When Keyon comes out, he asks, quietly, 'Why say you're okay when you're not okay?'

I shake my head. We'll only be alone for a second more.

Zoe plunges through the door, staring at her camera. 'That was awesome. I can't wait to edit this vlog.'

EB —

'It was sweet and intense'? That's all I get? Zoe hasn't done it yet so she's no help. YOU ARE THE ONLY PERSON I PERSONALLY KNOW WHO HAS DONE IT AND WOULD TALK TO ME ABOUT IT. Do you feel like Mark owns a piece of your heart now, that you'll never get back? Do you think it's possible to have sex and then be able to let it go and be your old self or is it a forever thing that changes you? What does it feel like to be in love? ALSO PS I DON'T THINK YOUR DAD IS IN ITALY.

I backspace over all that and start again.

EB —

Do I want him to be my boyfriend? Good question. We went out to brunch with Zoe and then the three of us hung out (this is my new 'free' life), and everything about it felt like he was my boyfriend and some things happened that felt serious (not physical things, emotional things. interpersonal things that are hard to explain) and after we dropped Zoe off, Keyon was kinda like 'did I do something wrong?' because I guess my body language was . . . argh I don't know.

He didn't do anything wrong. He paid for my food and put his arm around me and stuff and there was this kiss unlike all his other kisses and I should have been ready for things to change, should have thought about this A LITTLE BIT before now — but I didn't and my head was elsewhere to be honest. Blah blah blah anyway BORING I don't know. Benefits will continue to be limited.

And maybe I've been kidding myself about the 'friends' part. Maybe he already is my boyfriend. Why is it so confusing? I guess things are a little more clear when the guy gives you a necklace that says 'love'!!!

Yes I guess my family will survive without me. And your mom will without you.

Can I tell you that it's been my secret dream since I was eight to be an only child? Talk about guilt.

So your dad is in Italy RIGHT NOW?

Does he happen to have a twin brother who runs the gallery with him?

Sorry that didn't work out.

— Lo

Yes: Ugly but warm blanket my grandma knit me last Christmas.

No: Paper cuts from my filing job — quitting that next week.

Maybe so: A long-distance boyfriend?

THURSDAY, AUGUST 8
NEW JERSEY

When my mother calls me down to dinner on Thursday and pulls a steaming pan of chicken Parmesan out of the oven, I want to scream. It's like the whole world has suddenly gone mad for Italy. All week, everywhere I turn, there's the boot to kick me in the face. There are features about great Italian travel deals in every newspaper and magazine that crosses my path. Every show I watch on TV seems to have some reference to Italy or Italian food or Sicilian wine. So as much as I've tried to put the fact that my father is on this spectacular vacation out of my mind, I can't.

Yes, Lo, he is in Italy right now!

I haven't answered her e-mail yet, but not for any specific reason. I've just been busy, mostly spending time with Mark, and then thinking about Mark during the time I'm not spending with him. And anyway, our e-mailing has sort of settled in nicely and things don't feel so urgent all the time. I'm happy about that.

247

Then I feel newly irked about the e-mails my parents have been exchanging. I say, 'My so-called father's probably having chicken Parmesan in Italy right now. Did he mention his big vacation plans in his e-mail to you?'

'He did not,' Mom says, straining the spaghetti over the sink. 'Must be nice.' She slides the pasta back into the pot but then she just stands there, facing the window, not turning around.

For a really long time.

The steam fills the air like the house is on fire.

'Mom?' I finally ask. 'You okay?'

I know what's coming. I've been waiting.

'Yes.' She is wiping away tears. 'I'm fine.'

She takes a plate from the cabinet and puts some spaghetti on it, then hefts a piece of chicken out of the pan and puts it on top of the pasta. 'You're welcome to say 'told you so,' if you want.' She deposits my dinner in front of me.

'What do you mean?' I ask, even though I know.

'It's over.' Now she's fixing her own plate. 'The married one.'

'I'm sorry, Mom,' I say. 'Did he say why?'

I really *really* don't want her to know it has anything to do with me.

'No, he didn't say why. He didn't say

anything. He just stopped returning my calls. Stopped texting. It's like he died.' This gives her an idea. 'Maybe he *died*?'

'Mom,' I say. 'I am pretty sure he didn't die.' Though I sort of wish he had. Who goes around treating people like that?

'I'm pathetic.' She slides into a kitchen chair. 'How did I get to be so pathetic?' She starts crying.

I go to her side. 'You're not pathetic, Mom. You just . . . ' I am not sure what to say that won't make things worse. 'You may be trying too hard. You should, I don't know, let things *come to you* or something. Maybe you should take a break . . . from dating? Regroup? Take a vacation?'

She smiles and says, 'Where? *Italy?*'

'Anywhere.' I twirl my spaghetti and try to think of a place I'd want to be. I say, 'Anywhere but here.'

★ ★ ★

It's early when we're done with dinner so I ask if I can go out for a while, to the mall. I want to try to find a present for Mark, though I still don't have any idea what it might be. At the last second I decide to text Justine and Morgan to see if either of them wants to come along. Justine and I still haven't been able to find time to get together and it's starting to really weigh on me. I'm sort of relieved when they both say yes. I guess it makes me feel like I still belong. Then a text from Justine comes through — We're actually at my place — and I feel sort of sick.

I pull up in front of Justine's house and they're out the front door before I even put the car in park so I don't bother. They get in and we're off toward the mall with a quick exchange of 'heys' and then Justine says, 'Everything okay?'

I don't want to get into it; how I feel like they've dropped me entirely just because I broke up with Alex, just because I'm going away to college and they're not. I say, 'Yeah, of course. Why?'

Justine shrugs and kicks off her flip-flops and puts her feet up on the glove compartment. Morgan laughs in the backseat and says, 'But don't you sort of hate the mall?'

'I need a present for . . . that guy.' I swat at Justine's feet and she puts them down.

'Wow!' Morgan says, laughing again. 'Must be serious!'

'Yeah,' I say, annoyed by all her laughing. 'It sort of is.'

I take my right hand off the wheel again, reach for my necklace, and hold it up. 'He gave me this.'

Justine leans over for a look and says, 'Holy crap!'

Morgan pops forward to get a glimpse. 'That is intense.'

'Yeah,' I say, letting go of the necklace.

'So what are you going to get him?' Morgan asks.

'No freaking idea.'

★ ★ ★

Justine sees Alex and Karen Lord coming out of the food court, before either Morgan or I do, and says, 'Uh-oh.' They're face to face with us and we can't reroute or do anything about it.

'Hi, EB,' Alex says, and he drops Karen's hand. She responds by sliding her arm around his back, near his waist, and now I'm the one who wants to laugh.

'Hi,' I say to Alex. Then, 'Hi, Karen.'

'Hi,' she says, rolling her eyes like she couldn't be bothered.

'Hey, so good luck in California,' Alex says. 'You know, if I don't see you before you go.'

Twenty days. That's all I have left. It suddenly seems crazy. That's less than three weeks!

'Thanks,' I say. 'Good luck to you, too.'

I look pointedly at Karen Lord and wonder

251

if I get across what I'm going for. Namely, *Yeah. Good luck with that.*

'You beaching it tomorrow?' Karen asks Justine and Morgan, and my friends both look painfully awkward and mutter things like 'Maybe' and 'I'll text you.'

Then, with strained looks all around, we seem to agree that the interaction has come to an end and, without any more discussion, we're all on our merry ways again. 'That was weird,' Justine says.

'Yeah,' I say.

'Totally.' Morgan spies the Hallmark store and says, 'I need a birthday card,' then drifts in.

Justine and I linger by a front window display of all sorts of back-to-school fanfare and she says, 'So you know what else is weird?'

'What?'

'We're already moving on. Before we even have to. Why is that happening?'

'I don't know,' I say. 'Maybe it's easier. Less pressure to have some big final hurrah.'

'Maybe.' She seems to be studying the sign that says PENCILS, BINDERS, AND GLUE, OH MY! 'It's almost like you and me are too close. Like *sisters* close. Sometimes I'm not even sure I like you that much anymore, but I still love you.'

For a second it's like she's kicked me in the stomach but then I realize that she's right. The fact that she gets it, too, feels like a miracle. Morgan has gotten on line for the cashier and Justine shouts to her, 'Meet us next door.'

Morgan nods. The line is pretty long.

'So if I'm a sister you don't really like, what does that make Morgan?' I ask, and Justine shrugs, then says, 'A cool cousin?'

I smile.

'So tell me about this guy,' she says, wandering into a gadget-y store. 'What are we in the market for?'

'I don't know.' I'm studying a chessboard display near the front of the store when I say, 'What do you give a guy when you've already given him your virginity?'

Justine's mouth drops open; she has a massager of some kind in her hands. 'You did not.'

I think I smile. 'Oh yes I did.'

And then I did it again, too. The other night. Under the boardwalk! Such a cliché! For a second, I wonder if and when I'll do it enough times that I'll stop counting. Then I have a feeling of vertigo, like I'm on some crazy high slippery slope. Does this mean I'll never refuse a guy sex again? I don't think so, but I'll need to watch that.

Right?

'Holy shit.' Justine puts the massager down and grabs on to a built-in shelf along the wall, like she needs support, or to catch her breath. 'I never thought you'd do it before me. Never in a million years.'

'Sorry to disappoint,' I say with some snark, because this isn't about her. But maybe I'd feel the same way if I were her? Until I lost my virginity, I sort of resented people who already had; people like Morgan. I always wondered how they'd found the guts and the opportunity when it seemed unlikely I would ever find either of those things.

'Where? How was it?' She is tailing me as I wander deeper into the store.

'The Moonlight Motel,' I say, right as I find a noise machine display.

'You cannot be serious!'

'Why not?' The floor sample machine is turned on and it's making a white noise sound. I hit a button and switch it to 'Ocean,' then listen to see how authentic it sounds.

'No, I mean, that's awesome!' Justine grabs my arm but I am far away, lost in the waves. 'I love the Moonlight. It's so old-school. It's just . . . I'm looking at you and it's like you're this totally different person.'

I hit the button again and it switches to 'Heartbeat' and I turn it up, maybe a little too loud, and it feels like it's somehow in sync with my own heart, which seems to be pounding so hard that someone could maybe even hear it if they were standing next to me.

I don't want to be a totally different person.

'I'm still me,' I say, but Justine has already walked away. She has climbed into a big leather recliner, where she is testing out some fancy-pants pillow, and I swear, if we weren't in a public place, if Morgan weren't on her way across the store to us, I'd run over and climb in next to her for a hug.

⋆ ⋆ ⋆

Mark texts me later that night, asking How's your mom?

I write back: He didn't break it off. Only stopped calling.

He writes back Sounds about right. A-hole.

The whole thing feels sour, which I hate, and I have no idea what to say in reply so I sit there in my room, not quite sure what to do with myself, and he writes Missing you.

That, at least, is easy to reply to. I text Ditto. See you tomorrow?

He sends back Yes please. Will consult list for task to cross off.

G'night, I write. And I think hard for a

second about someplace we can slow-dance, or a fight to pick, or what to buy him, but nothing comes.

Dear Lo,
Only twenty days to go. It's funny. I'm having a hard time keeping myself in the present now that I know I'll be gone in a few weeks. I find myself drifting and thinking of other people I know and wondering what they're doing. Like I try to picture your final days in your house with your family, and I wonder what my mother's days are like, when she's at the office or an open house and I'm not around, and I wonder what my dad's doing right now, six hours ahead in Italy. (Yes, he is there now. He was already there when he wrote to me.) Probably drinking wine and having the time of his life. I wonder if I'll stop all this envisioning of other people and places after I move? I'm not making sense.

The situation with Keyon does sound confusing. (And yes, the necklace is a nice reminder that Mark reciprocates how I feel about him, and since I have this idea that we're permanently connected now, at least I'll always have this tangible reminder of the fact that it was . . . lovely? (Not to get all British sounding on your arse.) I've actually been trying for a while

256

now to think of a present for him because 'Buy each other a present' was on that list we made of stuff to do this summer. Now I feel more pressure. I even went to the mall with Justine and Morgan, but I came home empty-handed. (My ex, Alex, was there with another girl. It's funny how little it bothered me. I wonder how things would be different if I didn't have Mark.)

BUT ENOUGH ABOUT ME!

I don't know. In the friends with benefits scenario there is the friends bit and then the benefits bit. In the boyfriend/girlfriend scenario, it seems like there's sort of this third element, the swoony bit that has you thinking about stuff like getting married and all that jazz, right? So, for example, handholding is, perhaps, a clue as to more than just benefits? I am not sure, though. I've never been in a friends with benefits scenario.

My mother's affair has ended. He stopped calling her. No explanation. (Classy, right?) That makes my life officially, well, drama free! Thank God for that. I think I've seriously had enough drama this summer to last a lifetime. I want to turn off the Soap Opera Network now please.

Being an only child isn't so hot, trust me. I'd kill for a sibling because, for example, when my mom's old and senile I'm the only one who's going to be around to play bingo with her in the nursing home.

— EB

Yes: A swimsuit.

No: Winter parka. (Right?)

Maybe: I was strangely drawn to this noise machine I saw at the mall. Could come in handy if our dorm neighbors party hard . . . or if you snore.

(Do you snore?)

(I really hope you don't snore.)

FRIDAY, AUGUST 9
SAN FRANCISCO

It's 3 AM-ish. Sleep is not happening. And not just because P.J. snores.

It's been a somewhat shitty week.

Things have felt weird with Keyon. The weirdness is coming from me, I know, not him. I haven't handled it right. I've actually been kind of a jerk, answering his e-mails with really short replies like — Sorry so busy! More later! — then not writing more later. At work, I've run away from any moment we might have alone, any opening for a real conversation. He's asked me to go places this week, to check out some Goodwills, to take a run around the polo field, or otherwise hang out, and I've been claiming responsibilities at home. Which I no longer actually have.

What I *actually* have is plenty of time on my hands. To think.

And a lot of this waking up at night and staring into the dark, like now, listening to my sisters breathe and snore, to the L rumble down the hill, to the occasional car drive by. Mostly to my own thoughts.

I want to go online and delete my entire e-mail in-box, cancel my account, toss the laptop off the Golden Gate Bridge. E-mail is nothing but trouble. Without it, I would be walking into my dorm room in a couple of weeks and meeting a total stranger and starting with a clean slate, instead of knowing about her sex life, and her mom's sex life, and her emotional life, and everything else.

And I wouldn't be in the position of having to decide whether or not to relay the news flash: Her father is not in Italy.

Of course that wasn't e-mail's fault. It was my own fantastic idea to go to his stupid gallery and open this complicated can of worms.

I turn over onto my belly and smash my face into my pillow.

Why do people lie?

My little brothers and sisters lie so they won't get in trouble. But they're kids, it's natural, and they always wind up telling the truth because they feel so guilty you can see it all over their faces. When you get older and smarter, when you're not six, don't you figure out that lying only causes more hassle, more anger, more hurt?

One thing I can say about myself: I am usually a pretty honest person. I mean, I'll tell someone they look nice when them needing to hear it outweighs the truth factor. And, okay, I've lied once or twice about homework status or something to teachers. But about the important things, the things involving people's emotions and their lives and their concept of who I am and who they are, I try to keep it true. My parents have always been honest with me that way, and I guess it rubbed off. Which is why it's driving me crazy knowing I need to tell Ebb about going to her dad's gallery, and about him being there.

I need to be straight with Keyon, too, because avoiding him is another kind of a lie, a sin of omission, my grandma would say when she's feeling all spiritual and Catholic. I need to face Keyon and talk about what this is, so that two weeks from now we're not suddenly discovering that one of us thinks it's something with real potential and the other of us thinks it's merely a hookup.

And while I'm at it I should stop lying to myself. Because I know we passed hookup when his parents had me over for dinner. And that kiss at the gallery.

That kiss.

The memory of it is about to turn my early-morning worry into something more enjoyable, some Lauren time, when P.J. wakes herself up with an especially loud snore. The outline of her little body sits upright. She's disoriented, I can tell, and I know she's scared of the dark. I go to her before the wailing can start.

'Hey, Peej,' I whisper, and put my arm around her. 'It's okay.'

She nuzzles her warm head into me without saying anything. I slip under the covers with her and we lie back down, my nose against her hair, which is unbelievably soft and smells like baby shampoo.

Such a beautiful, simple thing.

I turn my nose away, because I think if I catch another whiff, I'm going to cry.

'I'll miss you, Peej.'

But she's already fallen back asleep.

★ ★ ★

Dealing with the Keyon issue seems the easier of the two things I have to face, since it's in person and immediate. As I hurtle my way toward the sandwich shop on the Hell Taraval, I promise myself I will not avoid this, or him, one more day. I should be using this time to work out what I'm going to say, but I can't get Ebb's stupid father off my mind. What possible reason could he have for telling her he's in Italy when he's not? What kind of a parent would do that?

I've had the thought all week that it could

262

be Ebb who's lying. Maybe despite her claims of not wanting drama, telling me her dad is in Italy is some way to make her life seem more dramatic and exciting than it is. Maybe her mom never was seeing her boyfriend's married dad. Maybe there is no boyfriend, and no virginity, or no loss thereof.

Maybe she is a psycho-compulsive-liar-roomie who is going to stab me in my sleep some night.

I'm grasping, I know. Trying to rationalize the option of pretending like I don't know anything about her dad, and pulling the plug on the friendship before it really gets started.

When I walk into the sandwich shop, Keyon is helping an early customer and barely glances at me. I go in the back to stow my messenger bag and put on my apron, and find Joe racking the bakery delivery. Despite my promise to myself not to delay, I've got cold feet and tie my apron as slowly as possible while I watch Joe work.

I wonder if Keyon will look like his dad when he's older. If he'll have that ashy gray hair around his sideburns, and if his cut abs will give way to a comforting little paunch, like Joe's.

'Need help?' I ask.

Joe turns, a loaf of rye in each hand. 'You can help me with my son.'

'Um, okay?'

'Found him in the kitchen at four this morning, halfway up to his elbows in my Cherry Garcia.'

I wait. Keyon was awake when I was awake, in the wee hours, both of us thinking our thoughts.

'No one eats my Cherry Garcia. Unless it's an emergency.' Joe racks the rye, and when he turns around I'm there to hand him two more loaves.

'Did he . . . say what this emergency was?'

'Didn't have to.'

We move on to the sliced sourdough. I remain silent. Because what can I say? It's complicated. And I don't know if I should even be talking about it with Keyon's dad.

'I'm not tryin' to take sides,' he says. 'Maybe you two changed your minds or what have you, or he did something stupid. Just don't let it fester.' Joe turns back to the bread rack. 'The longer it festers, the more I gotta spend on ice cream.'

I hand him two more loaves of bread, then go out front. Keyon is washing his hands.

'Your dad is really worried about his Cherry Garcia supply,' I say, sidling up to him at the sink. My stomach is kind of churny.

'What?' He reaches for a paper towel and

dries off. I watch his face. He really does look bothered about our lack of communication. The way a boyfriend would.

'I miss when we were making business plans for our Mr. Potato Head empire.'

I meant to make him laugh, I guess, or lighten the mood, but he's still got that bothered look on his face when he says, 'So you wanna go back to being . . . friends?'

And I realize that's exactly what it sounded like. 'No. I mean, that's not what I meant.' I turn on the water and wash my hands while Keyon watches. I think about his hands, and his hand holding mine, and how I like the way his skin looks next to mine, and about that very first kiss, in Yasmin Adibi's yard.

'You meant you're leaving in a couple weeks and so am I. I know. It's . . . ' He kind of kicks his toe into the rubber floor mat. 'It's bunk, is what it is.'

Honestly, he looks like he could cry. It stops my heart for a second, and it occurs to me: Maybe Key is going through the same stuff I am, about leaving home and saying good-bye — not only to each other, if that's what we do, but to everything that's always been the way it is for him. The sandwich shop, the hallway in his house with the pictures of him and his brother goofing around, his mom's cooking, his dad's gentle sort of toughness and rightness.

I put my arms around him in a hug, my hands still wet. He holds me tight and doesn't let go until we both hear the conspicuous throat-clearing of a customer.

EB,
Nineteen days.

Wow. I can't imagine what you're feeling now. I mean for me it's only going across the Bay. I can't even begin to know what it would be like to go even a few more hours further. Farther. Further?

Delete. Delete. Delete.
It feels disingenuous to make my usual small talk before I drop the bomb.

After work, Keyon and I sat in the back of the sandwich shop and split a piece of cheesecake and I told him about the whole Ebb situation. He thought for a minute, then asked, 'Would you want to know, if you were her?'

'Yeah,' I said instantly.

He tilted his head and raised his eyebrows. 'For real? Think about it. Think about how low that is. Your own dad telling a huge-ass lie that basically says: 'I don't want you.' Think about how it's gonna feel to her.'

I shook my head. 'I know it's going to suck. But I hate secrets.' I met his eyes, his warm eyes. 'That's something to know about me, okay?'

'Okay,' he said. 'It is known.'

Then we looked into each other's eyes and made contact. I don't mean eye contact. Something more. Communication. Like the kiss at the gallery. Telling me: This is not friends who make out, if I still had any question about that. This is more. 'Here's a secret,' I said, my heart hammering, and hammering again now to remember it. 'I like you.'

He smiled, dazzling but somehow shy, and after a second, said, 'That ain't a secret, Lo.'

We grinned some more, and finished our cheesecake, feet touching under the table. Eventually we stopped making googly eyes at each other and I said, 'I have to tell her. I just do.'

I start the e-mail again:

EB,

So I have to tell you something. I thought actually this might be better said over the phone but then I thought it's nice to have some time to think about how to react and stuff. You might be really mad at me. Just . . . don't shoot the messenger, okay? If I were you I think I would want to know this.

Okay. I don't think your dad is in Italy.

I went to the gallery last week and he was there. I'd seen a flyer at this coffee shop I always go to and I was all, 'Isn't that EB's dad's place?' and Zoe and I wanted to do something different, so we went. We were only there like five minutes and it didn't seem important. Then we went again this past Sunday to see this other artist and your dad was still there. I mean I guess I'm assuming it was him. He gave us his card. Neil. But maybe he has a partner who happened to be handing out your dad's card? He talked like he was the owner, though.

He's fit and good-looking for someone his age and has sort of a New York accent? Maybe he's having money problems and didn't want to tell you? Dads can be weird about money.

Why am I making excuses for him? I guess I don't want it to be true, either, that he'd lie to her like that. Hurt her.

I've been thinking all week if I should tell you. Maybe it's none of my business. Keyon thought maybe I shouldn't. But I feel like if I didn't tell you it would always be between us in this awkward way.

I'm sorry to add to the drama. If I did. Maybe there's an explanation.

Lauren

After sending, I get a message from my dad. In the mood I'm in, I tear up to see his name in my in-box, and imagine him down the hall, in bed and propped on pillows, e-mailing me.

Hon: Enjoyed our gelato date the other night. I just want to say I'm proud of you. For a lot of reasons. Also I've attached a picture of my foot.

He's such a weirdo goofball.
I love him.

SATURDAY, AUGUST 10
NEW JERSEY

I wake up to Lauren's e-mail on Saturday but I'm already late for work with Tim so I don't even have time to think about writing back right away, which is probably for the best. But the whole drive to work, I get increasingly steamed — at Lauren, for not telling me she'd met my dad when it first happened; at my dad, for being a liar, if he even is. There must be some kind of misunderstanding. It makes no sense.

Lauren says she's sorry.

But I don't want her to be sorry. I don't want anybody to be sorry. Not her, not my dad. Not my mother. Not even Alex, or Mark's dad. What I want is for everyone to, I don't know, get along. Get real. *Be* real.

When I arrive at the address Tim gave me, I sit in the car for a minute with my phone in my shaking hands. I don't know which one of them to e-mail first. Or if I should e-mail either of them at all.

Maybe because it's easier, because I'm in the habit, I pick Lauren.

I start typing. I am thinking about how she knows that I have no relationship with my father. How she knows I would love to stroll into his art gallery and have it not be horribly awkward. Does she think they're going to be buds? And she knew he told me he was in Italy. She's supposed to be my friend. Isn't she? Why didn't she *say something*? Confront him! I'm miles upon miles too far away to confront him but she was right there, in the flesh. And who does she think she is, telling me how to take this news, not to be mad at her? When I read what I've typed, it says this:

There must be some kind of mistake. And that's pretty fucked up that you did that.

I stop to take a deep breath and look at the words — I never use the f-word and it all looks sort of foreign — and I think what to say next but then I'm so angry that I just hit Send.

For a second I'm sick with regret . . . or something . . . but I mean it.

Fucked.

Up.

Then it's like some kind of truth spell has been cast on me and I can't stop myself from telling it like it is. Tim asks me around lunch-time if I want an early shift or late shift the next day and I tell him neither. I'm sort of done with this town and its gardens and I want at least a few weeks off from the weeding and clipping and mulching — time to, I don't know, stop and smell the roses? So I tell him I would like today to be my last day, if that's okay, and he grouses a bit but he gets it.

Later, Mark texts and asks if he can see me after work and I tell him no, that I need a quiet night to myself — maybe to pack or make lists or read or daydream, even if it's daydreaming about seeing him (though I don't tell him that last bit). I seem to suddenly realize that I can't live the next few weeks in a constant state of frenzy, like a passenger on a sinking ship.

And then, after work, I find my mother on her computer in the kitchen at home and I say, 'There's something I have to tell you. That guy I'm sort of seeing, Mark, it was his dad that you were going out with.'

Though we never talked about it explicitly — never named names — there was a part of me that assumed she connected the dots that first night, when I said I recognized him, that he had a son, but now, from the look on her face, I'm not so sure.

'Well, I hope he's a better man than his father is,' she says, sort of sadly.

I say, 'He absolutely is.'

For a second I think about bringing up my father — also no prize — but then she already knows that and I'm still thinking it's all just a big mistake.

I head upstairs to the shower and let the water run until it's almost too hot to bear, then wash off the brown from the dirt that seems to seep into my every pore during work hours. Afterward, I sit at my computer, hair dripping, and try to write an e-mail to my dad. But I really don't know what to say — *Are you really in Italy?* — and I find myself, instead, writing this long note to Mark.

I tell him that I love him.

That the time we've spent together in these past few weeks has meant so much to me.

That he'll never really know how badly I needed him to come along. At exactly this point in my life.

That I look forward to a million adventures with him, even if they never happen, even if we only manage a few.

And then I realize that this is also how I've felt about *Lauren* all summer, but I'm so furious at her I can barely think. This whole time she's been acting so morally superior about everything and now I find out she's been lying to me, and sort of stalking my dad?

What was that crap she was spewing about not being able to keep secrets from people she cares about?

I am pretty sure Keyon's dad would not approve.

She hasn't responded to the e-mail I sent this morning and I am sure she is hoping for me to write again to say that I get it, that I've calmed down and that I understand — to let her off the hook — but when I look inside myself I don't even see a glimmer of forgiveness.

I can't live with this girl.

Can I?

I save the e-mail to Mark as a draft — because it seems silly to send it to him now, when he has no idea why I'm getting all sappy on him — and I start to root around the Berkeley website. When I go to *Living at Cal*, then *Living with a Roommate*, I see a link for *Getting to Know Your Roommate* and click on that and start reading.

Roommates do not need to be best friends.

Good, because that ship has sailed.

However, we do expect you to be fair and honest, and to take responsibility for your own behavior.

My point exactly! Why didn't I visit this site earlier? Before things went horribly wrong?

I read on eagerly and the next part sort of

cracks me up. Because it's this long list of fill-in-the-blank icebreakers that they suggest will help you get to know your roommate better. Things like *If I were an animal, I would be a . . .* or *A food I would never want to eat is . . .* That's not how you get to know someone! And anyway, the ice between Lauren and me has already been broken. Shattered.

Fill in *this* blank: *Stalking someone's father is . . .*

Then I find a whole section about a Roommate Agreement — *This might have saved us a lot of heartbreak!* — but it turns out it's mostly about study habits and bedtime and cleaning and personal property, though there's a whole section called *Conflict Resolution* that makes me wonder why I ever thought having a roommate would be a good idea in the first place.

And then all of a sudden I am looking for a *Contact* tab.

So that I can write to someone in Housing and inquire about getting assigned a different roommate, or a single. But they don't make it easy. And who's to say a different roommate would be any better? Lauren may be a liar but at least she's not a drug dealer or a hippie freak. When I'm so irritated by the website that I can't bear to look at it another second,

I close my laptop, hard, and go downstairs. My mother is now under a throw on the couch, watching some Lifetime movie.

'Mom?' I say, and I can hear surrender or maybe just defeat in my voice. 'I need advice.'

She looks about as surprised to hear the words as I am to say them.

'I'll make us some popcorn,' she says, kicking off the throw, and I tail her into the kitchen.

SATURDAY, AUGUST 10
SAN FRANCISCO

. . . fucked up

The words blur on the screen. No one has ever used those words in direct relation to me or anything I've done. And I don't think Ebb should be using them now. I go over and over it, from my first impulse to check out the gallery to the circumstance that led me back the second time, to the decision to tell Ebb what I knew.

That first day was simple curiosity! Going back was Zoe's idea!

Lying about where he was is all on her *dad*.

. . . fucked up . . .

Seriously, Ebb?

Who doesn't check people out ahead of time anymore? Everyone Google-stalks crushes, new friends, siblings, potential employees. Facebook is like 98 percent about stalking, if you think about it, and somehow that's okay. But because *I'm* old-school, because *I* got off my ass and onto my own two legs and went physically to the gallery, now *I'm* 'fucked up'?

I bet every penny in my checking account

Ebb looked me up online that first day she e-mailed.

Which, by the way, was all her idea.

She started it.

Oooh we're gonna be best friends and we need a microwave and my mom's having an affair and I slept with my new boyfriend and I'm bringing my favorite socks!

Okay, Ebb. You want a friend and roommate who's going to lie to you and pretend nothing bad is happening when it obviously is, you want a roommate in denial — like your mom — that's great.

But it's not going to be me.

★ ★ ★

By Sunday, I make a shoe box in my head, put Ebb and everything about her into it, and shove it into the back of my mental closet so that I can enjoy my date with Keyon. A real one this time: at night, me and him, no Zoe. And he's meeting the parents, which is somewhat terrifying. All the kids are home, and all except Francis are running around like insane people.

'They've finally got their energy back after the flu,' Mom says, smiling, as if this is good news.

Dad is on his hands and knees, using the

278

mini-vac on the trail of crushed Cheerios that consistently appears between the kitchen and living room. 'Did you warn Keyon?'

'Yeah.'

And I warned *them* about Keyon.

It was this excruciatingly awkward conversation, for a bunch of reasons. One is that it's not the sort of thing liberal white people in cities like San Francisco are used to talking about. We're all so determined to prove how open we are, how down, how *so* not thrown off-kilter by things like interracial dating.

We are, though. Some of us. It's how it is.

Another reason: because of how my dad reacted.

Of course I've talked about Key before in the context of work and hanging out, but I haven't said anything more, and this morning my dad was all, 'Hey, I saw 'Lauren out' on the family calendar for tonight. Anything fun?'

'Yyyeah,' I said. 'Maybe we can talk about it when the kids are done eating.'

'Talk about what?' Jack asked. Unfortunately he asked it while trying to pour syrup and the syrup wound up about two inches to the left of his plate of pancakes.

'Jack,' Mom sighed, and got up to procure a paper towel.

Dad told the kids they could go watch a

DVD when they'd finished.

'Dora,' Gertie said.

Marcus frowned. 'I hate Dora.'

'*Hate* is a bad word.'

'You're right, Gertie,' Dad said. 'But let Marcus pick first this time, okay?'

When they were all settled, Mom bounced Francis on her knee and I told her and Dad about Keyon. 'That's who I'm going out with tonight,' I said.

At first I got strained smiles and quizzical looks, my mom saying things like 'I didn't realize you were dating . . . ' and 'Oh, I see, you're not dating but you're going on a date . . . ' 'So, more than friends but not officially a couple?' 'Oh, sort of officially a couple now?'

''Couple' is pushing it,' I said.

Dad stood up from the table and carried plates to the sink. 'But this isn't your first date,' he said, stating it rather than asking.

'Well, it *sort* of is.' I rationalized dinner at Keyon's parents' house, which mine didn't know about, as less than a 'date' and more like a 'visit.'

'You've been hanging out with him,' Dad said, 'in a boy-girl way, it sounds like.'

'He is a boy and I am a girl and we have been hanging out, yes.'

'Lauren, come on, you know what I mean.

You didn't want to tell us about this sooner?' His voice was loud over the running water as he rinsed dishes.

I looked at Mom. She had her nose in Francis's hair, what little of it there was. I caught her eyes and gestured with mine toward Dad, like, *Say something to him.*

'Of course we want to meet him,' she said. 'To establish a relationship, not to give you *permission.*' To Dad: 'Right, Doug?'

Dad flipped a dish towel over his shoulder and turned around. 'Keyon, huh?'

'Yeah, Keyon,' I said, knowing what he was asking. 'He's black, by the way.'

Mom said, almost too quickly, 'Not that it matters, honey.' She shifted Francis around so he faced her. 'We're just . . . surprised. It's been a while since you went out on anything like a date.'

'Yeah, I know. I thought you'd be happy that I'm having some fun and exercising my freedom.'

'You're totally missing the point,' Dad said; then, instead of explaining what that point might be, he tossed his towel on the counter and left the room.

Mom grinned at me, and wouldn't stop.

'What's so amusing?' I asked.

'I'm thinking about Grandpa, the first time I brought your dad home. You know Grandpa was one of the nicest men around. But he did *not like* Mr. Douglas Cole. He didn't have any reason not to, but simply the very idea of him — of *anyone* who might take me away from him, from home . . . It can be hard for some fathers. And mothers.'

'I've been on dates before, Mom.' Several. Mostly dances.

'I know. It's probably dawning on Dad that while you're across the Bay, we won't have any idea what you're up to and who you're up to it with unless you decide to tell us.'

'So he doesn't care about Keyon's . . . not-whiteness?'

'Oh, I'm not saying that. He might have something to work through there. But it's probably quite a bit more about sex.' Then Francis burped, and Mom put him over her shoulder, patting his back rhythmically while saying 'Sexy sexy sexy sex' with each pat.

'Mom, seriously? In front of Francis?'

'How do you think we *got* Francis?'

I groaned and rested my head on the table, immediately realizing I'd put it in a small puddle of syrup. 'I'm not having sex,' I said, using my napkin to blot the sticky mess. 'And I have no immediate plans to.' It surprised me, saying it aloud. And hearing it made me certain. 'Tell that to Dad before Keyon comes over tonight, if it'll make him act nicer.'

'My inner feminist says that's none of his business,' Mom said. 'It also wonders if you would like to talk about this sex thing with me now.'

'We had that talk four years ago.'

'I left a lot out.' There was a glimmer in her eye that made me nervous. 'So if you want more details and — '

'Um, *no*.' I got up before she could continue. 'I have to go wash syrup off my face. Immediately.'

She grinned again, like the whole thing was hilarious. I went into the bathroom, locked the door to prevent sibling invasion, and cleaned up. As I inspected my hairline for maple residue, I knew why I had said that I had no plans for sex with Keyon or anyone else:

I like the way I am. I don't want to change myself right now, in the way that I presume sex would change a person. Or at least the way a person thinks about herself.

With so many things shifting this year, I want to hold one thing steady, keep one thing exactly in the perfect place.

★ ★ ★

Keyon shows up right on time and there's immediate chaos.

Jack and Gertie run screaming to answer the front door. Jack opens it and Keyon gives him a big smile and says, 'Marcus, right?'

Jack shakes his head and walks away, dejected. Not the best start.

I put my hands on Gertie's shoulders. 'That was Jack. This is Gertie.'

'Oops.' Keyon bends down and says, 'Hey, Gertie,' and gives her a friendly shoulder-nudge.

She hovers around my leg, mute. 'She's shy with strangers,' I explain.

'It's cool. Me too.'

My mom comes in, smiling hugely, *hugely*, as if Keyon is there to announce she's won a million dollars. 'Keyon!'

Oh, lord. The force of her cheer is epic. And she gives Keyon this big hug.

I hope it's not as obvious to him as it is to me the lengths to which my parents are going to show how totally fine and not at all complicated it is that he's black. My dad is acting excessively jolly yet also not quite making eye contact with me. I don't know if Mom told him about the sex conversation, or if he's just being weird all on his own.

It's all slightly reminiscent of the way Keyon's mom talked and talked when I went to his house, and now I'm pretty sure she was as nervous as my parents are.

Worried that he'll try to fist-bump Keyon or something, I shove Gertie in my dad's direction. 'Will you round up Marcus and P.J. so we can say hi and then be on our way?'

He does, and we all stand around the living room for a while chatting and watching the kids run wild. Mom asks Keyon if he wants to hold Francis, and to me it sounds like 'You may be tall and black but we trust you with our infant!'

Maybe it's all in my head. Maybe I'm the one with the problem. Before he can say yes or no, I grab Keyon's arm and say, 'Well, we better get going . . . '

Finally, we're through it. Once we're in Keyon's car, he looks at me and asks, 'You okay?'

'Yeah!' I say brightly. 'Why?'

'You seemed nervous in there.'

I laugh self-consciously. 'Weren't you? Meeting the parents and all?'

'Nah, I don't worry about it.'

'I guess I've never really had a guy over to meet them.' I don't know why I'm lying. Good old honest Lauren, who, on principle, just *had* to tell Ebb about her dad! Here she is, lying to Keyon about this dumb little thing. The truth is that at the beginning of junior year Chris Manieri came for dinner a couple of times. But I don't want Keyon to think this race stuff means anything more than . . . whatever it means.

'And it's got nothing to do with me being black?' He says it with a smile, teasing.

I make a pretend shocked face and press my hand to my chest. 'What? You're *black?*'

He laughs, and reaches over to put his hand on my thigh, like he does all the time now, whenever we're in the car. 'Where we going?'

'Hey, you're the guy. You decide.'

★ ★ ★

We wind up at Nizario's, where there are some other kids from school and it's kind of hard not to join them, since the only empty table is a foot away from theirs, so we do. They're more from Keyon's circle than mine and seem a little surprised to see us together, but there we are, together.

I'm getting used to it. Getting used to it being true, and not only something that happens in a parallel universe that exists at the sandwich shop and in Keyon's car. Saying aloud we like each other: check. Meeting parents: done. On a date: yes.

Having the 'we're going to college in two weeks, what now?' talk . . .

We can no longer pretend this isn't

something that needs to happen, and soonish.

He holds my hand under the table while we wait for our order. I can't stop exploring his fingers with mine, each of them individually, the roughness of the cuticles and the smoothness of the nails. The landscape of his palm. The wrinkly part of his knuckles.

After we eat he slides his chair so it's touching mine and puts his arm around me. I press myself against him, too, and it feels good and right and safe, and is this what you feel after you know you like someone, and they like you, but before you know if you love them?

We drive down to Ocean Beach after dinner and sit in the car. I assume we're going to make out, but after a few kisses Keyon says, 'I ate too much pizza. My stomach is feeling kind of gnarly.'

So we talk.

Keyon tells me about his big brother, Joe Junior. How they used to get up to all kinds of nonsense when they were kids, driving his mom mad. 'When she'd had it with us, my dad would take us to work with him. Man, we loved that. We would sneak sourdough rolls and tubs of chicken salad and hide out in Pop's office during the rush and make ourselves sick on that junk.'

'It's weird,' I say, staring out at the fog

287

coming in over the water. 'I have all these brothers and sisters but I don't really know what it's like to have a brother or sister. I mean, they're all too young to do that kind of stuff with. Mostly it's like I'm an extra parent.'

'Yeah, I could see how it'd be like that.'

'Maybe when the kids get older, it will be different. But they're going to have all these experiences without me. They'll know every detail of each other's lives.'

'You're going to have a bunch of experiences without them, too. It's good. It's life.'

I snuggle against Keyon, with the emergency brake in my lower ribs, and we're quiet a long time. My mind drifts all over the place, from imagining what our kids would look like and if I could learn to do their hair right, to going over in my head the words I should use to break up with him in two weeks, and back to our wedding, or at least visiting each other in school . . .

'Do you know who your roommate is going to be yet at Chico?'

'Uhh, maybe? There's a letter around my house somewhere, I guess.'

'You were right about EB,' I say. 'I shouldn't have told her about her dad.'

'Pissed?'

'Ohhhyeah.' I bury my head in his shoulder and sigh. 'She's acting like . . . I don't know. The way you'd act if someone purposely ran over your dog or something. It wasn't like that.'

'Don't want to say I warned you. But . . . '

'You warned me.'

He touches my neck. 'Your intentions were good, Lo.'

'Apparently that's not always enough.' My back is getting all twisted, so I sit up and shift so that I'm leaning against the passenger door. 'I thought we were friends, me and her. Or getting to be friends. It proves my point about e-mail and all that. Like Zoe thinks she has all these 'friends' online, people who watch her videos and whatever — '

Her videos.

'Hello?' Keyon asks.

I will follow that thought later.

'Well, my point is you can't ever really know how it's going to be with a person until you meet them and hear how they talk,' I say, 'and see what kinds of expressions they make and stuff. You have to spend *time* with people. That's how you become friends.'

'Right.'

'I mean maybe this whole 'friendship' with her has been, like, an *illusion* from the beginning. What do I know? Maybe she chews with her mouth open or smiles too much, or not enough, or interrupts all the time . . . '

Keyon laughs. 'Or maybe she's just regular.'

I'm pulling out my mental EB shoe box now, digging through it. 'We told each other a lot of stuff. Stuff I don't even tell Zoe. I told her about you, for example. What happened at Yasmin's party.'

'Really?' He puts his hand on my neck. 'What did you think, that night?'

'I thought we kissed by accident.'

'A damn *tragic* accident.'

'And now look what's happened,' I say.

It hangs there. Waiting for one of us to put into actual words what's happened.

Keyon goes back to the EB issue. 'You telling her about me sounds like real friends. Even if she's a mouth breather.'

'I know, but now she hates me. She doesn't even believe me.' A problem I will soon solve.

His stomach makes a gurgling sound and he grimaces. We decide to go for a walk on the promenade, to help the pizza settle. Our hands cling together every second.

★ ★ ★

Zoe's YouTube channel is a confusing mess for someone like me who has spent maybe one hour on that site my whole life. I don't even know if she's done with the video she was making last weekend. Then I find one posted two days ago that already has over seven hundred views. How did she find all these people? How did they find her?

Anyway, I watch the video: *San Francisco Diary — Fine Arts Edition*.

A few minutes into it, there's Ebb's dad, smiling at the camera, talking about cash flow.

It makes me angry all over again, how he lied to her and the way she reacted when I told her. Like I was making it up or didn't know what I was talking about. I mean, why would I *say* something like that if I wasn't mostly sure?

I didn't expect her to be happy to hear it but I thought she knew me better than to think I'd tell her that news casually.

And I've been *open* with her, about stuff I don't tend to tell people.

Her dad is a dick. The end.

If she needs proof, here it is.

I find the 'share' link.

Maybe it is a mistake. Maybe this guy isn't your dad.
Maybe this isn't his gallery.

Send.

I wish I could say I did it to help her face the reality about her asshole father. To try to save our friendship and get everything into the open. To prove my good intentions.

But I know the truth: I'm mad at her over-reaction, and especially using those words, which I can't get out of my head, and I sent the video to hurt her, and the worst instinct in me hopes it really, really works.

MONDAY, AUGUST 12
NEW JERSEY

Lauren's e-mail is like poison. I feel it seeping into every molecule of my being, toxic. I see the words for what they are. I read the letters and assemble them into words that have a certain dictionary meaning. But somehow they look different to me, like there is a mirror layer of meaning that only I get. Her words look like 'told you so' or 'I know more than you do about your own father' or 'take that!'

No one could ever imagine that such a dopey video blog would cause someone so much pain — could they? — but here I am. Is she *trying* to hurt me? Is he?

My mother isn't home — I slept late — so I call Mark. I am crying when he picks up. I croak, 'Can you meet me?'

'Of course,' he says. 'Are you okay?'

'No, not really. Just meet me. The south beach parking lot.' I throw on clothes and tear out of there.

★ ★ ★

We park our cars side by side and go sit on a wind-worn bench on an empty stretch of boardwalk. He holds my hand while I tell him the whole story about Lauren and my dad; about the video and my last e-mail to her, everything.

'Why didn't you tell me when it was happening?' he asks.

'I don't know.' I am wiping away tears and more. 'It's like I'm embarrassed or something. Or was. I felt sort of dumb about how I reacted but this is how she responds? With a *video* of my dad? On some idiotic blog? It feels like she thinks this is a game or something. It's my life!'

He is still holding my hand. He is still not talking.

'I am *so mad* at her.' I am fishing for some support, some sympathy — no, empathy! — but he isn't offering any. Doesn't anyone get it? 'I mean, she goes into my dad's gallery and doesn't tell me for weeks? Then she sends me this video of him like she's got it all figured out?'

'She was probably just curious,' Mark says, finally. 'You told her the name of the gallery?'

I nod, like that has anything to do with anything, and I say, 'I'm sorry but it's weird.'

'I know, but think about it. Say you knew her dad owned a restaurant in Spring Lake or something. You wouldn't think about maybe going there?'

'Why would I? And if I did and he was there and he'd told her he was in Italy I'd say, 'Hey, Lauren's dad. Why'd you lie to your daughter and tell her you were in Italy?''

'You would not!' He is almost laughing.

'I would!' I feel certain of it.

He shakes his head. 'I looked him up. Your father. I Googled his gallery, found some pictures. How is that any different?'

'It just is.'

We sit there for a while then and I get this awful sense that he is trying to think of a way to handle me, like I am some insane person. I feel justified in that concern when he says, 'Are you sure it isn't your dad you're mad at?'

'Of course I'm mad at him,' I say. 'That's entirely beside the point.'

He puts his hands in his shorts pockets. Maybe I do sound insane. I wrap my arms around myself, like a straitjacket, trying on the feeling for size. 'How did I end up with such disastrous parents?' I shake my head. 'I mean, Lauren's parents sound amazing. Like normal, stable, loving people.'

'Well, mine are no prize, either.' He is looking at the water, not at me.

'At least you have relationships with both of them, though. My dad can't even spare a pillow and a sofa.'

He looks right at me when he says, 'Did you *really* think he'd say yes?'

I absorb his words and realize I've known all along that my father wouldn't come through. I look down and start crying and Mark slides an arm around my shoulders. How did I get to be so needy? So desperate that I thought a practical stranger would take me in? Like that would somehow make things better? I'm about to go out into the world on my own and I still have all these ridiculous ideas?

He says, 'Hey, at least she told you. What if she hadn't and you thought your dad was in Italy this whole time and kept this fantasy of becoming best buds or whatever?'

I have to wipe away tears and hold back a scream when I say, 'Whose side are you on?'

'Your side!' he says. 'Always. I think Lauren is, too.'

We haven't crossed 'have a fight' and 'make up' off our list yet and I was hoping we'd never get to it. But he is still talking and all I want is for him to shut up.

'She did the right thing,' he says. 'Even if it sucks to hear it.'

'She betrayed me!'

He groans. 'But not really intentionally, or I mean, not *maliciously*. And as soon as she knew something you needed to know she came clean.'

An older couple is walking by with a large, happy dog, and the sight of it — that big brown bounding fluffy thing, with its tail wagging and tongue hanging out of its mouth — makes me want to cry until I'm all cried out. After they pass, I say, 'I want you to be mad *with* me.'

Mark sighs. 'I am. At your sorry-ass father. Not your seemingly kick-ass roommate. She caught him red-handed. He can't bullshit you anymore.'

'What do I even say to her now?' I ask, annoyed that Mark is echoing stuff my mother said the other night.

'You say thanks.'

He's never going to get it. Two wrongs don't make a right. I stand up and say, 'I've gotta go.'

He gets up, too. 'Elizabeth, come on.'

I stand and face him. 'I want to be alone.' I have my car keys in my hand and am walking away.

'No you don't,' he shouts after me. 'You *called* me. You just want me to agree with you.'

'We're talking in circles,' I shout back to him as I open my car door and get in.

He comes to my window and knocks on it,

so I roll it down even as I put the car in reverse. He says, 'I'm not the bad guy here!'

'No, you never are,' I say. 'It must be nice to be so perfect. Maybe you and Lauren should get together.' I pull out and my ears are buzzing and they stay that way all afternoon, while I hole up in bed feeling sorry for myself.

★ ★ ★

I show my mom the video later that night, when she gets home from her first-ever Zumba class, and figure she at least will be as incensed as I am. Instead she is . . . disappointed? There is a funny nonchalance in her voice when she says, 'What an ass.'

'What do I do?' I ask her.

She is standing by the sink, guzzling water from a bottle. I swear I have never seen the woman drink water before.

She swallows and says, 'Call him. Make him explain. If it really matters. Or you pat yourself on the back for getting by all this time without him and move on.'

This is the same advice she gave me over popcorn, in addition to telling me to think hard about who I'm mad at before responding to Lauren or doing anything rash. It seems like ever since then she seems to be acting a bit more rational in general, almost as if my asking her to be the grown-up has turned her back into one. I wonder, though, if she's going to be able to take her own advice when I leave. Will she reward herself for getting by so well without me or backslide into misery?

It's not my problem. And it doesn't matter that no one else understands my anger but me. So up in my room, I search my in-box for the e-mail I got way back when, from Helen Blake in Student Housing. I open it, hit Reply, and dash off my message before I change my mind:

Dear Ms. Blake,
For reasons too complicated to explain, I am wondering if it is possible for me to get assigned a new roommate (someone other than Lauren Cole, as named in your original e-mail below), or a single.

Please respond at your earliest convenience,

Elizabeth Logan

After I hit Send, I open up Lauren's last e-mail and it gets me mad at her all over again. Because the snark is undeniable:

Maybe it is a mistake. Maybe this guy isn't your dad.
Maybe this isn't his gallery.

Maybe you don't have to be such a bitch about it!

I type Maybe you should mind your own business. Maybe we shouldn't be roommates.

And off it goes.

When I lie back on my bed, I stay very still and wait to see if anyone will respond right away, and to see if Mark will text me to say sorry or good night. Then I call my father's number, which I stupidly programmed when I got his e-mail — what a joke! — but he doesn't pick up and I don't leave a message.

When no new e-mails or texts arrive, I feel tired, as in exhausted, and also tired in general of people telling me what to think and how to feel. I've definitely had enough of that for one day. I turn my phone off and try to get some sleep.

SATURDAY, AUGUST 17
SAN FRANCISCO

I'm awakened by a hand on my shoulder and a whisper. 'Lauren.' It's my dad. He's got one finger on his lips and the other crooked and beckoning me up. I follow him, glancing out the window as I go. It's still dark out. Briefly, I wonder if I'm being called into a discussion about how he would prefer I not date Keyon, and in fact not date at all.

When we get to the kitchen, Dad clicks on the light. After my eyes adjust, they fill with tears.

'Dad.'

There's a fresh pan of cinnamon rolls on the table, and a glass of orange juice with the heart-shaped straw he got me for my seventh birthday. The rolls aren't homemade or anything — just those ones you get from the frozen-foods section of the grocery store. The same kind Dad used to make every Saturday back when it was the three of us, him, Mom, and me, before he started feeling like he needed to cook epic three-course breakfasts, before Mom started worrying about us eating

301

too much sugar, before Saturday mornings were overtaken by trips to Trader Joe's.

I look at him and he can see I'm about to lose it.

'My intention wasn't to make you cry, honey,' he says with a little laugh, putting his arms around me. That makes me cry harder and pretty soon I'm soaking the shoulder of his pajama top and afraid the tears will never stop. 'Lauren, Lauren,' he says, quiet. 'My first baby girl. It's hard to let go.'

And I know that's his apology for being distant from me since he found out I might have a boyfriend.

'I don't want to leave.'

Even as I say it, I know it's not true. There aren't words to say what I'm feeling, this mix of being so ready to strike out on my own and at the same time wanting to be ten again, eight, six.

Ready, not ready, it's happening in a week and a half. I can't stop it or hit the Pause button to figure out the mess that's been piling up. I clutch Dad's pajama top and a couple of more sobs escape.

'Shh. The goal here is time with only you, so let's not wake the rest of them.'

He smells like cinnamon rolls.

'I remember the day we brought you home,' he says. 'I looked at your mom and said, 'I don't want to mess this up.' We were like deer in the headlights. You were an alien. We were so . . . young.'

'You didn't mess it up.' My breath is settling down now. Dad tries to pull away but I hang on.

'Everything was new with you, for better or worse.' He forces me to lean back a little so he can look into my eyes. His face is so sweet, even with the saggy smile lines and receding hairline. 'We love all you kids — '

'I know.' My parents are good at telling us they love us. That's never in doubt.

'Let me finish. We love all you kids. But you've given us a lifetime of firsts, Lauren. I don't think you'll ever have any idea how special you are to me and your mom.'

I nod, to show I'm listening, to show I hear him. But I don't want to cry anymore, so I step back and wipe my face, and tease, 'You'll probably say the exact same thing to Gertie when she goes to college.'

He laughs, and tears a paper towel off the roll over the sink. I take it and wipe my face, blow my nose. Mom comes into the kitchen, squinting. 'I'm sorry,' she says. 'But I couldn't get out of bed fifteen minutes ago when I was supposed to.'

'It's okay,' I say, managing a smile. 'Let's eat.'

Later in the morning, I'm in bed sleeping off my juice-and-sweet-roll hangover while Gertie and P.J. play in the living room. I relisten to the voice mail Berkeley left me a couple of days ago:

'Lauren. This is the housing office at Berkeley. We wanted to let you know that your assigned roommate, Elizabeth Logan, has requested a change. Unfortunately, the only way to accommodate her request is to put you in a triple or a single. Please give us a call to let us know which solution is going to work for you.'

I haven't called back yet. Now that it's the weekend, there are just two more days to figure this out. Come Monday I have to make a decision. I also haven't responded to EB's e-mail. Everything is out of control, and I'm in full avoidance mode. I'm avoiding saying good-bye to Zoe, who's leaving for Seattle in four days. I'm avoiding talking about the future with Keyon. We're still hanging out, acting like boyfriend and girlfriend, and also acting like everything isn't about to change.

This coming week is our last at the sandwich shop, and I don't want to think about that, either, because it's become a crowded, mustard-smelling second home to me. Joe has already hired our replacements and they'll be training on Friday.

A major contributing factor to my avoidance can be summed up by one word:

Shame.

That I acted in anger. That I wanted to hurt EB. That I succeeded. That I haven't apologized.

Not for telling her about her dad, because I still think I did the right thing, but for how my motivation became proving myself right. It didn't surprise me when she dropped the maybe-no-roomies bomb. How else could she respond?

And shame to realize it's very possible I've taken the excellence of my own parents for granted. My dad made me freakin' cinnamon rolls. Hers acted like a weasel to get out of seeing her.

Shame is why I haven't told Keyon or Zoe about the latest episode in this drama.

'Shit,' I groan, and roll onto my side, pulling the covers up over my head.

Two seconds later, a small body lands on me and I stand — or lie — accused of 'saying a swear.' It's Jack. How did he hear me? Where did he come from? These kids are like ninjas sometimes. He pulls the blanket off my face and proceeds to burp in it.

'I love you, too, Jack.' His bedhead is

adorable, even if his burp smells like cat food.

'You said 'shit.''

'So did you. Now we're even.'

He knits his little brows together but cannot deny my logic. 'We won't tell,' he concludes.

'No, we won't.'

My phone, on the floor by my bed, rings. Jack looks at it, picks it up, and says, 'It's your boyyyyyfriennndddddd.'

'Give it.'

Jack giggles. I lunge out of bed and grab the phone out of his hand before the call can go to voice mail. 'Go away,' I say to Jack, clicking the Answer key.

'Hi?' Keyon says, confused.

'Not you.' I shoo Jack out and close my bedroom door behind him, then crawl back into bed. 'Hi.'

'How's my girl?'

Melt.

'Okay. Not awesome. But okay.'

'Anything you want to talk about?'

'Not right now.'

'Are you sure?' Keyon asks.

'Yeah.'

'Maybe you'll feel better after you hear this. Remember that radio you found at the Goodwill?' There's a touch of excitement in his voice.

'The Bakelite?'

'Yep. Guess who just sold it for nine hundred dollars.'

My jaw drops. 'No shit?' Then I cover my mouth and glance toward the door, hoping no minors heard that.

'Dude at the antiques store offered me seven-fifty at first, but I told him I knew it's worth over a thousand. We compromised.'

'Do I get a finder's fee or what?' He pauses and I think, *Oh, way to ruin a nice moment by talking about money.* 'Kidding,' I say. 'Good job on the sale.'

'No, no, here's the thing. I have this crazy idea . . .'

'Yeah?'

'You might not be into it, which is cool.' That edge of excitement in his voice has turned to something else. Something softer, more tentative. 'I'm kinda nervous even saying it but I gotta put it out there or I'll feel like a punk later.'

'Go ahead,' I say.

'The money . . . it could be, like, a special fund.'

'Yeah, to put back into the business.' I don't know why he's so nervous, seeing as we've already discussed this.

'No. Like. A visitation fund. A Key and Lo visitation fund.'

I sit up in my bed and stare down at the blue-and-white polkadot blanket. 'Really?'

'Unless you don't want to,' he says quickly. 'I mean, I got all kinds of other things I could do with four hundred fifty bucks. But I thought if we set it aside then at least money's not an excuse.'

Not an excuse. To not see each other. Which means we *will* be seeing each other. Maybe. 'We might have other excuses.' I say it like a flirt, like a tease, not like someone who actually expects to have any excuses at all.

'We miiiight.'

'But we might not.'

'That's what I was thinking,' he agrees.

I imagine him sleeping on the floor of my dorm room, next to my bed. Or in my bed. The two of us, in my potential single. How would that work in a triple? What if I get *two* roommates and they hate me? All these weeks I've been picturing Ebb as the one I'll get to like or not like or love or hate. Now . . .

'That money is probably worth eight visits,' I say to Keyon, to bring myself back to the present.

'I figured seven. Allowing for gas prices going up like they do.'

'They do.'

We smile at each other over the phone.

In the afternoon, I walk down to Ocean Beach and sit on the wall. The green-gray waves roll in, one after the other. It's a little cold today, not unusual for Ocean Beach in summer, but there are a few people with dogs, some walkers, a couple of surfers decked out in neck-to-ankle wet suits.

I pull my phone out of my pocket, along with the scrap of paper on which I scribbled EB's phone number. It was in that very first e-mail from Berkeley, letting me know my roommate's name and contact info. It's funny — not funny ha-ha, but funny-really? — to think about how upset I was that I didn't get a single, and now that I've been offered one I don't know if I want it.

What a shitty way to start college, in a fight with your roommate before you ever meet her! College is supposed to be a clean slate, a fresh start. How sad to go there with an already gossip-worthy past. EB can tell the whole story to her new roommate on their first night, and I'll be the surly, self-righteous bitch in a single who apparently doesn't want friends.

On the other hand, what if you could have a fight *and* make up before even meeting? In a way, wouldn't that make a nice, open path for the kind of friendship where you know you can get through anything? *Not* having to be brand-new. Letting something be on the slate. Something messy and slightly embarrassing but belonging to the two of you.

I punch in her number.

What if she answers? What am I actually going to *say*?

I hit the green Dial button before I can chicken out. It rings about a zillion times, and I swallow a lot before I get her voice mail:

'*Hey, it's EB. Leave a message. Or text me.*'

I'm so startled and mesmerized to hear the voice of this person I've been e-mailing all summer — a voice pleasantly alto and not Jersey Shore — that I just kind of breathe into the phone a couple of times, then hang up.

Stalker.

Or text me.

Okay.

Using my 9 key and predictive text, I manage:

That was me. Lauren. Should we talk?

After sending it I stay sitting on the wall, watching the ocean, and I think about friendship. Before EB came along, I'd barely given any thought to the question of that aspect of college. Of making new friends, and being a friend. I know I can't go through college the way I went through high school, with only one friend who really knew me and thinking that was enough. I think my dad might be wrong about only needing a couple of people to be close with. Not that I have to get online and be friends with everybody in my zip code, but I think a slightly bigger circle is better. That way, whichever direction you turn, there's a friendly face.

As much as I love to imagine being alone in an orderly lab, I also know you can't stay in there forever and expect to do good work. Life is one of those experiments meant to be conducted in a stimulating, messy environment.

So no matter what happens with EB, whether we wind up being best friends or merely good roommates or neither, I have to make sure she's not the only one on campus I share a connection with. I have to promise myself I won't use my family or work or studying as an excuse to avoid a social life.

I watch a seagull fly inches above the sand close to the water, and a guy running with his dog, and I smell the salt and the fog and I think, *Yeah, change is . . . good.* Certain things that don't change are good, too. Like the one person I've known and have let know me, for as long as I can remember.

I hit number 5 on my speed dial and wait to hear Zoe's voice.

SATURDAY, AUGUST 17
NEW JERSEY

It is a Saturday evening, eleven days from my departure date, when my mother pokes her head into my bedroom and says, 'Whatcha doing?'

There is no point denying it. 'Watching that video. You know. *Neil.*'

And looking for my phone, which I can hear but cannot see. It rang a minute ago, and from the sound of it, I have voice mail or a text.

'Elizabeth,' my mother says, sadly.

'I know.' I've been watching Zoe's blog a wee bit obsessively, trying to intuit some excuse or explanation, and feeling awful about the whole mess with Lauren but also feeling paralyzed.

Five whole days since we've communicated at all.

Eleven whole days until we meet. If we ever do.

After a few days passed and the sting of it all started to fade, I realized something: If two or three of the most important people in your life are telling you something and you are resisting it with everything you have, there is a distinct possibly that what they are saying is true. That you are wrong and just don't want to admit it. I guess I've been thinking an awful lot these past few days about fault and blame. Like whose fault was it that Lauren and I imploded?

I am pretty sure it was mine.

So I e-mailed Housing again on Thursday, and asked them to *please* disregard my initial e-mail, but they wrote back that Lauren had already been notified of my request and would need to be consulted. I've heard nothing definite about new assignments but can only assume it is happening, that I messed things up good.

My mother comes into my room and stands at the mirror and starts to put her hair into a ponytail, so I close my laptop and hunt for my phone more aggressively. It is probably a message from Mark, maybe about something new to add to our relationship to-do list. We made up — I took the lead on apologizing so maybe I'm maturing at least a little bit? — and have been working our way through the list like crazy people. In the past four days, though I have experienced continued failure on my search for a gift for Mark, we've been bowling and mini-golfing;

we've made out at the movies. We've officially picked 'our song' — though it's true that Mark sort of strong-armed that decision. I'd never heard 'Breathless' by Nick Cave and the Bad Seeds before but once he pulled me up to dance to it with shared iPod buds on the boardwalk, how could I refuse? We crossed off slow-dancing, too.

My mom looks at me through the mirror and cocks her head. 'Why don't you come to Zumba with me?'

I laugh, or snort. Some combination. Then I find my phone and see the text from Lauren. Should we talk? The very idea of it makes me feel winded.

My mother is standing up taller. 'You're not going to have very much fun in college, or in life, if you aren't willing to try new things.'

This new rational mom of mine is hard to argue with.

'Fine,' I say, and I study her clothing so I have a clue as to what to wear. 'I just need to change.'

I also need time. Time to figure out what to do. Do I call Lauren? E-mail? Text? And if I do, what do I even *say*? What is there to talk about if she's already been assigned a new roommate?

And so there my mom and I are, twenty minutes later, at the dance school above a high-end photography studio in town, where the windows are full of portraits of big happy families gathered on windswept dunes and color-blocked beach blankets. I am the only person under the age of maybe thirty in the room, which has one massive mirrored wall, but whatever. My mother is so beyond thrilled that I'm actually there with her that her happiness is sort of catching — or maybe I'm just happy that Lauren reached out, and that there might be a chance to salvage things after all. So when my mother introduces me around, I'm not as embarrassed as I thought I would be. For a second I even think that it *would* be okay if she came to California with me, to help me move in.

The Zumba teacher is a petite brunette named Meredith who looks around forty, with a medium-length brown bob and really white, straight teeth. She is wearing a cute sparkling top and genie pants and is so limber and lithe that I imagine she could actually contort herself into a tiny bottle or lamp. When the Latin hip-hop beat starts and the class begins to move, I try to follow along — at first just warming up with some basic steps — and I imagine myself being granted three wishes.

The first is for my mother to always be as happy as she looks here, dancing to this music that makes my ears feel like they're in a foreign country.

We've added arms; I am getting winded for real.

My second wish: for everything with Mark to end well, if it ends at all. No cheating, no lying, no bitterness. Please.

We're swinging hips; there is some turning.

And my third wish is this: for things with Lauren to be okay again. I know I can try to grant myself this wish, if I can grow up about it. As I whirl and sweat and try to keep up, I feel myself getting ready to make the call.

I am — there is no denying — a terrible Zumba dancer. No such thing as beginner's luck here. There is not a single move I get right, a single sequence that my brain remembers in the correct order. But it doesn't matter. My mother is smiling and I am laughing each time I goof up, and by the end of class I am wishing for one more wish. I wish my mother and I had started doing something like this together before now, before it feels like too little too late.

At home after class, we both guzzle a ton of water, then head for the den. We've been watching *Veronica Mars* again these last few nights and my mom cues up the next episode but then she says, 'You still haven't called, have you?'

For a second I wonder how she knows about Lauren's text, but she is not talking about Lauren at all. She is talking about my dad.

I shake my head and she plops down on the couch and pauses the show. 'No time like the present.'

So I go and get my phone and select my father's number. I am not sure what I even want to happen, maybe for him not to answer. But he does.

I say, 'Oh, hi. It's Elizabeth. Your daughter.'

'Elizabeth!' he says. 'Hi.'

I have a zinger I've been working on at the ready: 'I wasn't sure your phone would work over there. In Italy.'

There is silence for a moment, and I imagine he's trying to decide whether to compound his lie, maybe tell me about some international roaming plan. But then he clears his throat and says, 'I can explain.'

'I doubt it.'

He is quiet then, and I feel the need to get into specifics. 'My freshman roommate lives in San Francisco. She went to the gallery. In case you were wondering how I knew.'

'I'm sorry,' he says, and he clears his throat again. 'To be honest with you . . . '

'That would be nice,' I snap.

My mother raises her eyebrows at me as if to say, *Easy does it.*

But why should I go easy on him?

My dad says, 'I was caught off-guard when you asked to come stay here. I mean, I'm happy you'll be here for a few years, but I guess I haven't figured out what that means for me, exactly. Or for you or us.'

'Well, I haven't, either,' I say, and I feel tears start to form; my mother moves closer, puts an arm around me. 'But lying isn't going to help anything. And I mean, *Italy*? What the hell?'

'You're right,' he says. 'Of course you're right. And I'm sorry. I was supposed to spend the month there and it fell through. I thought anything else would sound . . . I don't know . . . like if I said I was busy at work or something . . . I'm really sorry.'

I have no words.

I feel worse than ever about that e-mail I sent Lauren.

My dad is the one who fucked up.

Not Lauren.

Not me.

'Why don't you come out a few days early?' my dad says, finally, but I think about my mother and all she's been through and is going through. It feels wrong to let him rob us of our final days together.

'That won't be necessary,' I say. 'I'm hanging up now.'

My mother pulls me into a hug, and I cry a little and she says, 'Oh, who needs him, anyway?' and then we decide to go ahead and watch the show. But the theme song gets me thinking about Lauren. So when the episode ends and my mother heads up to bed, I step out into the backyard and sit in one of the lounge chairs, its plastic bands cool against my skin. I call Lauren's number and I can hear it ringing on her end.

She has probably changed her mind.

She probably doesn't really want to talk. Or if she does it is only to tell me that she wants nothing to do with me once we get to school.

I lie back and look up at the stars — it's a Big Dipper night — and wait for disappointment to arrive, but then her voice comes through the phone — 'Hello?' — and, in spite of everything, I feel a skip of giddiness, like I've just seen a shooting star.

I sit up. 'Lauren?'

'EB?'

'Yes, it's me.' I am entirely too nervous, entirely too freaked out.

I hear voices, laughter, dishes, and she says, 'Hi, sorry. We're just sitting down to dinner so things are a little crazy.'

'Oh.' I close my eyes and imagine the scene — her big family, a bustling kitchen, kids ricocheting around the room. 'I'll be quick,' I say. 'I just talked to my dad, and you were right about him — but you know that — and I mean, well . . . ' I am botching it! 'Sorry I sort of suck at this. But I'm sorry. For my e-mail. And the new roommate request. I tried to undo it.'

'I'm sorry, too,' she says in a rush, like she's barely been able to hold the words in all this time. After a pause, she adds, 'For sending the video the way I did. It was . . . yeah, I'm sorry.'

I'm so relieved and also terrified that it's hard to find enough air to form words. 'Have you heard anything? Did you get a new roommate?'

'I just need one minute,' she says, away from the phone, then to me she says: 'They offered me a single.'

I'm afraid to ask whether she took it, so I say, 'Oh, well, that's good, I guess,' and I feel like I might cry.

There is an awful lot of noise on her end: happy shrieking. 'Sorry, I can't really hear,' she says. 'What did you say?'

'Please don't take the single,' I plead, but I don't think she hears because she says, 'Sorry, but can I call you later or tomorrow or something?'

'Sure,' I say. 'Of course.'

We hang up and I sit there and know that I

am too impatient to wait for her to call me later — I'll be asleep! — or tomorrow, so I open up a new e-mail and let words fly out of me. As I do, it's like I can literally feel the air around me being cleared.

Hey Lo,
So that was weird! Talking on the phone! I know you said you'd call me back but I have to go to bed and also I have stuff I want to be sure to say and e-mail is better for that.

I've been so angry. I guess you could tell that from my first response when you told me about meeting my father. I really felt like you'd betrayed me. But I know you thought you were doing the right thing. And I see now that you were. It doesn't matter. What matters is what happens next. And I don't want my deadbeat-dad drama to sour everything. And even though I didn't feel this way at first, I'm grateful that you're the kind of person who told me he was lying to me. I am sorry it took me a while to come around to that. I'm not even sure I can explain why I was so mad, I just was.

At the risk of sounding like a weirdo, I want to tell you how much our e-mails have meant to me in general. I really needed someone like you this summer. Someone on the outside who could look in with a different perspective. So even if we end up hating each other the second we meet — if we even ever do! — I want to say thanks. When I first sent you an e-mail asking about microwaves and mini-fridges, I don't know what I expected, but certainly not this.

I really do hope we end up meeting and becoming (staying?) friends but I've also been thinking so much lately about how in ten days I think I'll feel like this completely different person than I am now. In a lot of ways, I've been counting on that. A transformation. So I guess the person who shows up at college might not be the person who has been sending these e-mails.

I'm not making sense, I know. What I really mean is thanks.

(Have I said thanks yet? Because really I want to say thanks.)

And sorry. I hope you turn down the single. I already told them it was a big misunderstanding and to ignore my request so if you say that, too, maybe we'll still be roomies after all.

Many thanks,

EB

Yes: White flag.

No: F-bombs.

Maybe so: A copy of the official Berkeley Roommate Agreement. If we end up being roomies, we can either sign it or openly mock it.

When I hit Send I feel like a weight has been lifted. It is chilly out — I really want a sweater or a blanket — but I mostly don't want this feeling to end. I find the Big Dipper again, connect the stars in my mind's eye, and call Mark to tell him about Lauren and my dad and Zumba, and how maybe there's hope for me yet.

SUNDAY, AUGUST 18
SAN FRANCISCO

I'm in bed with my laptop on Sunday morning, and it's hard to tell from EB's e-mail whether or not she's still at least a little bit mad at me. In a way it sounds like good-bye. On the other hand, she wants us to stay roommates. Though I don't totally get how she could ever see what happened as some kind of betrayal, now that I've heard her voice e-mail feels different. Not quite so . . . final, I guess. She's a regular person, like me, leaving home for the first time, scared, excited, imperfect and trying to figure it all out.

Gertie runs into the room. 'Why are you still in bed?'

'Because it feels good.' My first instinct is to tell her to go back to the TV or whatever she was doing, but she bounces closer to my bed and her curls bounce with her, and that's impossible to resist. 'Come see.' I flip back the covers and scoot over to make room.

She climbs in and snuggles against me. Where did she get curly hair, anyway? Each of my brothers and sisters looks enough like my parents that no one would ever doubt we're all blood related. But they also each have some unique, mysterious physical characteristic that seems to come from nowhere.

Sometimes I think of them all together as a unit, a herd of creatures that need containment.

Other times, like now, I see the individual miracles that they are.

'What are you doing?' Gertie asks, her big eyes on my computer screen.

'Reading a letter. It's from my friend EB.'

'Eebee?'

'EB. Here.' I show her Ebb's sign-off. 'Do you want to see a picture of her?'

'Yeah.' Gertie's voice is whispery.

I pull up the picture Ebb sent, of her in a garden or park or something, standing under a tree with speckles of sun and shade on her face. Gertie leans toward the computer and touches Ebb's head, leaving a smudge.

'You know how me and you and P.J. share a room?'

Her curls nod.

'When I go to college I'm going to share a room with EB.'

After she thinks about that for a few seconds, she says, 'Me too?'

There's a rush of fluids to my nose and

eyes. I can't talk. Fortunately, Gertie loses interest fast when Jack dashes in to announce, 'Papa made pancakes.'

I close the laptop and take a big breath. 'We better get some before Marcus eats them all.'

Throughout breakfast my mom keeps asking — Don't I want to do something with Keyon? Wouldn't I like to go shopping with Zoe for a few school things? How about Dad and I go out to lunch? When she ambushes me outside the bathroom, a few laundry items clutched in her hands, and suggests I go get a pedicure, as if I'd ever done that before or expressed any interest in it, I've finally had enough.

'Mom. I want to stay home.'

I can see from her face that she's about to argue with me, maybe urge me to go hang gliding or explore my deeper self in a yoga class. I stop her by repeating, 'I want to stay home. I don't feel trapped. I don't feel obligated. I want to be here with you and Dad and the kids, and help you clean up the pancake mess. I want to change Francis's diaper and play Uno for hours with Jack even though he cheats.' My mom's perky mask is crumbling. My emotions start to let go, too. 'I . . . this . . . please . . .'

She drops the laundry and we more or less

weep in each other's arms for who knows how long. When we finally dry up and rejoin the family, we have exactly the kind of day I want to have: loud, messy, chaotic, hilarious, and maddening.

At one point, I think, *Well, this day is the last of its kind. Next weekend I'll be preoccupied with making sure I'm ready, and . . .* But as I watch P.J. lug Francis around the living room like a sack of potatoes, and Jack and Gertie actually being quiet during their DVD, I think maybe it's a mistake to think of anything as the 'last.'

School and my house are only an hour apart. Yes, I'll be busy, but I'll be here when I can and when I want. There are going to be hundreds of new kinds of days, and probably plenty of days that look an awful lot like this. I mean, I know it will be different. Maybe Ebb will come home with me on the weekends sometimes. Maybe other weekends I'll be at Chico to see Keyon. Maybe I'll get to go see Zoe in Seattle on a break. But home is always going to be home.

'Be careful, Peej,' I say as Francis dangles from her arms like a bewildered cat. P.J. brings him over to where I'm sitting on the floor and drops him unceremoniously into my lap. He keels to the left but I catch him before he falls over.

I lie back on the floor and balance my baby brother on my bended legs. He smiles. I hold his arms out.

We fly.

EB,
Thanks for calling me back and for your e-mail.

And for telling Housing to disregard your request. As soon as you said on the phone you didn't want me to take the single, I knew I wouldn't. (Even though if I went back in time to tell the Lauren who requested a single on my original application that we'd make this decision, she'd probably throw a fit.)

What you said was basically what I was waiting to hear . . . I mean, I didn't want to force myself on you!!

And, I'm sorry. I really am. I'd probably do the same thing again (only different) but I'm still sorry.

Prediction: We're not going to hate each other.

Like you (sort of) said, we've shared a lot this summer and I can't see the point in pretending like it never happened, and having to start all over with someone else. I think I'll stay out of the stuff with your dad for now and change the subject to:

PACKING.

I've been thinking about it tonight and mentally going through everything in my room and I can't imagine hauling all this crap across the country, let alone across the Bay. I'm feeling kind of overwhelmed so I think my strategy will be to do it in a few trips. Pack as if I'm going away for a week and then gradually figure out what I really need. It's different for me because, you know, all my stuff will be right here. It must be hard for you, leaving your life and your things so much farther behind.

Random: Pretty soon I'll start looking for work in Berkeley . . . on campus hopefully. Ideally doing something actually related to the sciences, and I don't count finding the perfect ratio of tuna to mayo, like at my sandwich job.

Tomorrow night, Zoe and I are going out and I will do whatever she says, even if it's karaoke, to make her happy. Later in the week me and Keyon will do something special. I don't know what. (Not THAT. Not ready.) I try not to think about all these good-byes too much.

The saddest thing that's happened is explaining to the kids that I'm leaving. I mean, we've been telling them for months, but little kids don't get things until they happen, so it's like, 'Lauren isn't going to live in your room anymore. Lauren is going to have her own room in a different house. She won't be here when you wake up, not every day like she was. Do you understand?' They nod their heads and then run off or ask if they can have crackers, so obviously it's not quite sinking in. Except today I told Gertie about you and she asked if she could be our roommate, too.

What makes me want to cry (or actually cry) is that when they finally realize that I'm not HERE, I won't BE HERE to comfort them.

I'm hoping to get to the dorms pretty early, but with traffic and potential kid problems it's hard to be sure. My dad is taking the day off work, and they're pulling Jack out of school so you'll meet all of them except the baby, Francis, who'll go to my grandma's. My parents think if the kids actually see me moving in they'll understand better what's happening. I hope you're ready for the mob.

Oh — sorry that I didn't call you back but here's what I think:

No more technology between us until we actually meet.

I'm imagining the moment we're all moved in and our families are gone and it's really US in our ROOM, starting college. You know?

Until then,

Lo

SUNDAY, AUGUST 25
NEW JERSEY

When Justine calls early and asks me to meet her and Morgan for a girls' dinner that night I decline, figuring my mom will want it to be just the two of us for Sunday dinner. But when I ask her it turns out she has to 'stage' a house she's trying to sell, and the job may run into the evening. It's a big listing for my mom, a three-million-dollar house on the beach, and she needs to fill it with hipster antiques and impractical white chaises to entice buyers. I call Justine right back and tell her dinner works after all.

That leaves me nothing much to do all day but pack for real. So after my mother heads out with some of our fancier soaps and the orchid I brought home from work at the beginning of the summer — 'For the master bath,' she says — I open my better suitcase and get started. When I can barely find any clothes I want to bring with me into my new life, I flop down onto the bed and call Mark.

'I was just thinking about you,' he says.

'Want to come over?' The simple act of talking to him makes me feel strangely alive, like I can feel my blood pulsing from the inside out.

'On my way,' he says. 'But I can only stay for a little bit. My mother wants to take me shopping for some dorm room stuff.'

When I open the front door for him a little while later, he steps right in and slides his arms around me and kisses me and kisses me; then he stops and asks, 'Is your mom home?'

I shake my head and he keeps kissing, taking a quick break for the stairs, until we're up in my room and my suitcase has been pushed off the bed. I feel daring at first, and then silly and a little bit guilty because my mom wouldn't approve. I pull away to catch my breath and he starts tracing circles with the hand he's slipped under my tank top.

'I need to pack,' I say. I wonder if Lauren has started, too. I am so beyond relieved that we are back to being roommates — Helen Blake has confirmed it — and though it has been hard to not e-mail Lauren this week, I think the no-technology idea is a good one. And anyway, I'm only here a few more days so it makes sense to really be *here*.

'Let's do it.' Mark rolls off me and gets up. He's entirely not bothered that we're not doing more.

It seems easier all of a sudden, the figuring out of what to bring. Mark sits on the bed, crossing things off my list as I pack them and also giving a thumbs-up or a thumbs-down to various pairs of jeans and tops and jackets. He only makes fun of the exhaustiveness of my list a little, like when he says, 'You really felt the need to write down 'clothes'?

'I'm going to miss you,' I say. Which is a way to test the waters, I guess. I've never said 'I love you' to a guy before. And if you don't count the word engraved on my necklace, he's never actually said it to me. He's flipping through my Berkeley stuff — course catalog, orientation materials, a printout of the original e-mail I got with Lauren's name on it. I take the printout from him and slip it into a folder that I'll pack. For some reason, I don't want to lose that printout. At this point, it almost feels like I should frame it.

I say, 'Hey,' to get his attention; then I sit next to him. 'I love you.'

He looks me right in the eyes and it's like I can see deep into him and he says, 'I know. I love you, too.' Then he stands up. 'Which is why it pains me to tell you I've got to go. But I'll see you tonight, maybe?'

I shake my head. 'Dinner with the girls.'

He groans.

'I have to.'

'Call me after?' He leans his hips into mine and kisses me.

'Sure.' It feels like good practice for saying good-bye for real.

* * *

My mother calls a little later and asks me to swing by the nursery and pick up some plants from Tim, who occasionally helps her out with stagings, and drive them over to the three-million-dollar house. I don't feel like I can refuse so I call Tim to tell him I'm coming and he says he's out on a consultation but that he set the stuff for my mom by the back door and left it unlocked. 'Be sure to lock up when you go, and hey,' he says. 'Don't forget to come by to say good-bye if you can.'

'I'll try,' I say, and I feel a weird sort of impatience to be gone already and not spending all the time I have left here *leaving*.

At the nursery I load up the plants — several of which are more like trees — and am about to leave when I notice a small bonsai tree near the register. Maybe it's completely dorky to give Mark a tree to remember me by, but I take one look at it, with its tiny twisting trunk — like two entangled limbs — and know he has to have

336

it. Or that I have to give it to him. Which may or may not be the same thing. I leave money and a note and lock up and go.

* * *

After delivering the plants and helping my mom figure out where to put them, I make a quick stop at home to shower and change and then drive down the beach road and wonder about whether this is the last time I'll drive this way before I leave. And when I'm about to pull into the restaurant parking lot, I find myself missing the turn and driving right up to the beach instead. I get out of the car, because I'm suddenly afraid that if I don't take a minute, the next few days will get away from me and I won't get to breathe all of this in. I stand there and study the ocean — dark and greenish against the whitish sky of dusk, where stars are about to appear — and I let my mind go blank. I want to very deliberately feel whatever it is I am feeling, and then that seems almost dumb, if not impossible, and I am a little bit late to meet the girls, so I go.

The lasts are going to keep coming now, hard and fast.

The last time I see the ocean.

The last time I see Mark.

The last time I sleep in my bed and wake up in my house.

The last time I drive this car.

The last time I walk through these restaurant doors . . .

It isn't until a few seconds after Justine shouts 'Surprise!' that I look at the faces around hers and see that they include Morgan's, yes, but also my mother's and Tim's and Mark's. Justine's folks are there, too, and Danny and Mitch, and even the Schroeders. Mrs. Schroeder is holding Vivian and comes up to me and says, 'We're not staying; we want you to enjoy your meal in peace. But we had to at least say good-bye.' Vivian dives at me and I take her and give her this huge hug and I think I'm going to cry but then the swell fades and I don't and I watch them go.

'You guys are amazing,' I say, turning to Justine and Morgan. I give them hugs and hold Justine's, especially, a little too long. Morgan says, 'Well, it was your mom's idea.'

So I go hug my mom and then I look over at Mark and see him looking up at the wall and blinking a lot and swallowing hard a few times. Fighting tears. Like me.

'Hey,' he says as I go to take the seat next to him, and he kisses me quick. I don't even need to look at the menu to know what I'm having. They make the best shrimp scampi on the shore here, so it's decided. I introduce Mark around, then, and he and Justine seem to hit it off, talking about how neither of them really knows what they want to major in yet. Morgan and Mitch start talking animatedly to Tim, though I can't imagine about what. Even Justine's boyfriend, Danny, who in all our time spent together has barely said more than two words directly to me, those words being 'Hey, EB,' seems to be chatty and having fun. He pulls me aside and says, 'She's really going to miss you, you know.'

'I know,' I say. 'Me too.'

Then salads arrive. 'I got you something,' I say to Mark as we sit down, and his eyebrows go up.

'It's a pony, isn't it?' His smile is tinged with sadness. His parents — both of them, together — are taking him out for a farewell dinner tomorrow and we have decided that it would be best if I don't go. I'm glad we never actually put 'meet the parents' on our list.

'Yes,' I say. 'It's a pony.'

Dinner comes soon after we're done with salads and my mother and Mark start to talk about Northwestern — when he's leaving, how he's getting there. Then she asks, 'And any plans to visit California?'

Mark looks at me. We haven't sorted out all

the details but we have a general game plan. Neither of us will do anything with anybody, no matter what, before Thanksgiving, at which point we're both going to come home to Jersey and check in about where we stand. If we're solid, we'll revisit the idea of defining our relationship. To my mother he says, 'We're going to let ourselves get settled before making any plans.'

'Well, that sounds wise.' She nods approval at me and I start to think that if my mother and I can find our way to Zumba, and to each other, maybe there's hope for me and Neil. Maybe we can have a kind of new relationship that breaks away from the whole wounded father-daughter abandonment thing. Only time will tell.

★ ★ ★

Mark stays with me when I say good-bye to everyone in the parking lot — the girls and I plan one final beach outing in the morning — and then I pop open the back of my car and pull out the bonsai, which I wedged between some random junk so it wouldn't fall over. I turn and present it to him. 'For you.'

He looks a little surprised and smiles a touch and then says, 'That is completely awesome.'

Still, I feel dumb. 'Do you really think so?'

'I do.' He seems entirely entranced as he takes it in his hands. 'All this time I've been thinking, *Please don't let her get me something boring like a watch or a pen. Please please please let it be something fun and cool and totally Elizabeth.*' He smiles. 'Or should I call you EB?'

'If you want,' I say, happy either way because it's all just me.

He holds out the tree and says, 'This is totally EB. And I love it.'

'Cross it off the list!' I say.

'Consider it crossed.'

I give him a quick kiss and ask, 'Anything else we should try to knock off tonight?'

He has the list on his phone so we lean against my car and look at it together. There's not much left. 'I have an idea that isn't on the list,' he says then. 'We can walk there, come on.'

So we head up to the boardwalk and toward the amusement parks, past shops selling taffy and stuffed sea animals, past the stands where you can throw darts at balloons or baseballs at stacks of milk jugs. Soon we are staring up at the massive swing ride. It has a top like a carousel, painted elaborately and lit with thousands of lights, and the chair swings hang from it on long chains. The ride is spinning right now, and the top has tilted so that the swings are really shooting up into the night, and just looking at it makes me sort of want to scream. Down below, on the mat where riders are loaded on, sit tons of pairs of flip-flops that were kicked off before the ride began.

'What do you say?' Mark says.

'You're serious,' I say.

'All this going-away-to-college stuff is starting to feel very grown-up.' He nods at the ride. 'This'll make us feel young again.'

I can hardly argue with that. So we go to a booth for tickets, queue up with some others, and then find two swings side by side, close enough where we can hold hands. I kick off my flip-flops and in a minute we're spinning. We start slowly, going round and round, but I can feel it, somewhere deep in my gut, when some new force starts to propel us out into the sky. Mark and I hold hands as long as we can but then the force is too strong and he laughs and I scream and we have no choice but to let go.

WEDNESDAY, AUGUST 28
BERKELEY

It's a little bit of a letdown. The room. I mean, after this whole summer and the e-mails and counting the days, in the end it's a dingy little box filled with wooden furniture from the early eighties. There are two of everything, matched:

Two desks. Two desk chairs. Two beds. Two closets. Two small bookcases. The Noah's Ark of living arrangements.

'So this is what I've been daydreaming about for months.' I laugh at myself. 'My room at home is nicer.'

'I wonder if this is what it looks like at Chico,' Keyon says, sounding like he hopes not. He goes over to the window, which faces another building, and opens it a couple of inches to let in the fresh air.

When I first told my parents I wanted Keyon to be the one to bring me across the Bay, they were upset and confused. I explained that I didn't want my entry into the dorms to be mobbed with kids and noise and all the stuff that comes with being a family of eight. But that I didn't want to be alone, either.

'Lauren,' Mom said, sounding frustrated, 'we only get to do this once!'

'Me too.'

'If you don't want the whole family, at least let Daddy take you.' At the same time, Dad said, 'You and Mom can go and I'll stay here.'

'I want it to be Keyon.'

Dad shook his head, clearly disappointed in me. But what could I say? All summer they'd been pushing me toward my freedom and now I wanted to claim it.

We went with a compromise.

Keyon brought me over and is helping me get settled before he has to go home and take care of his own moving stuff. Later, my parents will come with all the kids. They want to meet Ebb and make sure the room is secure and we aren't going to get snatched on the first night.

I join Keyon at the window. 'Nice view.'

He puts his arm around me, and I feel about a thousand times closer to him than I did at the fancy steak house we went to last night. There, we had candlelight, and the waiter kept coming by with different forks for the various courses and we were too out of place to really talk.

Here, it's simple and bright. Us.

'You'll see,' he says. 'Pretty soon it'll feel

like a home away from home.'

'Which bed should I take?' I ask, turning to face inside the room again.

'Hmm. You'd better let me check it out. Come here.' He takes my hand and leads me to the bed that's on the right as you come in the door. He stretches out and pats the very little bit of space left next to him.

I lie down and rest my head in the crook of his arm. 'This one's not bad,' I murmur.

'Smells a little dusty, Lo,' he says with an exaggerated sniff.

'That could be my hair.'

We laugh. Keyon pushes me out of the bed and we scuttle over to the other one and get into the same position. 'Now, this is a straight-up *bed*!' Keyon exclaims.

'Who's going to help you pick your bed, at your dorm?'

'I'll flag down some chick in the hall.'

'I don't think so,' I say. 'Maybe your mom will do it.'

'I know you didn't just say that.'

We're teasing each other but our voices grow softer and softer until we're silent, and as close as we can get. His body is so solid and warm and perfect with mine. About four seconds before I could fall asleep, he says, 'We'd better get your stuff up here before my car gets towed.'

I groan, because I want to stay exactly like this for about seventy-two more hours. He pulls me up until we're sitting on the edge of the bed, and he kisses the top of my head, and my neck, and my cheek. Everywhere but my lips and I think neither of us wants to. It would feel so serious, and only remind us that after we get me unpacked, we'll be apart for a while.

It takes us four or five trips up and down stairs to get all the stuff. The last thing, from way in the back of the trunk of his dad's car, is the microwave.

The microwave that started the whole thing with EB, and in turn started the whole thing with Keyon. 'Where should we put it?' he asks.

'I don't know.'

There aren't a whole lot of surfaces, and limited outlets. We try it on the floor near my closet, then on my bookcase, and finally settle for the corner of my desk.

'It's gonna get in your way,' Keyon says.

'Maybe.'

Then it's time for us to say good-bye.

★ ★ ★

Between when Keyon leaves and my family is supposed to come, I've got some time alone.

Now that my stuff is in here and I'm getting used to it, it doesn't seem as depressing. It could be something. We'll make it into something.

I venture out in the hall to see if there's a water fountain. A girl in cutoffs, Birks, and a Raiders sweatshirt walks by with an armload of books. 'Hey.'

'Hi.'

A Raiders fan, right down the hall. I shudder a little. But the books seem promising. They aren't textbooks, they are for-fun books. One drops. I pick it up — *Little House in the Big Woods* — and return it to her teetering pile.

'Thanks,' she says, taking it. 'I probably don't have space for these but when I was packing I . . . couldn't leave them.'

'My mom read those to me when I was a kid. I'm Lauren, by the way.'

'Hi. Violet. Nice to meet you.'

I point behind me, indicating my door. 'I'm right here. Waiting for my roommate and unpacking and . . . ' *Doing what every single other person in this building is doing.*

'Good luck. I'll look for you guys tonight at that thing in the lobby!' She walks off and enters a room several doors down.

Thing in the lobby? I'll check out the bulletin board later to see what that is. I know there's a ton of Welcome Week stuff but I've been too overwhelmed to sort it out.

The bathrooms are mildly frightening. Even in a house with my five brothers and sisters, I could at least close the door.

Back in our room, I'm overwhelmed again at the sight of all the stuff I need to find a place for. Hopefully Ebb is good at organizing and maybe decorating. I close the door and lie down again on my bed, and smell the faintest whiff of Keyon. It would be easy to have a major cry right now, but that's not the first impression I want to give my roommate, or the way I want my parents to find me.

I take a few pictures of the room with my new phone and zap them off to Zoe, then commence with the unpacking. In a laundry basket full of linens, I find something small and rigid wrapped in a hand towel.

Zoe texts: I can't believe you successfully messaged me pictures!! My little LoCo is all grown up. xoxox.

The thing wrapped in the towel is a photo frame, the kind that holds two pictures with a hinge in the middle. One is of me and my mom and dad at my high school graduation, the three of us squinting into the sun. My dad's mouth is sort of contorted because, as I remember it, he's trying to explain to my grandma how to use the digital camera.

The other is a Sears portrait of all the kids, which my parents had taken at Christmas.

Jack and Marcus have gel in their hair, and P.J. and Gertie are wearing ribbons. Francis is just a bobble-headed newborn.

My mom must have done this for me, and packed it. I stand there and stare at the pictures for a while, smiling, then set the frame on the desk next to the microwave.

I can't wait to see them again.

I can't wait to meet EB.

To go to my first class.

To talk to Keyon after he goes to his.

And wake up tomorrow in this room.

I'm ready.

WEDNESDAY, AUGUST 28
BERKELEY

In the cab, I'm sort of giddy about, of all things, the trees. Palm. Eucalyptus. I-Don't-Even-Know-What. I could seriously start laughing about how different the trees are from what I'm used to and for a second I consider telling the driver to redirect to Muir Woods, so I can see some redwoods, too, right out of the gate. But then he turns the radio on and the way the traffic and weather reports, and the DJs' voices, sound so foreign, so new, distracts me from the trees. The day continues to feel like some kind of bizarre-o out-of-body experience. But the tears, at least, are gone.

I felt the first cry coming when Justine stopped by the house, super-early, to give me a hug and wish me good luck.

The next was when I went up to the beach, just me and my surfboard. Something about seeing the ocean — *my* ocean, *my* beach — for the for-real last time before leaving made me well up. And when I paddled out, there weren't many breakers so I just sat there, straddling my board, taking it all in. I know California has an ocean; I know I'll be back in a few short months for a visit. Still. I closed my eyes, and bobbed and took some deep breaths and felt so very small and let a few of my tears slip into the vastness.

The third was when my mother squeezed my hand at the airport. We had stopped near where I had to get on line for the security check. It was time to say good-bye.

'I'm so proud of you,' she said. 'For leaving me.'

'I'm not *leaving you*, Mom,' I said. 'I'm just going away to college.'

'I know,' she said. 'But still.'

We'd talked about her maybe going on standby, but decided it was an awful lot of money to spend on a trip that would end the same way this moment would end, with good-bye. I can handle showing up on campus by myself. What I am having a harder time dealing with is the thought of her being alone when she goes home. I made her promise not to watch any more *Veronica Mars* until I'm back for Thanksgiving; then I made a wish about that three-million-dollar listing. Her commission would be huge, enough to get her to an Italian villa — or anywhere she wanted to go.

We hugged and I got on the line and she

left and I felt a sort of dread but also relief that that part was done. Then Mark texted me — I love you — and I cried again.

And then the mind-body disconnect kicked in.

There's me putting my bag on the belt.

There's me putting my shoes in a bin.

There's me walking through the metal detector.

There's me putting my shoes back on, grabbing my bag, then using the restroom.

There's me buying trail mix and a magazine.

There's me finding a seat at the gate.

There's me boarding, and falling asleep.

A text from Mark — Miss u already! — calls me back into myself, into the cab. I write back Me too.

So very much.

I decide to put my phone away for a while. I said I'd call him later, and I will.

For a moment I let myself replay last night — *our* last night. For now, at least. Mark came over and watched some *Veronica Mars* with me and my mom, and then when she went to bed we stayed up and went out into the backyard and lay on a blanket in the grass and looked at stars. And kissed. And more. And it was so lovely and sad that, afterward, we both cried a little but laughed because it seemed silly to cry about being so happy, so lucky, so in love. Then he threw his hands up at the sky and said, 'Why, God, why?'

I laughed and said, 'What are you talking about?'

'Why did I have to meet you now and not like four years ago or something?'

I found the Big Dipper more easily than ever before right then, like it was lit specifically for me. 'I don't know,' I said. 'I think maybe this all happened exactly the way it was supposed to.'

'Oh, you do, do you?' He turned and kissed me sweetly. 'Well, here's hoping you're right.'

And I realized that I never answered Lauren's question about whether it's awkward when Mark and I talk about this stuff.

But that's okay. I'll tell her in person.

As the cab speeds along, I study billboards and street signs — all so unfamiliar — and feel even more certain that things are happening for a reason.

I try to picture what Lauren's doing right now. Whether she's in the room waiting for me and whether she's already picked a bed or desk or whatever it is we've got. Maybe she's making soup or a Hot Pocket in the microwave and figuring out where we'll put the mini-fridge once I get it. I hope her family is still there and that they'll all welcome me with hugs and say they've heard so much about me and I'll say 'Me too. Me too.'

I climb out of the cab in front of the address I've written on a slip of paper in my pocket and I see a girl struggling with her suitcase at the front door, and I wonder if it's Lauren. But then she disappears into the building before I can think to call out, and anyway I am pretty sure the hair color was wrong.

I pay the driver and look up at the building's windows to see if there's a face there, someone waiting for me. But I don't see anything or anyone so I lug my suitcases over to the door and go in and take the elevator to the fourth floor. I consult my paper again, then go down the hall and find room 402. The door is closed, so I put my bags down and fix my sweater and push my bangs to the side in an attempt to look more presentable, though, really, it's too late for that.

Lauren already knows me, flaws and all.

I've got a rock in my jeans pocket, and I take a second to reach in and run my thumb over it. It's the surprisingly heavy one I took that day at Mark's, and this morning I grabbed it off my bedroom windowsill at the last second on my way out the door. Whenever I look at it I know I'll be reminded of him and Froggy and the letter telling me who my roomie would be and the Moonlight and Zumba — *all* of the surprises of this past summer, the one before everything changed.

I take a deep breath and knock and wait, and then I realize it was stupid to knock. It's my room, too. I hear footsteps inside as I reach for the doorknob and my breath catches as I grab on. I am not even sure who does the turning, but suddenly the knob is moving and the door is clicking open.

Here we are.

ACKNOWLEDGMENTS

From Tara:
I'd like to thank my agent, David Dunton, a most excellent resident career adviser; my husband, Nick, who continues to be an amazing bunkmate in life; my rambunctious housemates Ellie and Violet, even though they're useless at picking up after themselves; and most of all Sara, whom I effectively tricked into writing this book with me.

From Sara:
Thanks to my agent, Michael Bourret, with whom I've shared a lot, if not a room; my one and only roomie, Gordon, who puts up with my loud music and never complains about the hair in the shower drain; and especially the intrepid Tara, who started this whole thing and made sure it got finished.

Together, we'd like to thank campus admin for seeing us through to freshman year: Julie Scheina, who led the way; her lovely assistant, Pam Garfinkel; and the whole Little, Brown Books for Young Readers team. We bestow a sorority pin on Varian Johnson for a valuable early read. And classified thanks to our favorite secret society, BOB.

We do hope that you have enjoyed reading this large print book.

Did you know that all of our titles are available for purchase?

We publish a wide range of high quality large print books including:
Romances, Mysteries, Classics
General Fiction
Non Fiction and Westerns

Special interest titles available in large print are:
The Little Oxford Dictionary
Music Book
Song Book
Hymn Book
Service Book

Also available from us courtesy of Oxford University Press:
Young Readers' Dictionary
(large print edition)
Young Readers' Thesaurus
(large print edition)

For further information or a free brochure, please contact us at:
Ulverscroft Large Print Books Ltd.,
The Green, Bradgate Road, Anstey,
Leicester, LE7 7FU, England.
Tel: (00 44) 0116 236 4325
Fax: (00 44) 0116 234 0205

Other titles published by Ulverscroft:

PRECOCIOUS

Joanna Barnard

They say your school days are the best of your life. But everybody lies . . . Fiona is (un)happily married when a chance meeting with her former teacher Mr. Morgan plunges her headlong into an affair. But as their obsessive relationship grows ever darker, Fiona is forced to confront her own past. She first drew close to Henry Morgan as a precocious and lonely fourteen-year-old, and their relationship was always one which she controlled — or did she? Are some of the biggest lies Fiona has told been to herself? Has Henry Morgan been the love of her life, or the ruin of it?

THE LITTLE KIOSK BY THE SEA

Jennifer Bohnet

Meet Sabine, desperately fighting to save her little kiosk from closure whilst turning down her friend Owen's proposals, time and time again. Cue Harriet, returning to Dartmouth after thirty years, haunted by the scandal that drove her away and shocked by a legacy that threatens her relationship with her journalist daughter. Enter Rachel, the mysterious newcomer who has an unexpected chemistry with a local widower, and who sets in motion a chain of events she could never have predicted. One thing's for sure — as the autumn tide turns, there'll be more than one secret laid bare . . .